TRUSTING HER HERO

DARE TO SURRENDER
BOOK FOUR

DANIELLE PAYS

Edited by: Jen McDonnell, Bird's Eye Books
Cover by: Maria @ Steamy Designs

www.daniellepays.com

Prologue

Ten years ago.

"Hey, thanks for having me, but I got to head back." Wilder began to straighten up the dollar bills in front of him.

Chase laughed. "You can't stay away from that wife of yours, can you?"

No, he couldn't. But tonight, she likely wouldn't be home yet. She'd gone out for happy hour with her friends and knowing Kate she'd stay until the pub closed.

He understood that he and Kate were young, and she wanted to let off some steam, but dammit, every weekend?

Maybe a change of scenery will help, he considered, staring at the pile of cash he'd won in tonight's poker game.

When Kate got home, they could talk about using it to take a little vacation somewhere. That actually sounded great; they needed to get away from the daily grind.

He glanced up to see most of the guys smiling at him. All but Martin.

He shrugged. "Sorry, guys. Hate to win and run, but —"

"No, he doesn't. Enjoy all our money, asshole," Martin said, grinning now.

Wilder gave them a wave, then headed out.

On the short drive to their apartment, he came up with possible vacation destinations. Once he got inside, he grabbed a pen and paper and wrote it all down. By the time he got to the end of the list, though, his eyes were heavy.

His latest construction job kept him so busy that, by the weekend, all he wanted to do was sleep.

With a massive yawn, he headed to the bedroom, deciding the vacation conversation could wait until the morning. But when he turned on the bedroom light, he found Kate in bed, already asleep — with Scott Fisher.

No. This can't be real!

Kate should still be out drinking. And Scott? They both hated the man.

He rubbed his eyes and opened them again.

Nothing had changed.

His heart hammered in his chest. "What the fuck is going on?!"

At his shout, Scott jumped up, quickly grabbing the sheet to cover himself; the asshole was naked.

Wilder glanced at Kate. She was on her stomach, her back bare except for her bra strap.

She stirred, tugging the blanket up to cover herself. "Wilder? Come to bed. I'm tired."

What the fuck?

"Kate, what the hell is going on? You slept with Scott Fisher?"

She sat up and grabbed her head. "Fisssher?" He could *see* her confusion as she slurred.

Dammit. "You're drunk, aren't you? You seriously got drunk and brought a man home?"

Just a few feet away, Scott picked his pants up off the floor and hurriedly put them on, stumbling in the process.

"Sorry," Scott said as he caught his balance.

His fist was moving even before he had time to think about it.

Scott cupped his nose. "Fuck! I think you broke it!"

"Get out!"

Scooping up the rest of his clothes, Scott ran out of the room.

Wilder grabbed a duffel bag and began filling it with his own clothes.

"What's going on?" Kate sat up. "Was someone here?"

Oh, that was rich. As if she hadn't brought the guy home.

He moved to the bathroom and grabbed his toothbrush, razor, and shampoo, shoving them all in the bag. It would probably leak all over his stuff, but he didn't care. He had to get the hell out of there.

"Wilder, what are you doing?"

He spun around to see Kate standing beside him, wearing panties and a bra, holding her head.

"Hangover hit already? Good."

Yeah, it was a childish thing to say, but he couldn't help it. He was about to lose his fucking mind.

"I knew you liked to party, but sleeping with Scott fucking Fisher?" He dropped the bag as he took a deep breath. "We made vows to each other and you—"

She shook her head. "No, I was at the bar with Harmony and Tabitha. They left with two guys, and I was going to call a cab home, but then Scott said he'd give me a ride home after one more drink."

Wilder slammed his dresser drawer shut. "You've got to be kidding me. That man has been coming onto you since we got married."

"No, I had the drink, but I don't remember anything after that. Wilder, you have to believe me, I wouldn't sleep with him. I wouldn't sleep with *anyone*. I love you!"

Kate was crying, and when Wilder snatched his other jacket off the hook on the back of the door, she raced to him and grabbed his arm.

He jerked away. "No. I have to get out of here."

"Wait! Wilder don't go. You have it all wrong."

He stopped and was unable to help the chuckle that burst out as he turned back to her. "I have it wrong? I came home and found my wife in bed with

Scott Fisher. The man was naked, and you practically are."

She flinched.

"Yeah, that's what I thought." He stormed through the door, slamming it as he left.

He had driven halfway to the next town before he realized it. Where the hell was he going? The last thing he wanted was to see or talk to anyone.

Turning the car around, he drove to his parents' house. He could sneak in and sleep in his old room, then tomorrow, he could decide what to do.

Everything and everyone he loved was in Fisher Springs. But he couldn't stay here — not after tonight.

So where do I go?

Chapter One

"Your parents sure fucked up." Wilder's friend Dane shook his head, wearing a smirk.

He may not be his friend for much longer.

"Excuse me?"

Dane took a sip of the coffee he held as he sat on the edge of Wilder's desk in the Summit County Sheriff's Office. "They name you Wilder, and your brother William."

Wilder crossed his arms. "So?"

"Well, based on all those stories you told me about your brother last weekend, *he* should have been named Wilder."

God, last weekend. What a shit-show.

He'd gotten a voicemail from his little brother, William. William was getting married to his long-time girlfriend, Holly, in Fisher Springs and really wanted Wilder to be there.

The problem? Wilder hadn't been back in Fisher Springs in ten years — not since that fateful night he discovered the love of his life had cheated on him.

The image of her in bed with someone he'd thought she hated had torn him apart for *years*… to the point he had changed his last name to his mother's in hopes that his ex would never track him down.

He'd thought he was over his anger, seeing as it was a decade after the fact, but the memory of that night came back, and right after he got off the phone with his brother last weekend, he'd found himself at the gym, beating the hell out of a punching bag.

When Dane had come in and seen him, he'd pulled him away, but by then, Wilder's knuckles were already bloody. He hadn't worn gloves, wanting to feel the pain.

Dane was the only person Wilder had opened up to about what happened with his ex-wife. Well, his brother knew; hell, that whole town knew.

And that was another reason he had no desire to go back.

"And you are such a stickler for rules, you should have had the stuffy name William," Dane continued, unaware that Wilder was lost in his own thoughts.

" 'William' isn't stuffy, you motherfucker."

Dane tossed his hands in the air. "Hey, I mean no offense. Just an observation."

Wilder shook his head and stared at his desk, which was currently covered in four stacks of files.

As a detective with the Summit County Sheriff's Office, he had his fair share of cases — which included a ridiculous amount of paperwork. Unless he wanted to pull another late night, he needed to get to work.

"Coleman, in my office," his captain barked at him.

His breakfast churned in his stomach. It was too early for the tongue lashing he was about to get.

Wilder followed Captain Nelson into his office.

When he entered, he discovered that, by contrast, the captain's desk was immaculate. How the hell *he* didn't have a stack of papers waiting for him, Wilder couldn't understand.

The moment the door closed; Wilder started his defense. "Captain, I should be caught up on the paperwork later this week."

"Sit down. This has nothing to do with that."

Wilder let out a breath of relief and sat. But then his attention was directed to another man in the office.

"Coleman, this is Detective Dillon Simpson with the King County Sheriff's Office. Detective Simpson, this is Detective Wilder Coleman."

Simpson stood and shook Wilder's hand. The man appeared young for a detective… or maybe he just had a babyface. He was also several inches shorter than Wilder.

"Good to meet you, Coleman. It says on your application you went to Fisher Springs High School?"

Just the mention of his former hometown had his stomach in knots. How the hell was he going to face everyone at his brother's wedding?

Maybe I won't go.

No, that would be a jackass move, and his brother deserved better.

He had about five weeks to figure it out.

Simpson was staring at him, and he realized he hadn't responded yet.

He gave an uncomfortable cough. "Uh, yes."

'Have a seat Coleman," his captain directed.

Wilder sat down and Simpson took the chair next to him.

"Do you go back to town much?" Simpson asked.

"No, I left ten years ago and haven't returned."

Simpson frowned.

Nelson leaned back in his chair. "Why'd you leave?"

"I was married. It didn't work out."

The captain nodded. "I'm sorry. Do you keep in contact with anyone there now?"

Wilder shrugged. "Only my little brother."

"Does he know you're a detective?" Simpson asked.

Wilder looked over at the man, and his eyes caught on a file in Simpson's lap. *Ah.*

This wasn't some friendly get-to-know-you conversation; something was going on in his old town.

He pursed his lips. "He does, but I swore him to secrecy years ago. He hasn't told anyone. Not even our parents."

Nelson's brow furrowed. "Why did you swear him to secrecy?"

"Like I mentioned, I was married. I didn't want my ex to find me."

Nelson shared a look with Simpson, and Wilder shifted in his seat. He really wasn't comfortable talking about his personal life.

"Was she a stalker?"

"No. I'd just rather not see her."

"I hope for your sake she moved out of town."

Wilder braced himself. Whatever was coming wasn't good.

He glanced between the two men. When neither spoke, he asked, "Why? What's going on?"

Detective Simpson cleared his throat. "Our office has an ongoing investigation into the distribution of meth in our county. We were recently given a tip from a reliable source that a rival group wants to take over the distribution in Fisher Springs, and they've made a threat."

Meth in Fisher Springs?

What the hell had happened since he left? The town was small and full of families—at least, it used to be.

"Simpson is an old family friend," the captain explained, "and when he mentioned that town, I thought it sounded familiar. So, we've come up with a plan."

Oh no. Wilder groaned. *This can't be happening.*

His captain confirmed his fears. "We'd like for you to go back to your hometown. Undercover."

He took a deep breath, trying to find the words to decline without risking his job. There was no way he could just pop back into town like nothing had happened.

"I didn't leave on the best of terms," he hedged.

Simpson and Nelson exchanged another look, then Simpson leaned forward.

"This threat endangers the entire town. I'm sure you must have family or friends you care about there?"

That was a low blow, but yes, he had family there. William and his fiancée. And his parents — though he hadn't spoken to them in ten years.

Part of him hoped that maybe if he went to William's wedding, he could change the relationship with his parents.

As far as old friends, his first thought was Kate.

No, I'm not going to go there. Besides, she's probably left town with some guy by now. She talked about living in the city often enough.

Nelson spoke up in the silence. "I overheard Dane saying you were invited to your brother's wedding... That's perfect."

Well, shit.

Saying no was getting harder and harder. Could he really go back to Fisher Springs?

He took another deep breath. Yes, he could. The more he thought about it, the more he was certain Kate had moved on by now. She'd always said she wanted to leave that town; It was him that wanted to stay. That should have been his first clue how mismatched they were.

Shaking off the thought, Wilder asked, "What exactly do you know?"

Simpson held up the file from his lap. "This is for you. We don't have a lot of details, but what we do have comes from an informant who lives in that town. He says a man named Jerry Blight is responsible for all the meth in Fisher Springs."

Jerry Blight? "I don't know the guy."

"I'm not surprised. According to the background check we ran, he doesn't live there—and he never has."

"But you're sure he's the guy behind it all?"

Simpson shrugged. "That's what our informant told us, and I trust him.

Wilder made a mental note to read over Blight's entire file. If he was bringing drugs into town, he had to be stopped.

"There is something else you need to know. That rival gang that wants to take over distribution? Blight isn't taking them seriously, but the FBI has been tracking them long enough to know they will follow through on their threat."

"The FBI is on this?"

Simpson swiped at some lint on his pants. "Yes, I've worked with them on and off over the years. When I found out the threat is coming from the Bannons in Idaho, I ran it by one of my contacts at the agency. They've been monitoring them for years."

"Coleman," the captain started, "Blight has been given until July fourth to clear out. If he doesn't, the gang will bomb the town."

"Bomb? Did you say *bomb*?"

Nelson nodded.

Shit.

"But everyone will be hanging out in the town park for the annual July Fourth festival! They'll be easy targets."

Not to mention, William's wedding was scheduled for July fifth, so even more people would be at risk, with guests coming in that weekend for the festivities.

He released a sigh. "Sounds like I have no choice but to go back."

"Glad to hear it," Nelson gave a nod. "We rented an apartment for you in town."

Wilder gaped at him. "An apartment? Am I moving back?"

"You will go this weekend and stay through July fifth."

That's over a month. Fuck.

Going back for a wedding was already going to be hard enough, but to go back and live there?

Wilder swallowed. This wasn't going to be easy.

"But tell people you're there to stay," his captain added. "We've got some references you can use to get a job in construction."

"Construction?"

Simpson turned to him. "The tip we got is that a build site might be the location where the drugs are being delivered. It could help if you get a job with the contracted firm."

"If that doesn't work out, tell everyone you've returned to help with your brother's wedding."

He held back a scoff but didn't even try to hide the sarcastic edge to his voice. "Wedding Planner Wilder," he muttered. "Yeah, they'll buy that."

No one in Fisher Springs would believe for a minute he would help out with someone's wedding—not even his little brother's. Not after the shit-show that had been his marriage.

Chapter Two

"Thank you so much for all that you've done for us," Holly said.

Kate took a bite of her cotton candy, savoring the sugary goodness. She allowed herself one of these sweet treats only on Memorial Day weekend each year, when the main park in Fisher Springs was set up with carnival rides, games to win stuffed animals, and booths selling snacks.

"Of course. I'm always happy to help," she grinned. "Despite your wedding being mere weeks away, it looks like everything will go well."

Kate had agreed to assist Holly with some wedding details so that she and William could save on costs. Kate didn't mind; in fact, she enjoyed it.

"My favorite part was the cake tasting. I'm sorry William wasn't able to participate, but I have to say I loved stepping in for him. I swear I can still taste the strawberry cake."

Holly laughed. "I appreciated having you there. According to William, *'cake is cake.'*" She rolled her eyes.

"Cake *is* just cake," William insisted, appearing behind Holly. "And see? You were able to decide without me."

He wrapped his arms around Holly's waist and kissed her cheek. She spun in his arms and returned the kiss.

"Family event, here, you two," Kate warned.

She was happy for her friend, but of all the men in the world, why did she have to fall in love with William? He looked too much like his older brother with his deep blue eyes and dark wavy hair.

It was hard to watch the two of them sometimes; it reminded her of what she'd had once upon a time… before the love of her life refused to trust her, and left town with her heart.

Ugh, she had to shake the bad mood she was in. Ever since her birthday party at Brannigan's Pub last weekend, she'd been in a funk. In the middle of the festivities, she had looked around and discovered she was the only single person in the room — well, her and Scott Fisher, but that asshole hadn't been invited to her party. He just happened to be at the pub at the same time. Unfortunately, it was a public place, so as much as she'd wanted to toss him out, she couldn't.

Maybe it was seeing Scott that had set off her funk. After all, it was his fault her husband had left her ten years ago.

Since then, she'd dated here and there but those were all fleeting attachments, except for with Mitchell last year.

While she'd enjoyed her brief fling with the FBI agent, she'd known he wasn't forever material. He had been clear that he was only in town for an investigation, and that was fine with her. But that was the first time since her ex-husband that she'd allowed herself to be with one man for more than a few days. And she'd liked it.

A bit too much.

"You, okay? You're frowning while holding cotton candy," Holly said.

Kate sighed. "Yeah. Just tired. I didn't sleep well last night."

Holly bumped her with her hip. "I'm sorry. It was the wine, wasn't it?"

After trying all those yummy cakes yesterday, they went back to Kate's house to taste wines for the wedding. They ended up opening four bottles and drinking a lot of them. After William had picked Holly up, Kate tried to sleep, but her mind kept going back to Wilder. Something that had been happening ever since she'd overheard William tell Holly that Wilder hadn't responded to their wedding invitation.

"It might have been the wine," she lied.

"I know what would make you feel better," Holly said with a wink. "A man. Did you hear that Colt Fisher is back in town? He's an attorney now,

bought Mr. Anderson's practice. He's right over there."
She nodded to their left.

Is she kidding?

"No thanks. Aside from the fact I'm off the market for now, I'd never give a Fisher the time of day."

"Off the market?" William grinned. "Are you seeing someone?"

Kate shook her head. "No, I just want to focus on my designs for now."

"Does this mean you got the contract?" Holly asked.

Kate smiled. "It does. Martin called me yesterday. I have a lot of work to do, coming up with the landscaping for all the homes in his newest development."

"That's wonderful news! Congratulations!" Holly hugged her.

"Thanks. Hey, I'm going to find the bathroom. I'll meet you after?"

"We'll meet you at the beer garden."

"Sounds good."

Kate needed a moment. The smile on William's face when he thought she might have moved on was too much. Although she never asked him, she knew he talked to his brother and was all caught up about his life.

Odds were that Wilder had remarried and now had a large family somewhere. That had been his dream. And while part of her wanted to know, part of her knew it would tear her apart to hear. But maybe it would help her finally move on and take a risk trusting someone again.

Wilder had obviously had no problem turning his back on her, and here she was ten years later, still unwilling to give her heart to another man.

Okay, seriously, I have to snap out of it. Focus on anything else.

Taking in the crowd at the carnival put a smile on her face. Honestly, she loved everything about Fisher Springs. And after winning the contract with Martin's company, her landscape design business was going to take off. Then she could quit the diner.

While she loved working there, her back and feet were done with standing for long shifts.

After exiting the restroom, she almost ran into Chase and Harmony.

"Hey, stranger."

They were holding hands. Yep, everyone was coupled up. In her other hand, Harmony held a large stuffed tiger.

"Hey! Good to see you guys. I see you are enjoying the games."

"Whatever," Chase said.

Harmony laughed. "He's just sore that I beat him at Skee-ball."

"I'm not sore. And it doesn't matter because I'll beat you at the most important game here."

"Oh yeah, what's that?"

"The batting cage." Chase grinned.

Harmony rolled her eyes. "The one thing he knows he can win at. Hey, are you here with Holly?"

"Yes, I'm supposed to meet her and William at the beer garden."

"Beer garden? Well, let's go!" Chase said enthusiastically.

The smell of kettle corn wafted in the air as a group of teenagers ran by them laughing.

"Tabitha!" Harmony yelled.

Tabitha smiled at them from a booth that had a large poster for Fisher Springs Bank behind her. She felt bad for their friend being stuck in a booth working instead of having fun with them.

"I have something I need to talk to her about. Go ahead, I'll catch up." Harmony waved them off.

"Sounds good," Chase told her.

As she headed toward her friend, he put his arm over Kate's shoulder. They'd been friends since high school and were more like brother and sister than friends.

"I want to plan a romantic weekend away for me and Harmony," Chase revealed when they were out of earshot. "Has she recently mentioned any places she wants to go?"

"Hmm. She did say something about wanting to stay on a houseboat sometime."

"Shit. That sounds expensive."

Kate laughed.

As they rounded the corner of the beer garden, she heard Holly's voice.

"Wow, you haven't changed a bit."

A moment later, William laughed in response to something Kate didn't hear. Then she heard Holly again.

"I didn't expect you to be here. I'll be right back." Her head was turned as she moved, and she walked right into Kate.

"Oh, Kate! I'm sorry. Come with me." Holly looped her arm through hers and pulled her away from Chase.

"Kate?"

No. That couldn't be *his* voice.

Nausea rolled through her as she shook her arm loose and stepped around Holly.

Wilder.

Her body tingled, and she felt lightheaded. Damn, was she going to faint?

Taking a deep breath, she studied him. He looked the same, except there were some light lines around his eyes. They weren't smile lines, though; he didn't smile at her. No, pain emanated from his gaze and pulled at her heartstrings, just as it did that fateful night.

She took a step back.

She needed air; being this close to him hurt too much.

Kate continued to back up, then finally turned and walked as fast as she could toward the carnival rides. Her car was parked in the lot on the other side, she just needed to get there.

"Kate, I'm so sorry." Holly caught up to her at a jog. "I didn't know he was coming here today. William didn't either."

Kate picked up her pace. She had to get out of there. "I was bound to run into him someday. Honestly, I can't believe it took ten years." She sniffled.

Dammit. She was crying.

Ten years.

Ten years she should have had with him, but no, he'd refused to believe her. After all they had been through, one bump in the road, and he'd left.

Guess he never loved me like I thought he did.

"Kate."

Him again.

She stopped and heard his footsteps drawing nearer. His gait was different from Holly's, who stood quietly to the side.

With a deep breath, Kate turned around. A traitorous tear fell down her cheek.

His eyes tracked its movement before coming back up to hers. "Kate."

Was that regret she saw in his eyes? No, only indifference.

She squeezed her eyes shut. Because of this man, she'd never had another relationship. How could she, after he'd cut her so deep? It wasn't worth it.

"Holly says you're helping her with the wedding?" Wilder asked.

Her eyes popped open. "I am."

"I'm just going to go back to William," Holly said lightly, then she tiptoed away.

Wilder stared out toward the carnival rides.

God, he has the same gorgeous blue eyes and those long, dark lashes.

She wondered if he was remembering all the years they had come to this festival. All the years they'd ridden the Ferris wheel and made out at the top.

When he turned back to her, he was frowning. "We will likely see each other over the next month. I can be civil if you can. For their sake."

For their sake? Civil? Had this man ever loved her? He was being so cold, and his words felt like a dagger in her chest.

She wanted to scream at him, but no, she wouldn't give him that. Instead, she took a deep breath. "Sure. I think I can manage."

He continued to stare at her.

"Anything else?" she asked.

He shook his head.

They hadn't seen each other in ten years, and he had nothing to say to her?

He probably hasn't even thought about me before now.

That thought crushed her.

Without another word, she pivoted on her heel and got the hell away from Wilder. Once she'd made it a safe distance, she let the sobs come.

Chapter Three

Wilder unclenched his fists as Kate stormed off. *Shit.*

He'd not been prepared for that. He knew coming back to town meant he would run into people from his old life, but he'd convinced himself that wouldn't include Kate.

But living in denial had brought him to standing there like an asshole, his heart nearly pounding out of his chest.

She was more beautiful than he remembered. Her dark hair was longer and hung in waves. But what gutted him were those brown eyes staring up at him as they welled with tears.

Ten years might have passed, but the moment he'd seen her, all the pain had returned.

Looks like it did for her too.

But what surprised him even more was that he missed her. Seeing her against the backdrop of the carnival rides, memories had rushed back to him. She wasn't just his wife; she'd been his best friend. And damn, he missed her.

But no, he wouldn't let his heart go there again. Not after what had happened. He was done with relationships.

Unfortunately, with Kate still living in Fisher Springs and helping with his brother's wedding, there was no way he could avoid her.

Well, fuck. At least she'd agreed to be civil.

He huffed to himself. *Civil.*

He couldn't believe the words even as they were coming out of his mouth. They sounded so cold. But hell, he had to remain detached. After he'd left, he was a shell of a man. He couldn't let her break him again, couldn't afford to be anything more than civil.

And he was only doing that much out of respect for his brother and to get through his investigation. As far as the case went, he had no idea who all could be involved, so rubbing anyone the wrong way would be a huge mistake.

But seeing her so cozy with Chase had brought back his anger. She looked so wrong under his arm. Hell, she'd look wrong to him under anyone's arm.

Is she with Chase now?

At least he was a nice guy. Or, he had been.

Maybe he should have asked William for an update on Kate before he came back. At least then he would have known what he was walking into.

Frustrated at himself — at the whole damn situation, really — he made his way back to Holly and his brother, as well as Chase… who was kissing a redhead.

Wait, is that Harmony? What the fuck?

His brother was staring at him. "That looked intense."

Wilder tore his eyes from Chase to look William in the eye as he assured him, "We'll be fine. Don't worry about your wedding."

But he did look worried. So did Holly.

"If I'd known you were coming, I wouldn't have asked for her help," she said, her brows knitted.

"No offense, brother, but why *are* you back in town so early? The wedding isn't for a month," William said.

Wilder didn't hear his question. He was focused once more on Chase and Harmony.

When the couple finally detached from each other, she was beaming at him.

"Are you two together?" Wilder asked.

Chase grinned. "We are. A lot has changed since you left."

Wilder glanced back the direction Kate had gone. *Maybe not so much has.*

He hadn't been sure how he'd react the first time he saw Kate again, but jealousy had not been on that list.

"I can see that," he told Chase finally, then turned back to William. "I'm sorry, what did you say?"

"I asked why you are in town a month before my wedding."

Wilder wanted to tell his brother the truth, but until he knew who might be involved with Blight, he'd have to keep the fact he was there undercover close to his chest.

He shrugged. "I thought I could help out with anything you needed. I didn't realize you already had Kate."

"Actually, more help would be wonderful," Holly said. "I've been really stressed out, trying to get everything done — in addition to getting the shop ready for my two-week absence for our honeymoon."

Dammit, I guess Wedding Planner Wilder is making his debut after all.

He gave her a tight smile. "Just let me know what you need."

"I will. Thanks. Do you by chance know how to sew?" Holly asked.

William laughed. "He sewed up my arm once when we were kids. Does that count?"

Wilder chuckled at the reminder.

When they were boys, his brother had climbed a tree and tied a rope to the highest branch he could reach. Then he held onto the other end, thinking he could rappel down the tree holding only the rope. He fell the last four feet, but by some miracle, didn't break anything. Instead, he suffered a deep cut on his arm.

Horrified that their parents would find out, he'd begged Wilder to sew it up. Doing his big brother duty, Wilder had dug into his mom's sewing kit, retrieved the black thread, and had begun stitching

William up when their mother caught them in the bathroom.

"That had to have hurt like hell," Wilder rumbled, shaking his head.

"It did, but I feared the punishment, so I kept quiet."

Holly looked William up and down. "Where was this cut? I've never found any large scars."

William pointed it out. He'd gotten lucky; Mom had taken him straight to the emergency room, and they'd stitched him up correctly. He ended up with only a small scar.

"But why would I need to know how to sew?" Wilder asked, trying to steer the conversation back on target.

"Oh," Holly grinned. "I'm looking for someone to sub for my quilting class while I'm gone."

Wilder shook his head again. "That wouldn't be me. I have no skills in that department."

She shrugged. "Never hurts to ask."

"You teach quilting?" he asked, realizing he didn't know what Holly did for a living.

"Yes, it helps attract business to the quilt shop."

Ah. He nodded. "William mentioned you opened a new shop in town."

"I did. Through the Needle. It's been a blast getting to do what I love all day."

Wilder wondered what Kate did for work and if she loved it. She'd worked at the local diner after they were married; she always said she loved talking to the customers each day, especially the regulars.

He smiled, recounting some of the stories she'd share at the end of each day.

"Okay, who's ready to go on some rides?" Harmony asked as she led Chase toward the Ferris wheel.

Wilder didn't reply. Being at the carnival was the last thing he wanted right now. It held too many memories of him and Kate.

But he had to admit it was the perfect chance to get reacquainted with his old town before the real investigation began.

But can I do it without running into too many people I know?

There would be questions, and after his brief conversation with Kate, he wasn't in the mood to give any answers.

He was a dumbass if he thought he could avoid running into people he knew in a small town. Or dodge all the questions.

First, he saw Kate's mother. Fortunately, he was able to duck behind a guy selling cotton candy before she spotted him. Then he saw Lily, Kate's little sister; he hadn't recognized her at first, but William clued him in when Lily glared at him and didn't say a word.

He was relieved when the sun finally set, thinking the darkness would hide him, but no such luck. He'd just finished eating a corndog and tossing the wrapper in the garbage when he ran smack into Kate's father, Frank Waters, the mayor of the town.

"Wilder? Is that you?"

"Yes, sir."

The man's expression went from surprise to anger. "Why are you back?"

Wilder sighed. *He still hates me – possibly more now.* "I'm back for my brother's wedding."

"But that's over a month away. Are you staying until then?"

Not that it was any of Frank's business, but sometimes answering his questions was easier than arguing with him.

Wilder sighed. "I am."

Frank nodded. "This is just a visit, right?"

Wilder shrugged. "I'm still deciding."

The mayor crossed his arms. "You destroyed my daughter. I hope you don't plan on talking to her while you're here."

Don't talk to her? Does he know his daughter is helping Holly with the wedding?

"I'll try my best," he bit out, then shoved past him to walk back to his friends.

He had destroyed *her*? Kate's family had obviously gotten a different version of reality. Truthfully, it was Wilder who had been destroyed.

But he and Frank had never seen eye to eye. The man had even tried to talk Kate out of marrying Wilder all those years ago because he never thought him good enough.

Shaking off the memory, Wilder made it back to the table.

"Since the wedding is in the Chanler mansion's garden, we can invite up to one hundred people," Holly was saying.

"One hundred?" Wilder echoed in surprise. "There aren't enough hotel rooms in town to accommodate that many."

"I was worried about that too, but Mr. Smythe offered up the vacancies at his RV resort. So far, we have twenty guests who said they would love to stay there. Plus, the hotel gave us all the rooms they had available. Between that and Lauren and Nick taking on fifteen guests at the Chanler mansion, and all of my friends taking in a guest or two, we were able to get accommodations for everyone who wanted to be here for the Fourth of July celebration."

Wilder ran his hand over his face. *Shit.* That was a lot more people than he had predicted. A lot more potential casualties.

His job was to protect everyone in town from the bomb that was supposed to be placed in the heart of the weekend's festivities. Safety grew harder to attain as the guest list got longer. Simpson promised he would have bomb-sniffing dogs on site starting July third, but could Wilder trust that?

Not a chance in hell.

"Are you sure you want that many people? Wouldn't something smaller, more intimate be nice?" Wilder asked.

William frowned. "Wilder, the invitations have already gone out, and most have RSVPed."

"I thought you only set a date a week ago."

"It was over a month ago," William said.

A month? Shit. Had he put off calling his brother for that long?

"Hey, let's take a walk." William was by his side.

"Sure."

Once they were out of earshot of the group, William stopped. "Are you all right?"

"What? Yeah, I'm fine."

William nodded. "Kate looked as though she'd seen a ghost earlier. Did you two ever talk after you left?"

Wilder shook his head. "No. I sent the divorce papers, she signed them, and that was it."

He'd never talked to his brother about what happened. Hell, he'd never talked to anyone. It was the last thing he wanted to replay in his mind.

"That was it?" William scoffed.

"What?" Wilder knew his brother well enough to know the man had something to say.

"At the time, I had no idea what you were going through, but now that I'm about to get married, I can't imagine walking away from Holly like that and never looking back."

Wilder's eyebrows shot up. "Even if you literally found her in bed with another man?"

"Did you let her explain?"

"The situation was pretty self-explanatory."

William shook his head. "I'm sorry. That had to really suck, but I still can't understand how you never spoke. Didn't you want to know why?"

Wilder gave a wry laugh. "I didn't need to. Kate liked to go out drinking, and that night, she took it too far."

"Shit. All of it sucks. But can you tell me one thing?"

"One thing," he relented. "And then can we get off this topic?"

William nodded.

"Okay."

"I've always wanted to ask you this but figured you'd hang up on me over the phone."

Shit. I'm not going to like this.

"Why the hell is Dad so angry with you?"

He's right. I would have cut the call short.

He flattened his lips. "He disagreed with how I handled things."

That was the truth, for the most part.

"I thought it was because you changed your last name. I heard about that one for a while," William said.

"That's part of it."

His dad chose to take it as the ultimate insult that Wilder had switched to his mother's name, instead of trying to understand why he'd done it. But all that boiled down to…

"Dad thought I should have given Kate another chance."

William nodded but said nothing.

Wilder rolled his eyes. "I'm guessing you do too."

William held up his hands. "I didn't say that. But I think we can both understand why Dad would."

Wilder sighed. Yeah, the man had a *very* different view of marriage than his sons did.

"Wow! Is that really you, Wilder?" a voice asked from behind him.

He spun to find Bridgette Pearlman wearing very short shorts and a tank top. She still looked like the cheerleader she was in high school, with her hair in a long blonde braid. She hadn't given him the time of day when they were teenagers, but clearly her taste had changed, given the way her eyes now scanned him up and down.

"Hey, Bridgette," he said warily. "Yeah, I'm back for my brother's wedding."

Something banged into his shin.

"*Ouch.*" He glanced up to see his brother staring at him with wide eyes and thinned lips.

Oh shit, was he not supposed to mention the wedding?

"William, you're getting married? To Holly? Oh, I can't wait!" She clapped her hands and turned back to Wilder. "Do you want to go on the Ferris wheel with me, Wilder?" Her eyes raked over his body again, leaving no doubt what she wanted.

"Uh, maybe a raincheck?" he suggested clumsily. "I haven't seen my brother in quite some time."

"Sure. We should get together this week." She pulled her phone out from her tight back pocket. "What's your phone number?"

"What?"

Her smile grew like he had said something funny. "Your phone number. I'll call you so you have mine."

He caught his brother's eye and the fucker looked away, suppressing a laugh. Glancing back to her with discomfort knotting his stomach, he said, "Bridgette, I'm afraid I'm between phones at the moment. But I'm sure I can get your number from Holly, right?"

Her cheeks flushed. "Sure. I'll see you around."

Once she was out of hearing range, William burst out laughing.

"I was about to kill you for telling her about the wedding, no way in hell is she going, but then you said you were 'between phones'. Seriously, brother, that was the biggest blow-off."

"Why didn't you want her to know about the wedding?"

William winced. Then he glanced around before his gaze came back to Wilder's. "We hooked up a few times. It was before Holly, and she knows. But then Bridgette tried to get with me again after I made it clear I was with Holly. Let's just say you don't want to put those two in the same room."

He frowned. "If she was with you, then why would she want me?"

Shit, what was he saying? He'd already forgotten what a small town this was.

Again, William laughed. "You're the shiny new toy in town."

Wilder shook his head.

"You've been gone a while, but nowadays, there aren't too many single folks around here—especially men. So be ready. I'm sure Bridgette won't be the only one hitting on you."

"Not interested. I'm here for your wedding, and that's it."

"Well, you go ahead and tell the women that." He gave a wink. "Let's head back."

William turned to walk back to the group, but Wilder didn't follow.

"You go ahead, have fun. I'm going to call it a night."

"Okay, well, thanks for hanging out with us for a while. Oh, before I forget, I've got an appointment for my tux fitting. I'll call and see if they can squeeze you in too. It's tomorrow at four."

Resigned to his fate, Wilder gave a nod. "Sure thing. Just let me know."

He was halfway to his car when yet another familiar voice called out to him.

"Wilder? I heard you were back."

Scott fucking Fisher had the nerve to talk to him after what he'd done?

Silently, he spun around, not bothering to mask the pure hatred he knew must be in his eyes.

"Hey, have you seen Kate?" Scott asked. "She's looking good, isn't she?"

Oh, no the fuck he didn't.

Wilder swung as hard as he could, and Scott Fisher went down with a thud, both hands holding his face.

Wilder couldn't help his smile as the other man cursed and groaned on the ground. He resumed the walk to his car, rubbing his knuckles.

They'd hurt like hell tomorrow, but it was worth it.

Chapter Four

Kate's shoulders tightened as her little sister Lily walked into Lucky's Diner the next morning. She glanced over at Harmony, but she was busy with other customers. There was no avoiding Lily.

Lily had sent a text saying they needed to talk. Kate knew what about, and it was the last thing she wanted to discuss. But she couldn't avoid her sister, considering she was in the middle of her shift, and they were just past the lunch rush so there weren't many other customers at the moment.

Kate wiped down a menu then placed it on the clean pile. *'As long as they aren't sticky, they are clean enough.'* That's what Logan always said.

Something she and Harmony never agreed with.

"How's my favorite sister?" Lily asked as she sat at the counter.

Kate laughed. "You mean your only sister?"

Lily grinned. "Still my favorite."

They'd grown a lot closer since Lily had moved back to town—a move Kate believed to be a miracle. As far as Lily had been concerned, the further from this town she could get, the better. She'd also had an ex she'd been trying to avoid… but life had a way of throwing funny curves. Now, her and her ex, Ryker, were back together, and Kate was happy because her sister was staying local.

Lily grew serious as she watched Kate work. "Wilder is back in town. Have you seen him?"

She growled low in her throat.

Ever since his reappearance yesterday, everyone had been asking her about him—as if she were his keeper and knew why he was here and how long he was going to stay. Several had even asked what he had been up to the last ten years.

Kate wondered the same thing. Then she thought about *her* life over the last ten years.

Not a lot had changed. When he left, she had been working at the diner; here she still was, ten years later. But she *had* started her own landscape design business, and while it hadn't really taken off yet, it did make her some money.

Slapping down another 'clean' menu, Kate snapped, "Yes, I saw him. He's here for his brother's wedding, and that's all I know."

Lily leaned back and arched a brow.

Kate exhaled through her nose. "Sorry. I've been getting a lot of questions."

The bell over the door rang, and in walked Scott Fisher. Well, a beat-up, hungover version of the man.

Not that he looked that good to start with.

God, she hated him. And why the hell was he coming in and staring at her?

"What the fuck happened to you?" Logan rumbled, coming out of the back.

"I saw Wilder last night." He was still staring at Kate. "Let's just say he's still mad."

"Don't look at me like I care," Kate scoffed, a tightness in her chest. "Logan, I'm taking my break now."

She spun around and stormed past everyone, through the kitchen, and out the back door. Then she sucked in a deep breath.

Why the hell had Wilder punched Scott after all these years?

Does that mean he still has feelings for me? Her stomach fluttered with hope.

No. Wilder hated her. She knew that much. And the part that really sucked was she didn't do anything wrong. But he wouldn't listen, wouldn't believe her.

She took another breath.

And her stomach had no business fluttering. Even if her ex-husband wanted her back, he'd hurt her too deeply. That was in her past. She'd moved on.

Hadn't she?

"Hey, how are you doing?" Harmony stepped up beside her.

"Not great."

Harmony nodded. "Logan said you ran out after seeing Scott. I have to say… it's kind of nice to see that someone finally punched that asshole."

Kate laughed. Her friend was right.

Harmony joined in, then griped, "Just because he has the last name Fisher doesn't mean he's contributed anything to this town. Damn, why do the older folks treat him so well?"

Kate shook her head. "They don't know him. They only know his father."

"Well, maybe they'll hear he got his ass handed to him by someone who knows him better."

"And how would they hear?"

Harmony grinned. "Witnesses. A few people saw what happened, and you know how that kind of thing spreads through town. When I stopped at the Cozy Croissant this morning, Adele told me all about it."

Kate's hands flew to her face. "Oh no. What are they saying?"

"That Wilder's back and pissed. Bets have been placed on how long it will be before you two are back together."

"No. No, no, no. Not happening."

"No? What if he says he wants you back? You were so in love with him."

"Yes, that's just it. *I* was in love with *him*. Clearly it wasn't mutual, because he wouldn't even listen to my version of the events. He believed *Scott*. I had to explain my side in a voicemail—and he never called back! The divorce papers came two weeks later."

Before Harmony could reply, Logan leaned out the back door.

"Hey, you two ready to come back? A big group just came in."

"Break's over," Harmony muttered with a sigh, then she turned and went back in.

Kate took one more deep breath and followed, hoping Scott wouldn't still be inside.

Scott had still been inside, but Kate was so busy, she was able to ignore him.

Well, at least she pretended to. But his presence had her tense for the rest of the day, so by the end of her shift, she just wanted to go home and take a long, hot bath.

Wilder would probably be surprised by that choice.

While she had been a bit irresponsible when she was younger, that wasn't her anymore; she'd saved up, bought a house, and was now working hard to grow her own business. She loved the diner, but it wasn't a long-term career option—not when she came home every day with aching feet and a sore back.

She smiled as her house came into view. It was that time of year when many of her flowering bushes were in bloom. She was so proud of the garden she'd designed for herself; she felt a little boost every time she got to see it. But her good mood soured when she spotted another car parked in her driveway.

Her mother's. Kate did her best to avoid conversations with the woman, but it looked like she wasn't going to be able to do that today.

Steeling herself, she stepped up on her porch to find her mom in one of the two chairs. As usual, her mother's appearance was flawless. She wore a yellow dress, and her medium-length hair hung in waves at her shoulders, perfectly coiffed.

"Good afternoon, Kate."

"Hello, Mother. To what do I owe this surprise visit?"

"Sit." The older woman patted the other chair.

Kate cautiously obeyed.

She had a pretty good idea why her mother was here. One topic they'd never agreed on was Wilder; her parents never thought he was good enough. They hadn't supported the marriage and were outright pissed when she and Wilder returned home from a Las Vegas vacation announcing to everyone that they had eloped.

Her parents consulted with an attorney to try to get the marriage annulled, but Kate and Wilder had both been eighteen, legal adults who wanted to be married, so her parents had no choice but to finally give up.

That was the beginning of the end of her relationship with them.

The final nail in the coffin was after Wilder left. The things her parents said.

She closed her eyes. No, she wouldn't go there.

"Rumor is that Wilder is back in town. Have you seen him yet?"

And there it was.

"Yes."

Keep it short and simple.

"I hope you aren't getting all swoony over that boy again. Lord knows he was bad news for this family then, and he likely still is."

Kate stood. "Exactly how was he ever bad news? He was hard-working and he treated me well."

Her mother scoffed and then also stood. "Treated you well? He left at the first sign of difficulty! You told him you didn't do what he thought, and everyone knows that Fisher boy is trouble, but Wilder left anyway. That's not how a man behaves."

He wasn't a man back then. He was still a boy.

Her thoughts startled her. She'd never been sympathetic to his response… but that *was* ten years ago. They were twenty-one then, but they had both been so young, naïve. Maybe he had changed.

She didn't give her mother any clue about where her thoughts had led her. "If you are here to warn me off of him, don't bother. He's still very angry with me, and I doubt I'll see him much."

Except that he's here for a month to help with the same wedding I'm helping with…

"I'm happy to hear that. Your father will be relieved as well." Her mom brushed off her skirt. "And I'd love it if you could come to Sunday dinner. It's been too long."

Kate stared at her hydrangea bush just off the porch, noting it needed tending. Her entire garden did.

She mentally marked it on her calendar for Sunday.

"I'll think about it."

She had no intention of going, but she wasn't about to start an argument on her front porch.

Her mom pursed her lips. "Okay. I guess that's all I can ask. See you Sunday."

Kate had to suppress her eye roll.

After her mother left, Kate went inside and tossed her purse on the kitchen table. Immediately, her cellphone rang.

Fishing the device out of her purse, she checked the screen and saw the caller was Martin Fisher. Just seeing his name reminded her of seeing his cousin Scott and his black eye earlier. She chuckled to herself before answering the call.

"Hello, Martin," she answered, heading to the cupboard for a glass.

"Kate, do you have time to meet? I need to make a change to your designs."

She frowned as she turned on the kitchen faucet. "What kind of changes?"

"Oh, nothing serious. I wouldn't want to alter your overall vision; your designs are fantastic. In fact, if this contract goes well, I should be able to put you on retainer for future projects."

Kate set aside her full glass and jumped up and down, barely holding back an excited squeal.

Martin Fisher's development company was growing, and there was no doubt a contract with him could fund her business by itself, paying all her expenses and then some.

"That sounds great," she told him after she'd composed herself.

"Good. I'm glad. Do you have time to discuss the changes over lunch tomorrow? Are you free?"

Lunch with Martin? She took a drink of water as she considered the invitation.

She'd dated him in high school briefly, before she'd started dating Wilder. In the years after her divorce, the man had asked her out now and again, but she always smiled and told him she wasn't the dating type, and he'd take it well enough.

But something about this lunch had her worried.

He must have sensed her concern. He assured her, "This would only be a business lunch, Kate."

She swallowed. "Okay."

I can do lunch. It's no big deal, right?

"I'll text you the details," he said with a smile on his voice. "I gotta go."

That was the happiest she'd ever heard the man.

I really hope he won't try to make this personal.

Chapter Five

Wilder had spent the weekend getting settled into his new apartment. This morning as he walked into the living room, he shook his head as he glanced around.

The place came furnished, but it looked like Simpson had just grabbed leftover items from the police station. Instead of a couch in his living room, Wilder had five chairs, lined up like they were in a waiting room. On two of the walls hung posters with inspirational quotes.

The department had basically assured he would never entertain anyone here. Hell, *he* could barely stand the room. He'd likely be spending his time in the bedroom so as not to risk going fucking nuts.

Although William might stop by…

He'd definitely comment on Wilder's taste in decor.

Then his mind flashed to Kate and what her reaction might be upon entering the apartment.

He sighed. He had to stop thinking about her.

Instead of ruminating further, he grabbed his phone and called Simpson. He was due to check in before ten am.

"Simpson here."

"It's Coleman. I'm settled."

"That's good."

He had to ask. "Hey, did you... pick out the furniture?"

Simpson laughed. "No, I asked an officer to pick up a few things, and he sent a photo after the fact. Sorry about that."

Wilder sighed. "Thankfully, this is temporary. It's just the job. Speaking of, now that I'm here, can you tell me who the informant is?"

Detective Simpson exhaled into the phone. "I guess it makes sense to tell you. It's Joey Dunin. Any chance you know him?"

Joey Dunin? An informant?

"I do, and that doesn't make any sense. He's the police chief's son. He was an officer here in Fisher Springs when I left."

What the hell has happened around here?

"Well, he worked his way up to detective. But according to him, once his mother died —"

"His mother *died*?"

That was a blow to the gut. Wilder had fond memories of Mrs. Dunin; she'd helped him and William more times than he could count. Whenever his parents would argue about one of his mother's affairs,

Wilder would grab William and head down the street to the Dunins. Mrs. Dunin was well aware of their home situation, and she always made the Coleman boys feel welcome.

Why hadn't William told him she'd died?

"Yeah, according to him and his father, who has bailed him out a few times—"

Wait, a few times?

"…his mother's death really took a toll on Joey. He didn't deal with it well. Then he broke his leg and was prescribed painkillers… He said it was all downhill from there."

I bet it was. Wilder sat down and rubbed his eyes. "I'm stunned. I knew Joey. He's the last person I'd ever suspect would get mixed up in something like this."

"Well, people can surprise you."

No shit.

"Joey's been a bit vague on his tips, unfortunately," Simpson continued. "But he mentioned that the drug deals go down at a housing construction site. I'm hoping the town is small enough you can figure out where that might be."

Wilder dipped his head. "I'll drive around and see what I can find."

He ended the call, and his mind drifted back to high school. Joey was a few years older than him, but he'd been nice to the underclassmen. Hell, he'd been nice to everyone.

Shit, his mom died and Wilder had no idea. He should have reached out after he left.

Too late now. And I have a job to do.

He decided a run was just what he needed to think through everything. He had to get his head on straight. Joey wasn't supposed to know Wilder was there undercover, so he needed to be ready to put on a poker face if he saw him.

After changing into shorts, he ran from his apartment to Main Street, cutting through downtown. Then he jogged over to the residential area behind Main Street. Not much had changed in town; there was a new accounting business, Harrow Accounting.

Looks like Mr. Anderson left his law practice to... He stopped jogging. *Seriously? Colt Fisher is an attorney now?* He laughed as he shook his head.

Not that he really knew the guy, but if the man had gone so far as to attend law school, he had more ambition than his brother, Scott.

Dammit. Now he was thinking of Scott, which made him think of Kate.

Stubbornly, he picked up his pace, though he slowed when he hit Main Street again, and a man watering a hanging basket caught his attention.

When he was growing up, a team of volunteers would hang large flower baskets every Memorial Day weekend, and then another team of volunteers would continue to water them throughout the summer. It looked like that hadn't changed, and the fact made him smile.

Truth be told, he missed it here. Working down in Summit County was fine, but he knew all these people, it was special. Well, until it wasn't. He couldn't have stayed, knowing the whole town knew what happened between him and Kate.

A heavenly scent drew his focus to Lucky's Diner and caused his stomach to growl. He was about to cross the street to check it out when Joey Dunin walked out of the diner.

Wilder abruptly spun and pretended to stare into the store window in front of him. Instead, he watched Joey in the reflection of the glass. His old friend was staring at his phone as he slowly shuffled down the sidewalk.

Certain the man was preoccupied, Wilder turned to get a better look.

Joey was a lot thinner than he remembered. And older. His face was worn more than it should be for a man in his mid-thirties.

When Joey rounded the corner a moment later, Wilder jogged the other way, back to his apartment. He wasn't sure why his instinct was to avoid Joey; he was going to have to face him sooner rather than later.

Doesn't mean it has to be now.

After he got home, he showered and ate a late breakfast. Then he did a quick search for new construction in Fisher Springs, hoping the housing development would be big enough to warrant a website.

He found it quickly: twenty-five new homes being built by Fisher Springs Development.

Not very creative with their name.

A quick review of their website revealed they had several projects around this town and the next one over. Maybe he should figure out who to contact for potential employment. When he clicked on the team page, he was surprised to see Martin Fisher staring back at him.

This is Martin's company? Well, shit.

He couldn't get away from the damn Fishers no matter how hard he tried.

He picked up a quarter from the kitchen table and rolled it across his knuckles and back. It soothed him. And right now, he needed soothing so he wouldn't drive over to Martin's and punch him in the face.

His phone buzzed with an email from Simpson. Attached were photos of what appeared to be a construction site, though the images were taken at a funny angle. If he had to guess, Wilder would say Joey was using his phone and trying not to be obvious about it.

As he flipped through the pictures, his eyes narrowed. The mayor was in some of the photos. *What the fuck?*

Was this Joey's way of saying the mayor was involved? Or did he just happen to be there?

Shit. How reliable is Joey these days? And if the information checks out, what is he getting out of this arrangement?

These were important questions, but he had to deal with one thing at a time.

After pouring his coffee in a to-go mug, Wilder headed out to the address for the housing development listed on the website. It was a road he wasn't familiar with, which was odd... he knew every road in Fisher Springs.

As he navigated to the area, though, he discovered a lot of new roads, until he found himself in the middle of a large, incomplete housing development. The front area had been cleared, and several cul-de-sacs paved. Toward the back were at least twenty homes in some state of construction.

As he continued down the main road, signs pointed him toward the model homes. Following their directions, he parked in front of one of the new houses.

He took a gulp of coffee as he thought through his story. It was plausible: he was back in town and considering buying a house as well as looking for employment.

Closing his eyes, he leaned back. No one would buy that. Then he had an idea. If anyone asked, he could lie and say he already saved up a down payment. With a resolute nod, he unbuckled his seatbelt and got out of his car.

The moment he stepped inside the house, he was assaulted by the scents of vanilla and freshly baked cookies. He discovered the source when his eyes landed on an entry table holding two burning candles.

"Good morning, are you interested in buying a house?"

Wilder turned to his left to find a man in a suit smiling at him. "I'm thinking about it," he lied.

How the hell would this place have anything to do with drugs going through Fisher Springs if anyone can pull up at any time to view a house?

"Fantastic. Come on in, and I'll show you what we have."

Wilder followed him into a home office that was well-decorated. Not that he knew much about decoration, but it was certainly nicer than what was in his own apartment.

The man showed him photos of three model homes. Smiling, he asked, "Do any of these interest you?"

Wilder scratched the back of his neck. "Can I see each one in person? I can't really tell from the photos."

"Of course. You're welcome to walk around this house, then the other two model houses are to the south. Go take a look, and when you are done, come back here and we can talk."

The man stuck his hand out, and Wilder gave it a good shake.

"Thank you."

Wilder walked through each house quickly, glancing out the windows as he went. There wasn't much to see outside. He needed to get closer to the construction crew.

As he descended the stairs of the last house back to the foyer, Martin Fisher was there.

"Wow, I heard you were back in town. Back for good, then?"

"Thinking about it. You know, hoping to mend some things with my family. Time will tell."

"Good. Happy to have you."

Although he had already done his research, he was curious if he could learn more.

"You involved in this project?" he asked.

Martin's lips curled up. "Yes, I am. I own the development company."

Wilder acted surprised. "Wow. That's huge, Martin."

Martin shrugged. "Yeah, I guess it is. And what have you been doing all these years?"

Wilder smiled. He'd rehearsed his story a few times and was ready. "Construction. You might recall that's what I was doing before I left. I'm actually looking for a job here in town too."

Martin nodded. "I do remember. Shame you left so suddenly. Sorry about Scott." His lip twitched.

Wilder gritted his teeth. That was one topic he had not planned on discussing. And why the hell was Martin bringing it up anyway?

"Saw it coming a mile away, you know," the man continued. "My cousin always had a thing for Kate."

What the fuck? Was he *trying* to piss him off?

"Oh wait," Martin's eyes widened. "Is that why you're in town? To win Kate back?"

Wilder took a calming breath, careful not to show this asshole that anything he said bothered him. "No, I'm not. Like I said, I'm here to mend my relationship with my family. I don't know if you heard, but my brother's getting married."

"That's good… about Kate. She's not the same girl you used to know. Not as innocent, if you know what I mean." Martin chuckled.

What the fuck was this guy's problem?

A woman entered the house. "Hey, Martin." Then she noticed the visitor. "Wilder? Is that you?"

She looked familiar, but he couldn't place her.

"Yes, it is."

She pulled him into a hug. "Oh my god, it's been so long!"

Her embrace caught him off guard, but he patted her on the back before he stepped back.

She was grinning. "You don't recognize me, do you?"

"I'm trying."

Martin laughed. "My cousin has changed a lot in ten years."

The woman elbowed Martin in the stomach, causing him to groan.

"Melia Fisher," she supplied. "I look a lot different than the last time you saw me."

She did look a lot different than she used to. Instead of a girl in pigtails, she was a woman wearing a fitted dress and revealing a decent amount of cleavage.

"Wow, you've changed."

In that moment, it struck him just how long he'd been gone. And he had to wonder how much everyone else had changed too.

"I have. You've been gone a long time. Are you looking for a home?" she asked.

"I'm thinking about it. I need to secure a job first."

She pulled a card out of her purse and handed it to him. "If you need a realtor, give me a call. It was nice seeing you again, Wilder."

Her eyes perused his body, and he shifted uncomfortably.

"Well, I should get going. I'll think about the house. Thanks." Wilder stepped around Martin and made his way toward the door.

"Wait!"

He turned to find Martin holding a card.

"Here's my foreman's contact information. If you're looking for work, he's a good guy to ask."

His foreman? Well, this could be a good lead.

He took the card. "Thank you. I think I will. Hey, do you mind if I look around the lots?"

Martin frowned. "It might be a bit muddy."

Wilder didn't respond, just waited silently.

"Okay," Martin relented, "but stay away from the construction areas. Liability issues and all."

"Sounds good. Thanks."

Before the other man could say another word about Kate, Wilder headed out the door, hopped in his car, and drove down to where the construction crew was located.

A couple of minutes later, he got out of his car and walked around, pretending to look at the lots while actually watching the construction workers.

Everyone was working hard. He saw absolutely nothing out of place. Taking stock of all the trucks and the supplies they held, he noted with dismay that it was all related to the houses.

What am I not seeing? Or did Joey give us false information?

Realizing he had more questions than when he arrived, he got back in his car and drove out of the development. When he figured he was a safe distance away, he pulled over to call Simpson.

"Simpson here."

"I went to the housing development and toured the model homes."

The other detective laughed. "Already thinking about moving there?"

"Ha ha. Anyway, I didn't see anything suspicious."

"Hmm. No delivery trucks?"

"All the trucks I saw were full of tools and building materials. I plan to go back and do some surveillance this afternoon, though."

"Sounds good. Let me know what you find."

"Will do," he replied, then hung up.

Hopefully, he wouldn't find Martin. Wilder would have to be careful with this investigation; too many people knew who he was, which meant he couldn't exactly sit in the open and play spy.

Chapter Six

Wilder closed his laptop and laid back on his bed that afternoon. He'd researched everything he could find on what Martin had been up to over the last ten years. The man had done well for himself. Though, Wilder couldn't help but wonder where Martin had gotten the cash to buy up all the property it appeared his company owned.

His stomach growled, urging him to take a break. Remembering the diner just a couple blocks over, he decided to walk over, and grab lunch to-go.

His hand was on the entrance of the diner when a deep voice came from behind him.

"Goin' to see Kate?"

He spun to see a large man with a beard and sleeves of tattoos. "Who are you?"

"Zach Brannigan. Good friend of Kate's."

What the fuck? Is this her boyfriend?

A wave of jealousy hit. The guy was good-looking and clearly possessive.

Wilder scoffed. "Don't worry. I'm not trying to move in on you."

He turned back and again grabbed the door handle, but Zach stepped between him and the door.

"Kate is workin' there. Maybe it's best if you find somewhere else to eat."

Fuck. As much as Wilder couldn't stand to be told what to do, the large guy had a point.

"There's a coffee shop up the block, Cozy Croissant. They sell food," Zach offered.

Wilder glanced in and saw Kate in a bright pink shirt and jeans, serving someone coffee. She looked good. He'd noticed at the festival; she was a little curvier. It made her hotter. God, she was still gorgeous.

The sight of her smiling at a customer cracked his heart open a little.

No. He shook his head, hoping to clear those thoughts. He couldn't let his mind go there. She'd crushed him; she'd known what his mom's affairs had done to his family, and Kate still did what she did. He couldn't trust her.

"Thanks for the advice." Wilder stepped back and headed in the direction of the coffee shop.

While Main Street still looked the same as it had ten years ago, the coffee shop was new, and he was curious what it was like. But next to the diner, before he'd made it more than a handful of steps, another business caught his eye. It was probably the display of women's lingerie in the windows. He slowed down.

Wait... is that a vibrator?

He glanced up and read the name of the shop: Love More.

What the fuck? Was this a sex shop on *Main Street*? There was no way.

One thing he remembered about this town was that the older residents, particularly the mayor, were insistent that everything look proper. They'd even stopped the high school cheerleaders from doing a car wash fundraiser because they were wearing shorts that were too short.

That had been a pity. He hadn't minded watching Kate all sudsed up and bent over the hood of that car.

He shook his head. *Stop.*

The memories kept rushing back. Memories he didn't want. He was grateful when he arrived at the coffee shop and could focus on his new surroundings.

As he stepped inside, he smiled. On each of the walls was a cartoon of a croissant. It was very creative and a great way to keep customers craving that doughy goodness. There was a scattering of tables throughout the shop. Up front, next to the cash register, was a display case with sandwiches and some baked goods.

He stepped up to the counter, and a blonde woman smiled.

"What can I get you?"

"I was looking for something to eat," he said as he glanced at the sweets on display.

A dark-haired woman stood up from behind the glass case. "I highly recommend the croissants. Adele here bakes them every morning."

Wow. That *was* tempting.

"Sure, that sounds great. I'll take a croissant and a regular coffee please."

After he paid, he spun around to leave but came face to face with the man he did not want to see. A black and blue eye stared back at him.

Scott fucking Fisher.

Wilder chose not to hide his smile at his handiwork. "Want me to make the other eye match?"

"Wilder. I'm glad I found you."

"Scott, didn't I make myself clear last night?"

Apparently not, because Scott motioned to a nearby table. "There's something I have to tell you and it can't wait."

Well, hell. It looked like Scott was going to keep tracking him down; might as well get whatever this was over with.

He sat at the table, and Scott sat across from him.

"What's so urgent?" Wilder asked.

"I never slept with Kate."

He jolted back; sure he must have heard him wrong. "What?"

Scott scratched behind his ear. It was something he used to do as a boy when he was nervous. "It was a setup. I'm so sorry. I ruined your marriage, and the guilt has been eating me up all these years."

Wilder's heart was beating so hard, it was almost all he could hear. "What the fuck are you saying?" he barked out.

A few heads turned their way, so he took a deep breath to calm down.

"I didn't sleep with her," the other man repeated. "Nothing happened. No kiss, nothing."

If what Scott said was true, then Kate had told Wilder the truth all those years ago. That voicemail she'd left that he'd deleted. The truth that he didn't believe.

But...

"You were in our bed with her. *Naked.*" He couldn't just ignore the facts.

Scott nodded and looked down at the table. "That night, Kate was at the bar with a couple of friends. Her friends both met guys and left Kate on her own. I ran into her as she was leaving. She said she was going to call a cab, and I told her the one cab in town was driving someone out to Davenport so it would be a while. I offered to buy her a drink while we waited."

"I don't think I want to hear this." Wilder stood up.

Scott reached out to stop him. "You do. Trust me."

Swallowing a lump of dread, Wilder sat back down.

"I put something in her drink," Scott admitted quietly. "She didn't know."

Wilder clenched his fists. "You drugged my wife?"

Scott scratched behind his ear again. "I know. I'm a terrible person. I'm sorry. But I helped her home, and by the time we got there, she'd passed out. So, I set it up like... well you know. You saw."

"She passed out? Nothing happened?"

Scott shook his head. Nothing happened."

"Why would you do that?"

"My cousin paid me to do it and threatened to beat me up if I didn't. The dude is strong, and I was afraid. I'm so sorry, Wilder."

"Your cousin? You mean Martin?"

That explained why he'd kept bringing Kate up when Wilder had seen him earlier.

"Yeah, he's had a thing for her since she dumped him back in high school. If it makes you feel any better, she's never given him the time of day."

Well, that did help, actually.

Scott scratched himself again. "That night, I knew when you would be home, so I timed the staging accordingly."

"How would you know that?"

"'Cause you were playing poker, and Martin was there. He texted me when you left."

The entire night came back to him. He'd walked in and seen Scott, naked, barely covered by the sheets, and Kate laying on her stomach, her back bare.

He'd never felt pure rage until that moment.

Kate had woken while he was yelling at Scott. She was slurring. Wilder had been convinced she was drunk and grew even more disgusted. All he could think about was how reckless she had been, always wanting to go out and party. It didn't carry any weight that she'd never even liked Scott; that didn't tend to matter when alcohol got involved.

After Scott had run out of there, Kate pleaded with Wilder, promising that nothing had happened and swearing she had no idea how she'd ended up in bed with Scott. Wilder hadn't believed her. He had been convinced she was lying.

Even after he left that night, he'd never returned her calls. Each time she left a voicemail begging him to listen to her... he ignored her.

Shit.

He had to talk to her. But he couldn't interrupt her shift at the diner; hopefully, she'd be home by the time he was done watching the trucks at the development.

His phone buzzed with a text from his brother.

William: *Word of warning about the tux fitting. Dad will be there.*

Shit! He'd forgotten about the fitting. He would have to find Kate after.

But first he had to get through seeing his dad... the man he hadn't spoken to in ten years. The man who said he'd handled everything wrong.

Looks like Dad was right.

Chapter Seven

Dad will be there.

That was all he could think about as he drove to the tux shop. Did his dad know he was coming? They hadn't spoken in ten years… He should have reached out and at least tried to resolve their differences.

Regardless, he would be civil. This was special for William, and he wouldn't be the one to ruin it. But damn, he wished he could talk to his brother alone.

Everything Scott had said weighed on him. If it was all true, then Wilder had really fucked up.

The night he'd found Kate in bed with Scott, he'd packed up what he could and gone to his parents' house. Sitting at the kitchen table with them the next morning, he'd uttered the words he never thought he would.

"I'm filing for divorce."

His mom had inhaled sharply, and his dad shook his head.

"Wilder, don't make any rash decisions," his dad cautioned.

"This isn't rash. I thought about it all night, and there's no other option."

His mom stood up. "I'm calling Father Miser."

Of course, she was. Wilder resisted rolling his eyes. His mother relied on Father Miser for everything; so, did his father.

Once his mom was out of the room, Wilder lowered his voice. "Dad, I would think you of all people would understand, with what you've gone through with Mom. I don't know how you've done it, but I can't."

It was no secret that his mother had carried on a years-long affair with their neighbor Jerry. Wilder saw the hurt in his dad's eyes every morning she would come stumbling back home.

"You don't know how it is between your mother and me. I'm not as innocent as you think. But we made vows, we were married in the eyes of God — just like you and Kate."

"Kate broke those vows last night."

"You can't toss her aside over one mistake."

Wilder jumped up. "She slept with another man!"

His dad stood too. "Yes, and it was a *mistake*. The poor girl was here this morning, looking for you."

"She was?"

"Yes. It's clear she feels awful. I told her you'd call her after breakfast."

Wilder clenched his jaw. "You shouldn't have done that. My mind is made up." He walked to the door.

"Son, you don't turn your back on family. And Kate is your family."

Wilder didn't even respond, he just walked out—a decision he always regretted.

His father hadn't spoken to him since.

Whenever he would call that first year, his mom would tell him they couldn't talk now, and hang up. William tried to run interference, but all they'd tell him was that until Wilder fixed what he'd done, he was on his own. So Wilder stopped calling.

That had been ten years ago.

As he parked the car beneath the bright afternoon sun, he took a look around. The tux shop was in the neighboring town of Davenport, and not much had changed here in the past decade, either. He found that comforting.

"Hey, Wilder?"

He turned to find William jogging toward him across the parking lot. "Hey."

"I want you to know that I had a long talk with Dad this morning. He says he will be civil."

He winced. *Civil.* That's what he'd said to Kate. "Wow. Just what every son wants to hear."

His brother clapped him on the shoulder. "I'm sorry. I know what he and Mom did really sucks. I've tried to reason with them, but all they'll say is they don't believe in divorce."

Wilder shook his head. "Pretending I don't exist goes deeper than not believing in divorce."

He'd lived the last ten years knowing his parents were alive and choosing not to speak to him. It hurt. But what could he do? He wasn't going to cave just for them.

Of course, in the end, his dad had been right about one thing: he'd acted too rashly. Maybe if he'd stuck around, he would have realized the truth sooner.

"Ready?" William asked.

"No, but let's go in anyway. I can't wait to see my little brother in a tux."

"You could have seen that at *your* wedding. I still can't believe you two eloped."

Wilder laughed humorlessly. "Like her parents would have given her a wedding with me as the groom."

"Oh yeah. I forgot what assholes they were to you."

William pushed the door open, and their dad stood in front of a mirror, beaming at the reflection of himself in a tux. Wilder was stricken by how much he'd aged.

"William!" Their dad spun around, and his eyes caught on his oldest son. "Wilder?"

The man was thinner than he had been, and his dark hair was much grayer and thinning on the top.

Wilder swallowed. He should have stopped by his parents' first. It was hard to not hide his shock. "Dad."

His father frowned, then turned back to William. "Great color choice on the cummerbund. The blue matches the Loprete men's eyes."

A jab at Wilder for changing his last name. Wilder bit back his disappointment. He wasn't sure what he'd been expecting. He was a fool if he'd thought his dad would rush to him with open arms.

"Wilder, what are you doing for work?" his dad asked.

"Construction." He looked at William, who arched a brow.

Yeah, his brother wanted him to come clean to their parents. Maybe after the wedding, he'd consider it. After he solved his case.

His dad nodded as he stared at himself in the mirror.

The tailor was taking measurements, pretending not to be listening to every word. "We'll need to hem this up a little."

"Nonsense! I've been a thirty-two inseam all my life."

The tailor glanced from William to Wilder. Wilder shrugged.

The slight man cleared his throat. "Mr. Loprete, it's common to lose a little height as we get older. I'm sure that's what's going on."

"Are you telling me I'm *shrinking*?"

"Dad, I'm sure those pants were a little longer than thirty-two to begin with. Let's let the man do his job."

Dad finally smiled. "You're right. We have other things to talk about. Have I told you how happy your mom and I are that you are getting married? We can't wait for grandchildren."

Wilder swallowed. He and Kate would have had kids by now. How different his life could have been. Should have been. He had to talk to her and apologize for his mistake. But first, he had to get through this fitting.

"Good afternoon." A young brunette walked up to them. "Which one of you is the groom?"

"I am," William said.

"Right this way. I have your tux in room three. And you," she swiveled to Wilder and smiled, "are in room two."

Wilder stepped into the room she indicated to find a tux already hanging on a hook for him.

"Are you back in town for good, then?" his dad asked through the wall.

Wilder stilled. His dad was *voluntarily* talking to him? Maybe having the fitting room wall between them helped.

"Uh, I'm thinking about it." He cringed as he told yet another lie, but it was part of his cover story.

Although, it really wasn't a lie. The truth was he wanted to stay and have another chance with Kate. He stilled. Where the hell had that thought come from?

He shook the thought away, needing to focus on his brother's wedding. He removed his jeans and put on the tux pants. They fit pretty good.

"Does this mean you've finally realized your mistake?" his dad prodded.

Wilder closed his eyes. Well, so much for focusing on the wedding. He had to tread carefully before they got into an argument. *I am here for William.* He had to remind himself of that over and over.

Yet, what was there to argue about? It turned out his parents had been right.

He sighed. "My mistake about Kate?" He removed his shirt and put on the white button-up.

"Yes. You should have given her more time," his dad insisted.

Wilder leaned his forehead against the mirror. "You're right. I shouldn't have left so quickly."

When he gathered himself and pushed his door open, his dad was standing on the other side in a similar white button-up and tuxedo pants—but his fly was open.

"Uh. You forgot..." he waved his hand toward his own crotch, hoping his dad would get a clue.

The older man glanced down then zipped it up. Bringing his gaze back to Wilder, he smiled. "Are you saying what I think you're saying, son?"

Wilder gave a small nod. "I made a mistake."

His dad's smile lit up his entire face as he pulled Wilder into his arms. "I'm so happy to hear that. I have no doubt you can fix this. That poor girl hasn't been serious about anyone since you left. Rumor is she's just too heartbroken."

Wilder swallowed. *Is it possible that's true?*

Hell, it was for him.

"I'm not so convinced I can fix it," he hedged. "I saw her. She hates me. I doubt she'd want to be friends again."

Wilder frowned. *Friends*. Was that what he wanted? All he wanted? The more he thought about it, no, it wasn't all he wanted. He wanted back what they had. But could he convince her to try again?

"Yes, but you know what they say. There's a fine line between love and hate."

"As much as I hope you're right, all I see from Kate now is hate."

His dad patted him on the shoulder. "Well, it's a good thing you have me and your mom on your side, then. Don't worry, we'll fix it. Your mom will be so happy to hear this."

"No, Dad. This is my life; I need to fix it."

The other man sighed. "I know. I only want you to be happy, Wilder. I'm so sorry I never reached out. I was so angry at first, and then it seemed like too much time had gone by..." His eyes welled up.

Shit, he'd never seen his dad cry.

"Maybe we can work on things now," Wilder offered.

His dad nodded and pulled him in for a hug. "I'd like that. And don't worry about Kate. Your mom and I will give you two a little nudge."

Wilder chuckled. The man was so stubborn. He knew there was no talking him out of it. He could only hope whatever he was thinking wouldn't cause more problems between him and Kate.

His dad pulled back and arched a brow. "Then we can discuss the issue with your name."

Wilder smiled. "Okay. But I'm going to focus on Kate first."

"Of course, you are." His dad shook his head, then pulled him in for another hug. "I'm so happy you're back Wilder."

As he stared at his reflection in the mirror, he realized he was happy to be back too. Now he just had to convince Kate to give him another chance.

Chapter Eight

"I can't believe you got to leave work early, but I'm happy you did," Kate said.

Tabitha dropped her bag into the back booth at Brannigan's Pub then fell into her seat. "Me too. Especially on the day after a holiday weekend. It's a rarity to get out before five."

Tabitha worked at the bank in Fisher Springs, and as a manager, she often had to stay past closing to do whatever it was she did there.

Kate took on a mock-serious expression. "Lily still doing a good job, or do I need to give her a talk?"

Tabitha laughed as she pushed her blonde hair over her shoulder. Lily was a teller at the same bank, and Kate knew she was a hard worker, but she liked to give her sister a hard time.

"I'll let her know you're checking up on her. She'll love that."

"Tell her if I hear any complaints from you, I'll make her go skydiving."

Tabitha's eyes widened. "Have you gone?"

Kate nodded. "Several years ago."

"Damn, you'll try anything, won't you?"

Kate smiled to herself. There had been a few years when she was open to trying anything. But as she'd gotten older, those sorts of things held less appeal. Now, she craved the very life Wilder had once wanted: to be settled down with someone she loved and maybe have a child or two.

"Considering even I know about Lily's fear of heights, I'm sure that threat will work," Tabitha said.

"Here you go." Zach Brannigan placed two glasses of beer on the table.

"Zach, I haven't seen you in forever," Tabitha said before taking a sip of her drink.

"Been busy with the pub and Jessie."

Every time he mentioned Jessie, he got a dopey look on his face. It was cute.

"I'm happy for you, you know." Kate nudged him. "I'm glad it all worked out for you two."

Zach scratched his beard. "Me too. I still worry about some of the cases she takes on, but I know she's more than capable of handling anything that comes her way."

Jessie had come to Fisher Springs as an FBI agent working on a case. She and Zach had traveled a bumpy road, but they'd finally gotten their heads out of their asses and figured things out. Now, Jessie was a private investigator with an office of her own.

At first, Kate didn't think she'd get much business in a small town. Boy was she wrong. She doubted that Jessie had planned on so many cases involving cows, though.

The squeak of the door grabbed their attention as a group of four men walked in.

"I gotta go. Enjoy."

"Thanks, Zach." Kate took a sip of her beer as she took in the pub.

Not much had changed in the years since Zach had taken over. Being the owner of the only pub in town meant he didn't have to do too much to keep things interesting.

It was usually pretty crowded by nature, but right now, it wasn't, and Kate was appreciative. She knew what Tabitha wanted to talk about, and she didn't need the whole town overhearing her business.

But two hours and two drinks in, Tabitha still hadn't mentioned Wilder's name. Fortunately, she had a new boyfriend and was more interested in talking about him, her boss at the bank whom she was angry with, and kayaking—apparently, her boyfriend loved it, and they went every chance they had.

But, having had her fill of these subjects, Kate was about to excuse herself for the evening when Tabitha leaned in.

"Are we going to talk about it?"

"About what?"

Tabitha rolled her eyes. "Please. The whole town is taking bets on when you and Wilder will be back together. You got any inside information for me? I'd love to win."

Kate waved to Zach then grabbed a paper napkin from the holder on the table and began to fold it.

Tabitha put her hand on Kate's. "He's got you wound up I see." She nodded to the napkin.

Kate nodded. She was more than wound up. Wilder's arrival in town had her on edge. Feelings she hadn't felt in years were resurfacing and she wasn't sure how to deal with them.

"You want another?" Zach asked, approaching the table.

Kate glanced at Tabitha. "Yeah, let's do one more round."

After Zach left, Tabitha arched a brow.

"We're not getting back together." Kate shook her head. "You should see how he looks at me. Pure hatred."

"I'm so sorry. You should have let me kill Scott back then."

"I should have, but I thought I could get answers. I never understood why he did it. And what kind of grudge he'd have to hold to go to that level of cruelty."

"I always wondered if your dad was behind it."

Kate shook her head. "My dad is an asshole, but he wouldn't stoop to something like that. That would be 'unbecoming behavior' for the mayor."

Zach returned with two more beers.

"Thank you."

He gave them a nod, then gave them privacy.

Tabitha sighed. "Hey, do you have any idea why Wilder is back?"

Kate laughed. "With all the town gossip, you haven't heard? He came back to help his brother with the wedding."

Tabitha's eyebrows shot up. "Isn't that in a month? Why would he be staying for so long?" She picked up her beer. "Do you think he's moving back?"

Kate spit out the sip she'd just taken. She hadn't thought of that, but why *was* he here so long before the wedding? It was one thing to avoid the man for a month, but if he moved back? It would be impossible. And if he moved a family back with him...?

No. She was getting ahead of herself. There was no reason to think any of that.

"I have no idea why he came early," Kate finally said as she dabbed her mouth with the napkin she'd folded.

"Oh shit! You promised Holly you'd help with the wedding. Doesn't that mean the two of you will be working together?"

Kate groaned. "Yeah. I don't know how it's going to work, but I plan to stay civil." She cringed as she used Wilder's word.

The pub's door creaked open, and Tabitha sucked in a breath through her teeth. "Well, get ready to be civil."

"What?" Kate looked toward the entrance, and sure enough, there was Wilder, wearing a pair of well-fitted jeans and a tight T-shirt.

"Shit, Kate. He's really filled out. I mean, he was always hot, but now he's... wow."

Kate sighed. She had to agree. It wouldn't have hurt so much if he'd come back looking worse for the wear, but no, he had to look better.

She watched as Zach poured something from a pitcher and handed it to Wilder. Wilder then turned and walked straight to their table. His eyes connected with hers, and her whole body tingled.

That wasn't a look of hatred he was aiming at her; that was heat.

What the hell changed?

"Wilder, it's been a while," her friend greeted before she could.

He glanced at the other woman, and Kate saw the moment recognition dawned. "Tabitha?"

"The one and only." She stood up and pulled him in for a hug. "Welcome back to town." She ran her hands up his back, then pulled away. "Wow, you really are muscular now, aren't you?"

Wilder stepped back, and Kate had to stifle her laugh as Tabitha reached out and squeezed his chest.

He cleared his throat gruffly. "Do you mind if I have a moment alone with Kate?"

Tabitha grinned. "Not at all. I'll be at the bar if you need me." She grabbed her beer and walked to the bar, spinning around once to give Kate a thumbs-up.

Wilder slid into Tabitha's spot in the booth, setting his drink down.

"Is that iced tea?" Kate asked, nodding to his glass.

He smiled. "Yeah, some things never change."

His smile fell as he clasped his hands on the table and stared at them.

Kate was equally uncomfortable. Even though he was across the booth, this was too close. His scent wafted in the air between them.

After several minutes, she couldn't take the silence any longer. "I heard you punched Scott Fisher. Why would you do that?"

He glanced up, and all the anger in his eyes was gone. So was the heat. It was replaced by something else, something she didn't recognize.

"Because he's an asshole," Wilder said simply. "But I shouldn't have done it."

"No?"

He shook his head. "He tracked me down earlier today, said he needed to tell me something."

Kate closed her eyes. "Wilder, I don't want to rehash our past, if that's why you're here. What's done is done."

He reached across and grabbed her hand. Startled, she opened her eyes and stared at their connection. The air hummed around them, and her feelings for this man came rushing back—not that they'd gone all that far, honestly.

"Kate, I'm so sorry."

Her eyes moved to his. He was being sincere. "What?"

"Scott told me he set you up that night. He said he put something in your drink to knock you out."

The knot in her chest loosened. *Scott finally told the truth.* She'd known nothing had happened, but why had Scott set her up?

The hurt and confusion she felt for Scott only compounded what she felt for her ex-husband.

"But I tried to tell you I felt like I was drugged. I said that I'd never sleep with anyone. You didn't believe me!"

"I know." His voice cracked. "Kate, I'm sorry. I'm sorry I didn't believe you."

She scoffed. "You obviously thought pretty lowly of me to think I'd do that to you."

Her anger from all those years ago came back. The helpless rage that had battered at her when she'd received the divorce papers and realized he wasn't going to listen to her side of the story. She doubted he'd even listened to her voicemails. Because if he had, how could he throw away all the years of love they had shared?

He shook his head. "No, I thought the world of y—"

"Then what is it?" she snapped. "Tell me why you wouldn't believe the woman you claimed to love. The woman you *married!*"

She was yelling now and drawing attention, but dammit, she didn't care. How *dare* he come back to town and drop this on her?

"I'm sorry," he pleaded. "I was young, immature, too proud for my own good. I let my own pride get in the way of my marriage."

Kate stood, her blood too heated, her nerves too fried to stay seated.

His eyebrows shot up. "Wait, where are you going?"

"I'm leaving."

"Kate, please. We need to talk."

She barked out a laugh. "Oh, *now* you want to talk? Well, you're about ten years too late."

In one swift move, she grabbed his iced tea and dumped it over his head. Then she set his glass back on the table and stormed out of the pub.

Tabitha caught up to her about a block away. "Holy shit, Kate! I'm happy you didn't let him give you any shit, but—"

Kate stopped. "Please tell me you're not on his side."

Tabitha's brows shot up. "No, not at all. It's just that everyone in the pub saw, and you know how word travels fast around here…"

Kate dropped her shoulders with a groan. "Shit. My mom."

"Yeah. Do you want to go to my place for a while, until this blows over?"

While the idea of avoiding another confrontation sounded nice, there was no point; her mother would figure out where she was sooner or later.

"Thanks for the offer, but I think I'll go home. I need some time alone."

Tabitha pulled her in for a hug. "If you change your mind, call me."

She nodded silently and turned toward home.

One thing Kate loved about living in such a small town was that it wasn't a far walk.

Once she got to her house, she sat back on the couch and let her thoughts roam.

Wilder apologized. He knows the truth now. But what does that really mean? Are we supposed to become friends? Can I even **be** *friends with him?*

She grabbed a pillow, laid down, then let the tears fall.

Some time later, a knock on her door startled her. She sat up and glanced at her phone. She must have fallen asleep; two hours had passed since she'd left Wilder at Brannigan's.

The knock came again, louder and harder.

With a groan, Kate forced herself to her feet, went to the door, and opened it. Her mom walked in wearing a scowl.

Kate smiled brightly just to piss her off. "Please come in, Mother."

As her mother walked past her, she rolled her eyes. Then she spotted her neighbor, Mr. Finley, on his porch across the street, staring at her and shaking his head.

Either news traveled fast, or the man was sympathizing. Everyone in town knew she and her mother were not on good terms.

The older woman went to the couch and sat down. "Kate, dear." Her mother patted the couch for Kate to join her.

Kate followed but chose to stand. "Mother," she responded. "Two visits in one week. This is unusual."

"Word in town is that you and Wilder were together earlier. Is this true?"

"We sat together for five minutes at the pub and talked. We are not *together*. Nor will we be getting together. So please drop it."

She went to the kitchen and filled a glass with water from the faucet. When she returned, her mother was smiling.

That was never good.

"Do you know where he's been the last ten years?" she asked sweetly. "What he does for work? If he's married?"

Kate sat down on the other end of the couch. "No, I don't. We're not exactly on friendly terms."

Her mom sighed. "I supposed not with you pouring iced tea all over his head.

Kate laughed.

"You know, dear, you catch more flies with honey."

She finished her water and set down her cup. "I know, Mom, but believe me, I don't want to catch Wilder."

Her mom arched a brow. "I'm happy to hear that."

Of course, her mom would be happy to hear that. But the truth was part of her did want him. Well, she wanted what they had but that was gone.

"Well, don't worry," her mother sniffed in Kate's silence. "I'll go find out for myself what his plans are." She stood.

Oh god no. "Mom, don't. Please stay out of my business."

Her mom leaned in and gave her one of the light hugs she'd perfected as the mayor's wife. "Don't worry, dear. I know what I'm doing."

Kate watched her walk out the door with dread pooling in her stomach. "That's what I'm afraid of."

Chapter Nine

Sitting in his car watching Martin's housing development, Wilder chuckled to himself as he remembered the look in Kate's eyes as she poured the iced tea over his head yesterday. He'd forgotten how passionate she could be.

Passionate. Damn it, he missed that about her.

Hell, he missed everything about her.

He had too much time to think as he sat in his car up at a little park on the hill. From here, he could see the entire development including everyone that went in and out. And, as a bonus, the park itself was deserted; after those four cups of coffee, he really needed to piss.

He'd needed that much coffee to stay alert. He was bored as hell after spending most of the day reclined in his seat, holding up the current thriller he was trying to read but couldn't quite concentrate on. He was also sore from sitting too long. But he did record every truck and car that went in or out of the development.

Simpson had been right; there were quite a few deliveries. As Wilder logged the company names from the side of the trucks, he looked them up on his phone. They all appeared to be legitimate businesses.

Two trucks had no name—old, painted over Penske rigs likely purchased at auction. They definitely had him curious. Fortunately, he was able to get their plates, thanks to his binoculars.

Before he packed up for the day, he shot Simpson a text then called him.

"Simpson," he answered.

"It's Coleman. I got a couple of plates we should run. I just texted them to you."

"Good. I'll get right on that."

Wilder stared down at the development as the last of the construction workers drove away.

"Any more news on the bomb?" Wilder asked.

Simpson sighed heavily into the phone. "No, I've spoken to my FBI contact who's monitoring the Bannons. He hasn't heard anything about a bomb."

"A contact? Do you trust him?"

"I do. They've been tracking this gang for a while. He assured me if he hears anything, he'll call right away."

Wilder was relieved that Simpson at least had eyes on the gang. Not that he wouldn't but Wilder didn't know the man very well and didn't like not being in control of the situation himself.

"Okay, call me as soon as you hear anything," Wilder said.

"Will do."

He ended the call and pocketed his phone.

Wilder took a deep breath as he stared straight ahead. Despite closely watching the local traffic, he kept replaying that fateful night ten years ago over and over in his mind, especially how out of it Kate had been.

Then he replayed his conversation with Scott. When the other man had said someone *paid* him to do it, paid him to ruin Wilder's marriage, Wilder's hands had balled into fists, and he was so convinced he knew what name he was going to hear.

But it hadn't been Frank, as he expected. It wasn't Kate's father; it was Martin Fisher.

Wilder remembered that Martin had briefly dated Kate in high school. When she dumped him, Wilder took his chance and asked her out. Then they had stayed together until he left her.

But why would Martin wait all those years to exact his revenge? Was that what it was? Or had he wanted her? Had she dated Martin again after he left?

No, Scott said she hadn't.

And Kate said she hadn't slept with Scott, that the last thing she remembered was the drink.

Which checks out, because Scott admitted he drugged her... Fuck, she had been telling the truth, and I believed someone else over my own wife.

He ran his hand through his hair.

Fuck. She hated him, and rightfully so after what he had done.

He needed advice, and he only had one person to turn to. One person who knew him better than anyone.

He drove to William's place, rather than calling him and risk being put off. He knew his brother would be home by now.

"Wilder?" William answered the door, eyes wide in surprise.

"Sorry to stop by without calling, but I... I learned something, and I need to talk to you."

William gave a silent nod, stepping aside, and Wilder walked in.

This was the first time he'd been in his brother's home, and he stuttered to a stop. It wasn't what he expected. Oh hell, what had he expected? Of course, William wouldn't have it anything like the home they'd grown up in.

The furniture was modern in style and cream in color. Several throw pillows were strewn about in shades of turquoise and gray. A variety of houseplants stood near the windows, and above the fireplace hung a large photo taken in some unidentified forest.

"Where's your television?" Wilder asked dumbly.

"The media room. Why? What's going on?"

Wilder ran his hand through his hair. It was probably sticking straight up by now, considering how much he'd done that in the last hour.

He frowned. "The media room?"

"Wilder, you're scaring me. You look upset. What's going on?"

Letting out a breath, he said, "Scott Fisher told me he was paid to make it look like he slept with Kate, so he drugged her to pull it off. Nothing actually happened."

William's eyes widened. "Shit. Are you serious?"

"Sadly, yes."

"How's Kate taking this?"

Wilder picked up a framed photo off the mantel of William's fireplace. He and William were so young, both holding ice cream cones and sitting on the curb, waiting for the big Fourth of July parade to start.

"I don't know."

It was the truth. Yes, she had been pissed at him for not trusting her. But after the anger subsided, how would she feel? Pissed? Hurt? Upset at all that they had lost? Or was that just him? Maybe she truly had moved on.

William nodded. "Follow me."

He led Wilder to the kitchen, where there was a large island surrounded by stools.

"Sit," he pointed.

Wilder obeyed while William grabbed a bottle of whiskey and two glasses from a cupboard. He poured a little for each of them, then asked, "What did Scott tell you?"

"Just what I told you."

"Who paid him? Was it her father? I can't stand that man."

Wilder laughed without humor. "That was my first thought too. But no. He said it was Martin Fisher." He swallowed his drink in one go.

"No shit?"

He nodded. "Did Kate date him after I left?"

Scott said she hadn't, but at this point, Scott wasn't exactly reliable.

William crossed his arms. "I thought you never wanted to hear about her?"

Wilder poured himself another drink. "Yeah, well, that was before I found out I might have tossed aside the love of my life because of Martin fucking Fisher."

William considered his brother for a moment, then said, "She never dated Martin that I know of." Then he finished his drink.

Wilder pursed his lips. His brother likely didn't even know that Kate dated Martin in high school. Being two years younger, he hadn't been as aware of what went on with the senior class.

"Is she married now?" he asked, instead of pressing the Martin issue. "Or with someone?"

His brother shook his head. "I don't think she ever had another serious relationship. But we don't exactly travel in the same circles."

Wilder chuckled. "Small town. Kind of hard not to, isn't it?"

William shrugged. "I manage to not get too involved in town gossip."

That was something he understood; Wilder had been the same way when he lived there.

"But the bigger question here," William continued, "is what are you going to do now? Apologize to Kate?"

"I already did. Let's just say she's not in a forgiving state of mind."

William laughed. "Right. I heard about the iced tea."

Wilder cocked his head. "Thought you weren't involved in town gossip."

William shrugged his shoulders. "I'm not, but when it involves my brother, it's hard not to hear. Everyone wanted to talk to me about it."

"Great."

William clapped him on the shoulder. "Okay, so she's angry. That's understandable. Give her some time to cool down, then make your move."

"My move?"

William leaned forward. "You don't have a plan?"

"No, why the hell would I have a plan?"

"Hmmm," he grunted, releasing his shoulder.

Wilder knew that 'hmmm'. His brother was thinking something he didn't want to say. He sighed. "Spit it out."

William took another sip. "You came to town a month before my wedding... and I know you said you came to help..."

"I did."

William held up his hand to stop him from saying more. "I don't buy it. I know you, Wilder, and you want nothing to do with weddings."

Shit. Maybe he should have told him his real reason for being here.

Not ready to give it up just yet, he said, "I wanted to spend time with you. Is that wrong?"

"Of course not. But I think you're really here for Kate."

Before Scott had told him the truth, Wilder swore to himself that Kate was the last thing he wanted. But if he was being honest, he had to admit that the moment he saw her again, he realized how much he missed her. And now that he knew the reality of what happened that terrible night...

Yeah, I want her back.

Wilder sighed. He never thought anything would open his heart to Kate again. But here he was, heartsick with missing her, and feeling guilty as hell for being so stupid and not hearing her out all those years ago.

At least now, he could be honest about his feelings.

"I do want her back," he finally admitted out loud.

William grinned, his eyes glinting mischievously. "Yeah? What are you going to do to win her back?"

Wilder laughed, feeling lighter than he had in a decade. "Look at you, all about romance and shit. Who would have thought it, back when we were rolling around in the mud?"

"I'm a changed man thanks to Holly. Oh, hey, maybe Holly can help!"

Wilder shook his head. "No, I need to figure this out on my own. Thanks, though."

But what the hell was he going to do? With the wedding getting closer, Kate would get busier and busier.

Of course, that also meant he'd have more excuses to see her...

William clicked his tongue. "I'm surprised you came here without a plan."

"I came here to help *you*. I figured Kate had moved away. She used to talk about wanting to live in Seattle so we could enjoy the night scene."

"Really?"

"Yeah, it was a huge issue between us because I wanted to stay here. I loved small-town life."

William leaned back and crossed his arms. "Huh."

"What?"

"Well, it's funny you say that, since *you* ended up moving away, and Kate stayed here."

Wilder tossed back the rest of his drink. "She stayed here? The whole time?"

His brother gave a slow nod. "For the last ten years, Kate has been living in Fisher Springs."

She never moved away?

When he saw her at the carnival that night, he thought she had likely gone but then moved back for some reason. But she'd never left?

Why?

Chapter Ten

"Hey, Kate!"

She spun on the sidewalk to see a grinning Martin Fisher briskly walking her way. She had almost reached the Cozy Croissant and didn't need Martin getting between her and her morning coffee.

Martin was wearing his usual suit, but his tie was loose, and his jacket unbuttoned, giving him a rare *casual* look.

Her guess was he didn't have a morning meeting to rush off to.

Just my luck.

She didn't want to deal with him today. She was still too pissed at Wilder.

And Martin, for that matter.

He'd accepted her bid for the landscape design, but he kept putting off meeting with her. They were supposed to have lunch — at his request, even — but he'd canceled at the last minute. Now, it seemed the only time he was available was in the evenings, over dinner.

Fortunately, she had been scheduled to work at the diner every time he'd asked.

Martin finally caught up to her, carrying two coffees. "I thought you might want one," he said, offering her a cup.

Part of her was grateful; she'd been up half the night. Since Wilder had returned to town a few days ago, she'd had a hard time sleeping. Well, unless it was while crying on her couch, apparently. So yes, she needed the coffee.

But how the hell did he know she'd be here?

"You just happen to be carrying an extra for me?" she asked.

His cheeks reddened. "Uh, no. Not exactly. I've seen you go into the coffee shop a few mornings. Today, I got there first, and voila. Here it is."

Kate took a deep breath, then smiled and took the coffee. "Thank you." She took a sip, but the moment the cold liquid hit her tongue, she spit it out. "What the hell? This isn't coffee."

Martin looked puzzled. "No, it's iced tea. Word around town is you really like it but didn't get to enjoy it the other day." He grinned at her.

Word around town? That was her private business, not something she wanted broadcast to everyone.

Of course, it was her fault for dumping iced tea on Wilder's head in the middle of Brannigan's Pub...

She shoved the cup back into Martin's hands, hard, causing it to spill onto his shirt.

Martin growled. "Shit, Kate! I have to wear this to work."

"You're not funny, Martin."

She stormed down the street, wanting to get away before she blew up at him. *He's lucky he only got a few drops on his shirt. Jackass.*

Unfortunately, he didn't take the hint, as he was right on her heels.

"Sorry about the tea," he said. "But I do have something I want to ask you."

She stopped and swiveled around to face him. Might as well. The man was persistent, and she didn't want him chasing her all the way to Cozy Croissant. Because once she got there, she hoped to relax. In peace. With no mention of iced tea.

She sighed impatiently. "What is it?"

Martin tugged at his loosened tie. Then he gave her a half smile.

Oh no.

Kate braced herself. There was only one reason Martin would be this nervous; he was going to ask her out again.

He cleared his throat. "Do, er... Do you want to see a movie with me on Friday?"

"Are you asking me out on a date?"

"Uh... yes?"

Why the hell was he asking her *now*? Was he mistaking her anger for interest? Or was it because he'd heard about her drama with Wilder?

Now she was curious.

"I'm sorry, Martin. I'm not up for dating right now. As you know, Wilder is back in town, and my head isn't in a good place."

There. She didn't add that she would never date Wilder again even if he was the last man on Earth; she only needed Martin to think she would.

He ground his teeth, and Kate suppressed a smile, happy she'd hit a nerve.

"I didn't realize you still had feelings for Wilder," he gritted out.

She shrugged. "We were married. I think there will always be feelings there. Look, I hate to rush away, but I need to get a coffee before my shift starts."

"Oh, sure. It was good seeing you again, Kate. Hopefully, you'll be up for that date sometime soon."

She gave him a placating smile then quickly spun around and made her way to the coffee shop.

Did he only give me the landscape contract to get a date? What happens when I keep turning him down?

She would keep saying no, of course, but despite her repeated rejections, he wasn't getting the hint. She worried about what he might do when he finally did.

Once safely inside the coffee shop, she inhaled the delicious scent of freshly brewed coffee and baked bread.

"Kate! It's good to see you," Adele said as Kate walked up to the counter.

Adele was the little sister of, but nothing like, her boss Logan. Adele loved to push his buttons and opening a cafe in the same town as his diner might have done that on a big scale. If asked, they'd claim they weren't competing, but it wasn't until after Adele opened up Cozy Croissant that Logan ordered the fancy espresso machine for the diner.

"Good to see you too. How's business?"

"It's going great. Funny thing, we actually have had a run on iced tea today. Every time I ask someone what's going on, they say I need to ask you."

Adele was grinning ear to ear, so Kate was pretty sure she'd already heard the story.

"Ugh. Doesn't anyone in this town have anything better to do than talk about me?"

Adele laughed. "Nope. So, what's up?"

"I'm sure you've heard. Why make me repeat it?"

"She poured a glass of iced tea on that man that used to be her husband."

Kate turned to find Mr. Finley, her neighbor. "Mr. Finley, where did you hear that?"

The old man leaned against the counter. "Ruth told me. She said her son was in the pub when it happened."

Kate took a deep breath. "I see. Well, can you not spread it around?"

"Oh fiddlesticks. The entire town already knows, thanks to Mrs. Pauly."

"Well, how did she find out?"

"I told her. But I told her to keep it to herself. See what good that did." He walked away, shaking his head.

"He really doesn't think he's a gossip, does he?" Kate asked.

"Nope. I see you've had enough for one day, though, so what can I get you?"

"Thank you. Just a black coffee please."

Once Kate had her coffee, she sat down in the corner. She didn't really have a shift to get to, like she'd told Martin. And if he showed up at the diner for lunch, he would figure that out.

Her phone buzzed, and she couldn't help but smile when she saw it was a text from Holly. Focusing on the wedding was a much better option than stewing on the iced tea caper.

Holly: *William and I decided to have a joint bachelor/bachelorette party. We would like you and Wilder to plan it. I'll send you an email about what we're thinking. Oh, and I'll text you his number too.*

She reread it five times. There was no way the happy couple was asking the two of them to work together. It made no sense. It had to be a sick joke.

Kate: *Haha. Not funny.*

Holly: *I'm not joking.*

Shit. How the hell was she supposed to work with Wilder?

She took a deep breath. Either Holly or William, or both, were trying to get her and Wilder together. Damn, how big was the town's betting pool? Because money was the only reason she could think of for Holly to betray her like this.

Her phone dinged with Holly's follow up email, and Kate sipped her coffee as she read through it. Another ding on her phone, and Kate saw that Holly had texted Wilder's number. She rolled her eyes and read the rest of the email.

Double shit. There was no way she could pull this off without Wilder.

Is this really even what they want?

Kate leaned back in her chair as she thought it through.

What are my options? How can I appease the bride and groom while still avoiding my ex? Let's see… We can keep the party simple and divide the tasks that need to be completed?

She smiled.

Yes, that's it. We can do this and barely have to speak to each other.

Barely speak to Wilder. Then he'll leave town and she won't have to see him again.

Tears welled in her eyes as an ache grew in her chest at the thought of never seeing him again.

No, she was supposed to be mad at him. But in her mind, she kept seeing him sitting across from her at Brannigan's Pub when he said he was sorry. It was sincere and, in that moment, while she had been mad as hell, it also hit her how much she missed him. How much she missed talking to him, joking with him, and yes, even arguing with him.

As that thought sank in, she realized she *wanted* to work on this with Wilder.

Her smile fell.

He's getting under my skin again.

But had he really ever left?

Chapter Eleven

"Good news!" William was all smiles as Wilder walked up to his door.

"What?"

"I confirmed with the caterer that we will have plenty of iced tea at the wedding, so Kate can do her worst."

"Jesus Christ," Wilder muttered as he spun on his heel and headed back to his car. It had been three days since his talk with Kate and everywhere he went people were making iced tea jokes. If he heard the words *iced tea* one more time, he was going to punch something.

"Oh, come on now. Too soon?" William laughed.

Wilder held up his middle finger as he kept walking.

Everyone thought they were so funny with their iced tea jokes everywhere he went. At this point, he'd be happy if he never had iced tea ever again.

Somehow, William caught up and jumped right in front of him, stopping Wilder in his tracks.

"Stop. Seriously. I won't bring it up again."

"Good. I'm holding you to it. Now what was so urgent that I had to drop everything and come over?"

William suppressed a grin then looked away. "We should probably go inside."

Wilder narrowed his eyes. He was hiding something. "Spill it."

His brother grimaced. "Well, Holly thought it would be a great idea for you and Kate to work together to plan our bachelor/bachelorette party."

"No," Wilder said as he stepped around him to continue to his car.

What the hell were they thinking? Work with Kate? Kate couldn't stand to be in the same room with him right now. It would be best if he gave her space to cool down.

"Please, Wilder. You owe me one."

And that right there kept him from getting in his car and driving away.

He *did* owe his brother. He owed him a lot. When Wilder had left town after finding Kate with Scott, his brother was bombarded with questions from family, friends, complete strangers who thought they deserved to know their business. And even though William knew where Wilder was, he didn't give that information to anyone, allowing his brother time to get his head on straight.

Taking a deep breath, Wilder looked up at the sky. He wasn't a religious man, but right now, he needed a higher power to help him get through this.

He spun around. "Fine. I'll do what I have to, but Holly had better not be trying to play matchmaker. As far as Kate sees it, that ship sailed years ago."

William's face lit up with the biggest smile, and he pulled Wilder into a hug. "Thank you!"

"Are you sure this was Holly's idea? You seem a little too happy about it."

"Haven't you ever heard the saying 'happy wife, happy life'? This will make Holly *so* happy."

Wilder thought about that as he returned his brother's embrace. He and Kate had argued quite a bit that last year of their marriage; they hadn't been on the same page in terms of their priorities...

He hadn't kept her happy. It was that simple. If that night with Scott hadn't happened, something else would have come between them. Their separation had been inevitable.

"Hey? You okay?" William frowned as he pulled back.

No.

But there was nothing he could do about it now.

"Yeah, I'm fine." Wilder clapped him on the back as they walked back to the house. "Why don't you tell me what it is you guys want for your party?"

"Oh, Holly has it all written up. She'll send it to you. Basically, we want a joint party, so we have to go somewhere that can fit all of us. Brannigan's would be cool. Holly is pickier about decor and party games, though, you know."

"Party games?"

William shrugged. "That's what she said."

Wilder rubbed his chin. Hopefully, Kate would have some ideas about that, because if it were up to him, they'd be playing beer pong.

"Want a beer?" William asked, leading the way to the kitchen.

"No, I have to do some work tonight."

Wilder shut his eyes.

Shit.

He hated lying to his brother. But he was going back to the housing development to try to find work so maybe he could be honest about that at least.

"Work?" his brother grabbed a beer out of the fridge, opened it, and took a pull.

"I mean I have an interview," Wilder corrected quickly. "I'm trying to get a job in construction while I'm here."

William grinned. "Okay, I've been good and haven't asked about shit, but last I knew, you were a detective. What happened?"

Wilder had to decide: could he trust William? He really wanted to.

He sat in silent debate for a moment, then let out a breath. "All right, you can't tell anyone this. I'm serious."

The other man's eyes widened. "Okay."

Wilder lowered his voice. "I'm here on an undercover assignment."

"I knew it!" William crowed as he slapped the counter. "I *knew* you weren't just here for my wedding."

"Sorry I lied. I'm not supposed to tell anyone. And the case I'm investigating... I'm making no progress. I don't know who's involved and who's not—which is all the more reason for you not to say anything. And don't ask, I can't give you any details."

William took a pull of his beer. "I won't say anything. But I can't wait to hear about it after you solve the case. Something is going down in our little town. Who knew?"

"Okay, wipe that smile off your face. You know nothing."

William only chuckled. "Hey, did you hear about the poker game?"

Wilder plopped down onto one of the barstools. "Poker game?"

"Yeah, remember the ones you went to before you left?"

"They still do those?"

William shrugged. "Yes, but not weekly. Just when the guys can get together. There's one this Saturday."

Huh. A night off from everything would be nice. He needed to clear his head of all things Kate.

His brother continued, "If that's something you want to do, Martin Fisher is hosting, so you should ask him about it."

Wilder balled his hands into fists. He couldn't go one day without hearing that creep's name. It was bad enough his stakeouts had him watching the man fake-smile at everyone; of course, he was going to have to see it up close, if he succeeded at getting on the construction crew. Then he would have to exercise some serious restraint.

William must have seen Wilder's tension. "Shit. I'm sorry, I wasn't thinking. I shouldn't have brought him up."

Wilder shook his head, trying to get himself under control. It wasn't his brother's fault that hearing that asshole's name had him seeing red.

"You know," William floundered, "I can talk to the guys, and we can get a separate game going without him, sort of a welcome back —"

"No. No need."

The last thing he needed was for it to get back to Martin he was trying to set up a game without him. But damn, to have to sit all night staring at Martin's ugly mug, pretending they were buddies might be more than he could handle right now.

But Wilder had to remember he was here for a case, not to make friends.

"You sure? It wouldn't be a problem."

"No worries. I can be in the same room as Martin.

I hope.

Hey, I need to head out. I'll call you about this party, all right?"

"Sure thing."

Wilder found himself back at the housing development that evening to interview with Topher who led the construction crew on the development. The interview had gone well, and Topher had offered him a job. Hoping this would help him learn more about any deliveries coming and going, Wilder gladly accepted.

Afterward, he drove to the model homes. It was after showing hours, but that was fine. He was here to see one man: Martin.

Martin was in the main office. Wilder had seen him through the window when he'd driven by. Just seeing the man from a distance had pissed him off, so now he was sitting in his car up the street, trying to cool off before he ventured inside.

A few moments later, he reached for the door handle of his car, but another car pulled up directly in front of the office. Wilder watched in the rearview mirror as Frank Waters got out, then he turned around to check through the back window to make sure it was him.

It was.

Why is the mayor here after hours?

Though, he supposed it probably wasn't too odd for a politician to meet with a property developer.

Frank pointed a key fob at his car causing it to beep as the doors locked. Then he walked into the office, and Wilder's curiosity got the better of him. He exited his car, closing his door quietly. Then he made his way next to the house.

Wilder pressed against the exterior and then leaned toward the window to catch a peek at the two men. Fortunately, the men were staring at each other and didn't notice him.

Martin's face was red. Angry. Frank was yelling, but Wilder couldn't make out the words. The construction was too good; the room was soundproof. Then Frank pulled an envelope out of his jacket and handed it to Martin, who opened it and pulled out cash. A lot of cash.

Why would the mayor be paying Martin?

Frank turned and walked out the office door.

Shit, he's coming outside.

Wilder peeled away from the wall and looked for a bush to hide behind. There were none.

Why the fuck are there no bushes?

Hearing the front door open, he was out of time, and he ran toward the back of the home as fast as he could. He'd just rounded the corner when he heard the beep of Frank unlocking his car with his key fob.

Once he heard the mayor's car drive off, Wilder made his way back to the front door. He knocked, then entered.

"For fuck's sake, I told you no!" Martin yelled as he came out of the office that sat at the front of the house. Once he saw Wilder, he stuttered to a stop. "Oh, sorry. I thought you were someone else."

"Oh? Who?"

Martin waved his hand. "A landscaper. He keeps coming by and trying to push his services on me."

Wilder looked over his shoulder at the lots. They were all dirt, as none of the houses were complete yet. "A little premature, isn't he?"

Martin sighed and walked into the office. Wilder followed.

"Actually no. I've already contracted a landscape designer, and we're shopping for a landscaping company to make it a reality." He sat down and smiled at Wilder as if he hadn't completely blown up his life.

Wilder took a deep breath. Now was not the time to deal with that.

"What brings you by?" Martin prompted before he could speak. "Ready to buy a home?"

He chuckled. "Not yet."

Not ever, from this asshole.

"I heard the old poker games were still going on and you're now hosting them. I'd love to join."

Martin smirked. "You drove all the way out here to ask about a poker game?"

Shit. He wasn't going to make this easy.

"Aside from helping my brother with his wedding, I don't have a lot to do. It was no big deal to drive out here."

"Are you in town for the wedding? Or are you back for good?" Martin stared at some papers on his desk, trying to look disinterested.

This was a test; he'd already asked Wilder this the last time he was here.

Wilder crossed his arms. "I told you, I'm here to mend things with my family. I'm not sure about the rest yet."

Martin nodded and shifted his eyes so they were on the window. "So then why tour model homes and tell Melia you might buy a house?"

He shrugged. "Keeping my options open."

"You aren't trying to get Kate back?"

How dare he say her fucking name to me?

Though he knew exactly why that asshole was asking.

Wilder was happy Martin wasn't staring at him because he needed a minute to school his features. As much as he wanted to punch this guy, he needed to stay on his good side to get in that poker game.

Those guys talked more than one might expect; if he wanted to learn what was going on around town, that was the place to be.

Unclenching his jaw and dropping his hands to his hips, he finally replied, "No, not here for Kate."

After a beat, Martin met his gaze. "Good luck with your family. I'm afraid the poker game is full. But maybe we'll find room for you at the next one, if you're still in town."

What the fuck? He was excluding him? Wilder glanced out the window Martin kept staring at and he realized with the lights on inside, it was like a mirror.

Well, shit.

If Martin saw him glaring at him then that explains why he wouldn't invite him to the game. Trying not to reveal his disappointment, he rapped his knuckles on Martin's desk. "I'll let you get back to it, then." He walked toward the door, but the need for more answers made him pause. "Did I see the mayor leaving when I pulled up?" he asked as he turned back around.

A vein on Martin's forehead bulged at the realization that Wilder didn't buy his landscaper story. "Yeah, he stopped by. He was checking on the progress of the project. Something about wanting to tell his constituents."

Martin tugged on his loosened tie.

"And how is the progress?"

Martin cocked his head. "Why do you want to know?"

Wilder shrugged. "The mayor looked pretty pissed."

"He did?"

Martin stood and walked around the desk to face him. "Why are you asking about the mayor?"

It appeared he was used to controlling the room. But Wilder used the six inches he had on the man and stood tall. "I figure if I know Frank's business, I can keep away from it. I don't want to see him anymore than I have to while I'm here. He isn't my biggest fan."

Martin nodded. "He hates you for leaving."

"He said that?"

Come on, Martin, admit you talked to him.

Martin smiled. "I'm truly sorry about you and Kate."

Wilder bit his cheek to keep from saying something. He was pretty sure Martin didn't know that Scott had come clean about his family's involvement.

Martin continued, "But I find things usually work out for the best. You know?" He gave a smarmy smile that Wilder wanted to knock off his face.

The man wasn't sorry at all; he was actually enjoying the fact that he'd pulled one over on Wilder.

Or so he thinks. Martin had better hope he isn't involved in the drug trafficking in this town because I am itching to get my revenge.

Chapter Twelve

Kate hadn't spoken to Wilder since she poured iced tea on him last week. She was nervous about seeing him again but had put it off as long as she could. Holly texted stating Zach agreed to let them use his pub. The problem? The only date available was less than two weeks away. She and Wilder had to work on planning this party and that was why she was now sitting down at Brannigan's Pub, waiting to meet him.

For a moment, she'd thought against meeting here again, but then she decided she was more comfortable here. She'd spent a lot of time at the pub. She even took a shift every now and again so Zach and Jessie could have a night off together.

She wished she could take credit for initiating the 'civil' contact between her and Wilder, but before she'd gotten up the nerve to text him about the party planning, *he* had texted *her*. Apparently, Holly had given him her number as well.

Most guys would take a hint after having a beverage dumped on their head.

But Wilder had never been like most guys; that's what had won her over when they were younger. Seeing as that hadn't changed, she was worried about spending so much time with him on wedding plans and getting all 'swoony,' as her mother had put it.

Fortunately, she'd already figured out a great plan that had them meeting only once more, very briefly, to go over a few details. The division of labor was a pretty genius idea, in her opinion.

She'd even rehearsed what she was going to say to him to keep their meeting brief. She would say it and then hand him her new, revised list of tasks they each needed to complete for the party. But she wasn't sure she could go through with it. While her head told her she needed to keep her space with Wilder and limit the amount of contact they had, her heart wanted the opposite. Which was ridiculous. The man had only apologized to her. Nothing more. If she let her heart take control, she'd only get hurt again.

That was confirmed when he walked in the door, and she was caught completely off-guard. His eyes met hers and when he smiled, it reminded her of how he used to look at her back when they were in love. She gripped the table to keep from jumping up and running into his arms.

Wilder walked to the bar to order a drink and she took him in. He wore a black T-shirt that stretched across his chest, and jeans that fit just right. From this angle, she had a full view of his ass.

God, those jeans look good on him. Part of her wanted to know what he looked like under that shirt now, too.

She shook her head. *Shit, get it together.*

Yes, he was a good-looking guy, but he was the man that broke her heart. Maybe if she kept repeating that, she wouldn't forget it.

After Wilder got his drink, he spun around and located her, making solid eye contact again. His dark hair was combed back, and his eyes looked a deeper blue than normal.

Even though she knew she should look away, she couldn't. Then he smiled, and her stomach fluttered.

This is so not good.

As he sat down and the smell of his cologne wafted over her, she recognized that it was the same scent he used to wear. It brought back so many memories…

No, she was still pissed at him. They were only meeting to discuss the party, nothing else.

Never mind that when he ran his hand through his hair, it reminded her of when she would do it. His hair had been so soft… She wondered if it still was.

"Kate. You're beautiful."

She closed her eyes. "No. We are here to talk about the party, and that's it."

"Okay."

He leaned back, folding his arms, and she stared at the way his biceps flexed against his T-shirt.

How the damn thing didn't rip was beyond her. It was snug all over, almost like it had been fitted just for him.

"The party?" he prompted.

Her eyes snapped to his. He was grinning.

Damn him. He'd worn that shirt on purpose. But it wouldn't distract her.

"I see you didn't order iced tea this time," she quipped, her eyes on his beer.

He chuckled. "No, thought I'd try something new in case you decided to pour this one over my head too. A man can only take so many iced tea jokes."

She tried to suppress her smile, but he caught it.

"You're still a bit hot-tempered, aren't you?" he asked.

Her cheeks heated and she clenched her fists under the table. "No!" she said a bit too defensively.

Ugh. It would be easier if she'd planned this whole damn party herself. It was bad enough to have to sit across from Wilder in his sexy as hell T-shirt, smelling like heaven.

She closed her eyes. No, there was nothing good about him. He hadn't believed her, nor would he listen to her when it counted the most.

She only wanted to get through this meeting and go home.

Focus on the party. Not his biceps.

She cleared her throat. "I've devised a plan to simplify our coordination of this event. We each have a list of tasks. Assuming we each do what we need to, we only have to meet one more time before the party to finalize the details. Then we have the party, attend the wedding, and then you can leave."

"Trying to get rid of me already?" he teased.

She glanced up and locked eyes. "Yes."

He huffed. "You didn't let me finish that night, when you interrupted my story with that refreshing iced tea bath. There was more to it."

"I don't need to know." She handed him a printout of the tasks he needed to complete.

Wilder opened his mouth to object because she very much needed to know, when a loud group walked into the pub.

Both Wilder and Kate looked up in time to lock eyes with Martin Fisher. He frowned and gave them a quick nod before heading to the bar with his friends.

Wilder growled as he turned back.

Kate cocked her head, watching him. "Did Martin piss you off?"

Wilder drained his beer. "You could say that." He set the glass on the table and leaned forward. "Like I said, there's more to the story. You want to know *why* Scott set you up?"

"You know?"

He nodded. "He said Martin paid him to do it."

Kate's body tensed. *Martin paid Scott? Martin is responsible for ruining my marriage?*

No. This was too much. Martin was the key to her future. What the hell was she supposed to do with this information?

Her mouth went dry as she tried not to react.

Had it not been for Martin's meddling, would she and Wilder still be married? Would they be happy? Would they have the kids they'd talked about?

Martin robbed us of that life, of that choice.

"Kate."

She turned her attention to Wilder but said nothing.

"Martin doesn't know I know, and I'd like to keep it that way. All right?"

She frowned. "Why?"

Avoiding her gaze, he stared at his empty pint glass. "I can't tell you, but please, Kate, don't say anything."

She understood why *she* was avoiding confrontation with Martin; if she lost the development's contract, well, that was the only business she had right now. She had a lot to lose. But Wilder? He was only here for his brother's wedding. Why did he care about the consequences?

The old Wilder would have been livid and simply decked the guy. Hell, he'd decked Scott — *twice* now. So, what the hell was going on?

She let out an exasperated breath. "You need to explain. You punched Scott the first chance you got, but when it comes to the mastermind… what, you're letting him off?"

Wilder grabbed her hand, about to protest, but her eyes immediately went to their connection. It lit her whole body on fire, and she wanted nothing more than to crawl across the table and kiss this man.

She shook her head. Holy hell she needed to get a hold of herself. His presence, his cologne… it was all too much.

She yanked her hand away.

He stared at his now empty hand and sighed. "Listen to me, Kate. I'm not letting him off. You have to trust he'll get what he deserves. But he can't know yet that I know. Got it?"

Is Wilder plotting revenge? That's not like him.

Although, what did she really know anymore? Ten years could change a person.

But what did it matter? After the wedding, Wilder would leave, and she could get on with her life.

Get on playing nice with Martin. Ugh.

That was the last thing she wanted, but a necessity when the man owned the only company putting up new housing in their town. She had tried to advertise to individual homeowners in her hometown, but most weren't interested. Then Martin had suggested she put in a bid for the landscape design on his new development, she did.

Unfortunately, all the new construction going up in Fisher Springs and the neighboring Davenport were all under Martin's company. Until Wilder dropped this revelation, she figured she could deal with Martin and his advances. But now that she knew this? She wasn't so sure she could continue to play nice.

"Fine," she grunted. "I won't say anything, but how do you know Scott hasn't told him that he told you?"

"I can tell."

She wanted to know how, but before she could ask, he spoke again.

"Um, Kate? There's something I want to ask you."

It had better be about this damn party.

"What?"

"Your dad… Is there any chance he might be involved in something with Martin Fisher?"

She jolted back in surprise. "My dad?"

Why the hell would Wilder want to know anything about her *dad*? The two men had never liked each other. There was no reason to discuss him. Unless...

"Wilder? Are you just trying to put off dealing with this party?"

"No, I really want to know if your dad has involvement with Martin."

She leaned forward. "In case you forgot, I don't really have much of a relationship with my dad. That didn't change because you left."

He swallowed, and her eyes were immediately glued to his Adam's apple.

Why the hell does he have such a sexy neck?

"I'm sorry," he said.

She shook her head. "Don't be. If it wasn't my relationship with you, my dad would have found something else wrong with me."

Wilder reached across and put his hand on top of hers. This time, she didn't yank it away.

"Seriously, I'm sorry," he murmured. "I know how much you had hoped he could forgive you."

She closed her eyes, lost in the familiarity of his touch, his cologne... With Wilder being nice, it was all too much. But he had been the one who was there for her when her parents found out they'd eloped. Her father had been cold and distant even prior to that, but after she got married, it was almost as if she didn't exist.

"Stop. I can't take this, Wilder."

"Can't take what?"

She pointed at their hands. "This. You. I'm angry with you, I can't deal with you being nice to me."

He squeezed her hand, and then let her pull away. "I have so much to apologize for. Please let me, Kate. I've missed you so much."

He missed her? He didn't have the *right* to miss her. He was the one who left!

She blinked back the tears that threatened to fall. She would *not* cry over him. She had done enough of that when he'd left her without a single look back.

Willing her voice not to break, she told him, "Just do your tasks for the party," she said as she shoved the piece of paper with his to do list in front of him. "I'll text you to set up one more meeting. Then that's it. We have nothing else to discuss."

She stood, and Wilder grabbed her wrist.

"Please sit down. There is one more thing we need to discuss."

Warily, she looked around the bar. She knew she should leave, she did. But several people were watching them. Wilder's eyes were pleading. Maybe he was going to beg for her forgiveness.

"Fine." She sat and crossed her arms. She probably looked like a petulant child, but she didn't give a rat's ass at this point.

Wilder leaned forward and lowered his voice. "I know you said you don't have much of a relationship with your dad, but would you have any idea why he would give Martin a handful of cash. Do you have any idea what that might be for?"

He wanted to talk about her dad again? Tears stung her eyes. No. She wouldn't show him her disappointment. "I just told you I'm not close to my dad. I don't want to talk about him."

Wilder sat back and gave her a nod.

"Sorry. I understand."

How would Wilder have seen something like that? Unless…

"Are you following Martin? How do you know what he's doing?"

Wilder stared at the table. "I interviewed for a construction job at Martin's development."

Kate's mouth fell open. "You're staying in town?"

He shrugged. "I'm thinking about it."

Then he glanced up and met her gaze. "Would you mind if I did?"

She swallowed hard. Would she mind? Hell, she couldn't get her head on straight when she thought he was only here for a few more weeks but moving here? Permanently? It was too much to think about.

Avoiding his question, she asked, "You want to work for Martin?"

Disappointment flashed across his face but then he shook his head. "No, I would be working for the construction crew. Believe me, I don't want to work for that man in any way."

She winced. Neither did she but she didn't have a lot of choices right now.

"While on site, I saw your father give Martin a lot of cash. I then went to talk to Martin, but he thought it was your dad coming back, and before he saw who I was, he yelled, 'I told you no!' I'm curious why your dad would pay Martin in cash."

What *would* her dad want from Martin?

Unless Wilder thought her dad really was behind what Scott did, and believed he was pressing Martin to do it again.

God, that's probably it. He's so paranoid.

Whatever it was, she wanted no part of it. Right now, she needed to be alone to process that he may be back to stay.

"Like I said, I don't know his business. I have no idea what the two of them would be doing together, and frankly, I don't care. I need to go." Kate stood, grabbed her purse, then

walked out the door.

Wilder did not follow, and instead of being relieved at his absence, she was disappointed.

Chapter Thirteen

Kate slammed the loaded plate down on the diner table, causing a piece of toast to fall off and onto the floor. The couple startled and Kate winced.

"Sorry," she said to them.

"It's all right dear," the woman said.

Thankfully, they were regulars who knew Kate was not normally this pissy.

"Kate? A minute please?" her boss spoke up from behind her.

Great. Logan wants to talk to me. Probably about my shitty attitude.

It has only been a couple of days since she'd seen Wilder. A couple of days that she'd thought of nothing but seeing Wilder daily if he moved back to town. She really wasn't sure she could do it. What if he dated someone in town? What if he brought her to the diner? All of it made her sick to her stomach. And angry. Which was ridiculous because of course he'd dated other women over the last ten years.

Yeah, but she didn't have to watch it.

"I'll grab them some more toast," Harmony said as she put a hand on Kate's shoulder and gave it a squeeze.

"Thank you," Kate said then headed toward the kitchen grateful to be at the end of the breakfast rush. She found Logan in the locker area, leaning up against the wall.

He arched a brow. "What's going on?"

"I'm sorry. My ex is back in town, and he said some things that really pissed me off, and I can't stop thinking about it."

Normally, she wouldn't be so open about her personal business, but Logan wasn't just her boss, he was a friend. Everyone she worked with at the diner was more like family.

"Wilder? Yeah, Harmony filled me in."

I'm surprised he hasn't heard about it from all the customers too. She barely suppressed an eye roll.

She hadn't encountered one person that didn't know about the 'Iced Tea Escapade,' as the town now called it.

Logan took a deep breath. "From what I hear, he's going to be around a while. Perhaps we can find another way to channel your anger rather than slamming plates?"

Kate nodded. "I'm sorry."

"Don't be sorry for feeling. That's what makes us human. Just try not to scare any more customers." He grinned.

She smiled back. "Thanks, Logan. You're a good guy, you know that?"

He chuckled. "I know."

"Have you made your move yet?"

Logan's face flushed red. "*Shh!* No. And no one here knows about that."

She had to bite her lip to keep from telling him that *everyone* knew about his crush on Sophie, the best friend of his little sister Adele. She didn't want to shatter his illusion of privacy.

After a few drinks one night, Logan had confided in Kate that he had a thing for Sophie. But because of Adele, Logan hadn't made a move nor felt he could. Kate had tried to convince him he should with no luck.

Too bad, because Kate was pretty sure that Sophie felt the same way, based on the way they sparred with each other whenever she came in.

"Okay, you should get back out there," Logan told her. "And if you can't find a release for that anger, let me know, and I'll bring you with me to my gym."

"Wait, isn't that a boxing gym?"

"It is. Might do you some good to hit some bags."

Hmm. That sounded fun.

"I might take you up on that."

"Good. Now good luck out there." Logan winked as she headed out the double doors to the dining room.

Kate was able to stay calm for all of five minutes. Then her dad walked in.

He beelined straight for her and took a stool at the counter. "Kate, a moment?"

"I'm at work. I can't really talk."

She knew he could've called her on her lie; they weren't very busy, and no one was sitting nearby. She could easily spare some time — if she'd wanted to.

"This will only take a minute," he pressed.

She exhaled through her nose.

Watching her, her dad said, "I saw Wilder at the carnival on Memorial Day weekend, and I understand he's back in town. I hope you plan to stay away from him."

Kate laughed. "You're kidding me, right? I'm an adult. I'll hang out with whoever I want. I need to get back to work."

"Wait. Can I get a coffee to-go?"

Kate sighed then grabbed a to-go cup and set it on the counter.

Her dad's jaw ticked. "Kate, I'm afraid that family will reflect poorly on ours."

" 'That family'?"

Kate watched as her dad looked around then brought his eyes back to hers. "Like you said, you're an adult, so I'm sure you know about his parents' open marriage. Everyone in town knows." He scoffed and shook his head. "I'm so glad you are no longer with that man, otherwise the town would probably be saying the same thing about you two."

She turned her back to get the coffeepot and to hide the surprise she was sure was on her face. *Open marriage?*

Wilder had told Kate stories of how his mother had cheated on his dad and expressed his disbelief that his dad had stayed despite all that. But she'd never heard anything about an open marriage. She wondered if Wilder knew the truth.

She shook her head. It didn't matter.

"No worries, Dad. We are only being civil to each other to get through his brother's wedding. Then he will hopefully be leaving town." She started pouring coffee into his cup.

He leaned back. "Leaving town? You sure about that? I heard he got a job on Topher's construction crew. And he's not staying at the motel or his parents' place—he's renting an apartment."

She looked up at her father, astonished. He was serious. *Wilder mentioned an interview but he accepted the job? And an apartment? That doesn't sound very temporary.*

"Kate, the coffee!"

She glanced down to see she'd over-poured and now had a puddle on the counter.

She returned the coffeepot to its cradle and grabbed some towels. "Sorry."

After she mopped up the coffee, she raised her eyes to see her dad staring at her.

"Like I said," he rumbled, "you should stay away from him. He's nothing but trouble."

She knew her dad had never liked Wilder; that was no secret. But to actively try to keep them apart after all these years?

Why?

Her conversation with Wilder at the pub the other day came back to her. *Could* her dad have had something to do with Martin and Scott? She didn't want to believe it, but...

"Dad, what do you think of Martin Fisher?"

His face scrunched up, and he coughed a laugh at her fast change of topic. "Martin Fisher?" He frowned. "He's a good businessman, contributes to the community... nothing wrong with him."

"Yes, but do you like him?"

The man chuckled. "I'm a politician, I have to pretend to like everyone."

That wasn't really an answer.

She huffed. "Okay, what if I said I was dating him?"

His smile dropped. "No, don't date him."

Interesting.

"Why not?"

"I hope you're kidding, otherwise your taste in men has me deeply concerned."

"I'm curious if you would hate any guy I dated."

"Not all guys. I like that guy, Jared."

"The librarian's son?"

Her dad smiled. "Yes, that's the one."

Funny her dad would choose the one guy that wouldn't be into her.

She resisted the urge to shake her head. "I think Jared prefers men."

"Oh? Shame. I thought you two were well-suited for each other. Oh, I have to run. But please do me a favor and stay away from Wilder. I don't want to see you hurt again." He stood up and tossed a five-dollar bill on the counter, then he turned and walked out of the diner — leaving the coffee.

She chewed on her lip as she watched him go.

It was curious that her dad didn't like Martin for her either; it made her wonder what he knew. But what had her more distracted was the fact that Wilder had apparently moved back to town and gotten a job.

Why would he do that? And where has he been for the last ten years?

The next couple of hours went by quickly. Kate was deep in the middle of the lunch rush when Martin walked in and took the last empty seat at the counter.

Kate steeled herself then handed him a menu. "I'll be right with you."

At his nod, she grabbed the coffeepot and walked as far away from him as possible.

The desire to pour coffee in his lap was strong. How the hell was she going to act normal around him?

By the time she made it back to the counter, Martin had set down the menu and was staring off into space. She wondered if he'd smiled when Wilder had left town ten years ago. Was he happy about what he'd done? Or did he feel guilty?

"Know what you want?" She snapped.

"Are you and Wilder getting back together?"

She abruptly spun around, turning her back to him, and clutched the handle on the coffeepot, trying to calm herself. Then she set the pitcher down on the counter, dropped her hands to her hips, and turned back around. "Didn't you already ask me this?"

He shrugged. "That was before everyone was talking about how Wilder is back to stay."

She sighed. "No."

She wasn't going to give Martin any more ammunition.

"Good."

"Good?"

"Yes. Now let me take you out."

She frowned. "You're kidding, right?" Why the hell was he asking her out again?

He didn't crack a smile. "No, I don't kid."

"No, you just sabotage marriages."

Her eyes widened when she realized what she'd said.

Martin's jaw clenched, and his cheeks and forehead flushed hot. "Where did you hear that?" he asked evenly.

"Wilder told me."

Shit. She just couldn't stop!

"I think I've lost my appetite." Martin stood up and marched out of the diner.

Fuck!

Had she destroyed her business? Martin was the only contract she had.

There was no time to think about that. Her gut told her she needed to tell Wilder what she'd done.

She ran to the back. "Logan, I need to take a five-minute break."

Not waiting for his response, she pushed the crash bar on the back door and shot off a text.

Kate: *Accidentally accused Martin of blowing up our marriage*

The response was immediate.

Wilder: *You better be joking.*

Kate: *No, sorry. He asked me on a date again and I got angry.*

Wilder: *He asked you on a date? Again?*

She stared at her phone. That really wasn't what he should be focusing on.

Kate: *Yes. He keeps asking.*

Wilder: *Did you ever say yes?*

What the hell?

Kate: *Not that it is any of your business but no.*

Her phone rang.

"What, Wilder?" She knew she was being rude, but he was being ridiculous.

"Sorry. Just the idea of Martin moving in on you after what he did… it pisses me off."

She bit her lip. "Are you jealous?"

He sighed into the phone. "Yeah, I am. I'm jealous of any man you're with because as far as I'm concerned, I'm the only man who should have that honor."

Her heart was racing. She couldn't believe what she was hearing. "What?"

He didn't speak for a minute.

"Wilder?"

"This isn't how I wanted to bring this up, but we should never have split up. We should be together now. But I know ten years is a lot of time, and people change, so for now... would you let me take you out? On a date? Let's get to know each other again. Because dammit, Kate, I've missed you, and being near you but not being *with* you is driving me crazy."

Holy shit, that was romantic. But she was still angry with him. And how could she trust him again? She needed time to think.

"I'm not sure that's a good idea. Yes, a lot of time has passed, but that doesn't change the fact that when it came down to it, you didn't trust me. That hurt me deeper than you know. For now, let's just plan the party and get through your brother's wedding."

She heard him sigh. "Wilder?"

"Yeah?"

"I'm sorry I told Martin."

"Me too." He ended the call.

She stood there, unsure if she'd made the right decision in pushing him away. Part of her wanted to say yes to a date with Wilder. But if she did, what would have changed? If he didn't take her word ten years ago, what would happen the next time Martin tried to interfere with their relationship?

Because her gut said that man *would* try again.

Chapter Fourteen

Wilder dropped to the cement floor of the unfinished garage to take a break. Nearly a week had passed since Kate had told Martin she knew. A week that Wilder spent working on the construction crew right under Martin's nose. He'd sensed Martin watching him these last few days, probably wondering why he hadn't punched him the way he had Scott.

He wanted to. But he had to put this case first.

It had also been a week since he'd told Kate he wanted to try again, and she said no. He couldn't lie; that stung.

But he had to remember why he was here: in two and a half weeks, someone was going to try to blow up the town. And he had made little progress in finding out who.

Guzzling down the remaining water in his bottle, he realized he still had two hours left in his shift. Two more hours of lugging in bags of mortar into the bathrooms of the unfinished homes. But then he wouldn't have to lift anything until Monday. His muscles screamed hallelujah at that thought.

Topher was a nice guy, but he got a bit too much enjoyment from watching Wilder suffer. It had been a long time since Wilder had done hard labor and damn, he was sore.

At one point, his arms had started shaking while he was holding up the cabinet, and to explain, he had to tell the guys he'd been out of work for a couple of weeks.

They all nodded knowingly, but Topher nicknamed him Noodle — as in noodle arms.

"Noodle!"

He turned to find Billy grinning at him.

Billy was the loudest of everyone, cracking jokes every few minutes. The guys all laughed, even though the jokes really weren't that funny. Their overexuberance was the reason Wilder went out of his way to befriend the man. He wasn't sure if the others were scared of him or looked up to him for some reason.

"Yeah?" he called back.

"Follow me. We need you."

Please don't let this involve more heavy lifting.

He followed him inside one of the houses, to the laundry room.

"More cabinet work." Billy grinned.

Topher was standing on the other side of the cabinet. "Ready to lift, Noodle?"

"Yeah, let's get this done," Wilder said.

Together, they lifted the unit and held it to the wall. Wilder knew he was in trouble seconds later, when his arms began shaking.

"Are you almost done?" he spit out, trying to focus on holding up the cabinet.

"Just about," Billy said. "Oh damn. The screw bent. Let me get it out."

And just like that, Wilder's arms gave way, and he dropped his side of the cabinet.

Billy caught it from underneath, saving it, and he and Topher lowered it to the ground.

"You didn't have *any* screws in?" Wilder asked.

Topher laughed. "Nope."

Billy stepped up close to him. "I saw your arms jiggling and we've noticed you've been moving a little slower today. But we figured you'd be back to your old self by now. You sure you worked construction?"

Both men stared at him.

The hair on the back of his neck went up. Something was wrong. "I did. But I told you I didn't work for a couple of weeks. I took some time off to deal with some family stuff, so I'm a bit out of shape."

Topher narrowed his eyes. "You know what we do to guys who aren't quite in shape?"

Wilder glanced from Billy to Topher. Both were large men, and here he was trapped in a small space with them. He didn't even have his service revolver because he was undercover. And hell, he didn't think he'd need anything like that, working at a construction site that didn't appear to have any criminal activity.

Just this morning, he'd almost called Simpson to tell him he was certain Joey was feeding them false information. But now he wasn't so sure.

Topher took a step forward. "We make them… unload the truck. Now get out there, it ain't gonna unload itself." He and Billy laughed.

"Oh man, you should have seen your face!" Billy wiped his eyes; he was laughing so hard. "What did you think he was going to say?"

"Wait, I'm being hazed at a job?" Wilder wasn't quite sure he was reading this right.

Topher put an arm around his shoulder. "Nah, we don't haze. Think of it more as an initiation."

The man led him outside to a truck that hadn't been there before; it was one of the unlabeled ones.

Still trying to play it cool, Wilder laughed. "Tell me it's not those heavy as fuck bags of mortar."

Billy opened up the back. "Nope."

Staring back at him were wall-to-wall boxes.

"Nails?" he gaped. "You want me to unload nails?"

Billy grinned. "Yep."

Well, shit. These boxes usually weighed around fifty pounds apiece. Normally, that wouldn't be so bad, but damn, he was already sore.

He sighed. "Where do you want them?"

Topher nodded toward the open garage. "Just inside the doors."

"Okay. I'd better get to work."

Wilder grabbed a box and carried it into the garage, which was attached to a house that was almost finished. The garage itself still needed some work. The drywall still needed to be mudded, sanded, then painted.

It wasn't until his walk back to the truck that he realized this wasn't the closest house to the ones they were framing. He groaned, realizing the guys would probably ask him to move the nails two houses down on Monday.

"Hey, Topher," he called out.

Topher was standing next to the truck, staring at his phone, but he glanced up at the sound of his name.

"Wouldn't it make more sense to put these in that garage?" Wilder pointed two houses down, to one next door to the next three lots they'd be building.

Topher stared at him for a minute. "Nope. This is good." Then the man walked to the house Wilder had just pointed at.

Now that Wilder thought about it, he hadn't been inside that house yet. Maybe he needed to change that.

Two hours later, he'd unloaded all the nails. He'd taken his time, hoping everyone would be gone by the time he was done, and he'd be able to peek into that mysterious house. But no such luck. Topher never left the site, and Wilder couldn't stick around without raising suspicion.

"Noodle, good news!" Billy said as he approached. "The guys chipped in and got you a massage. Your appointment's in thirty minutes." He handed him a piece of paper with an address on it.

Wilder glanced up and arched a brow.

Billy laughed. "Seriously, this is legit. A lot of the guys go here."

Wilder nodded. "Thanks. I'll check it out."

The address was in Davenport; he needed to leave right away to make it on time. He hoped like hell this was a legitimate place.

On the drive over, he replayed the last week in his head. He hadn't seen anything suspicious; all he had to show for his time was a sore back. And now he was about to get a massage.

Shaking his head, Wilder parked then glanced again at the address on the paper Billy had given him. It was for an apartment building. With a furrowed brow, Wilder got out of the car and walked to the door. He buzzed the unit number that had been listed as a suite number. Billy must have written the address down wrong.

"Hello?" a woman's voice asked through the intercom.

"Uh, hi… I think I have the wrong place."

"Are you here for a massage?"

"Y-yes."

"I'll be down in a minute."

Wilder remained in place, though he was not too sure about this. He was concerned that his definition of a massage and Billy's weren't the same.

Before he could think too hard on it, a familiar blonde came out the door.

"Wilder?"

"Bridgette?"

"Are you here for the massage?" Her eyes lit up, and he *knew* this was a mistake.

"I'm sorry, I think I should go."

"Nonsense." Bridgette spun him around and began rubbing his shoulders. "You are so tense. Come up to my place, and I'll rub that out."

Wilder choked on air. Again, he wasn't exactly sure what she was offering, but after their run-in that first weekend he'd been back, he wasn't about to find out.

"Wilder? Is that you?"

Oh no. He turned to see Mr. Finley walking down the street.

"Not wasting any time, are you, son?" the old man sneered.

"Excuse me?"

"I see you around town with Kate and now here you are with this blonde vixen."

Oh god. It was not going to help his case if Kate's neighbor spread rumors about him and Bridgette.

"No, it's not what you think. Bridgette was offering me a massage, but I told her I need to go," he assured the old man.

Bridgette continued to rub his shoulders. "No, you need to come up to my place so I could work out these tense muscles."

Mr. Finley's bushy brows jerked up to his hairline. "A massage?" He glanced at Bridgette. "I'm not an idiot, I know what that's code for." He practically darted to his car.

"Mr. Finley, no, it's not like that!"

Wilder went to follow that man but Bridgette grabbed a hold of his shoulders.

"Let him go. Come upstairs."

He shook her off and went after Mr. Finley, but it was too late. The old man drove off before he could stop him.

Shit!

He debated calling Kate to ward off any rumors she might hear. It *was* an excuse to talk to her.

He reached for his phone.

No, he'd been going crazy not knowing what she was thinking this past week. He wanted to see her in person.

Chapter Fifteen

Wilder grinned when he saw he'd beaten Mr. Finley back to Kate's house. But then, knowing the old man loved to gossip, he'd probably stopped at the diner to share his latest scoop.

Practically holding his breath, Wilder pulled into Kate's driveway and walked up to her porch. He had to smile at the welcoming vibe the two chairs and single table provided.

When she didn't answer his knock on the door, he had a moment to worry that Mr. Finley had gotten to her after all. Her car was in the driveway, so she was likely home.

Maybe she's avoiding me.

Not giving up hope yet, he went around to the back, where he spotted a light on in what he presumed by the textured glass of the window to be a bathroom.

Well, he couldn't break in; that would only draw more attention and create more rumors. He was stuck waiting.

He walked back around to the front and plopped himself down in one of the porch chairs. When Chase jogged over a few minutes later, Wilder chuckled at how small the town really was.

"Wilder? Is that you?"

"Yeah."

Chase came up the walkway. "Is this a good sign, you waiting for Kate on her porch?"

Wilder grinned. "I'm trying to make it one."

Chase nodded. "Is that why you came back a month before the wedding?"

Wilder didn't want to lie to his friend, but he couldn't tell him the entire truth either.

"Not originally," he admitted. "But then Scott told me he'd only made it look like he and Kate had sex."

Chase's brows shot up. "What?"

"He said he drugged her and set up the bedroom, so I'd draw that conclusion when I saw it."

"Fuck. That's cold. Damn. I'd arrest the guy, but the statute already ran on that. Why would he do that? He never showed interest in dating her after you left."

Wilder ground his teeth. "Martin paid him to do it."

"Oh shit. I've seen Martin hitting on her. She turns him down every time, though, you have to know that."

"I know."

The front door opened.

"What are you two doing here?"

Wilder spun around and Kate was peering at both of them with her body hidden behind the door.

Chase nodded to her. "I just stopped for a second. I'd better finish my run." Then he turned to Wilder. "Good luck."

"Thanks."

When Chase went on his way, Wilder stepped up to the doorway and stood face to face with Kate. Her hair was wet, and she had no makeup on. She didn't need any. She was still stunning.

"Why are you here? Is it about the party?"

"No."

"Then leave." Kate began to close the door, but Wilder got his boot in the way.

"We have to talk. Can I come in?"

This was the closest he'd been to her since he'd been back, and the smell of jasmine hung thickly in the air. He closed his eyes. Was it possible she still used the same body lotion? It brought back a lot of memories he didn't have any business reliving right now.

Kate sighed. "I guess I'd better let you in. Mr. Finley called to tell me that you were loitering on my porch, and I'm sure he's still watching."

Oh shit, the old guy is home? Wilder spun around to see the old man standing next to his front window.

"About Mr. Finley..." he said.

He forgot his train of thought when he stepped inside and took in what she was wearing. Her silky robe complimented her curves, but when she bent over to move some pillows from the couch, it fell open just enough.

"Kate," his voice was husky. "Are you wearing anything under that?"

She glanced down then pulled the garment closed, tying it tight. "No, I'd just gotten out of the shower when Mr. Finley called."

He couldn't stop staring and his fingers itched to touch her.

"Wilder, why are you here?"

His eyes snapped up to hers.

"Right. About Mr. Finley, I saw him—"

"Please tell me you didn't yell at the poor man. I'm pretty sure he started that damn iced tea rumor, but he's harmless."

"No, I didn't yell at him—though I might have if I'd known all the iced tea jokes were his fault. But it's his habit of starting rumors that brings me here."

Kate walked to the sofa and sat down, wrapping a blanket around herself. "Are you worried what this town thinks of you now? Can't take a little teasing?" She quirked a brow.

Wilder sat on the opposite end of the couch. "No, that's not it. One of the guys on the crew set up a massage for me."

"Crew?"

"My construction crew. I'm working on the new development by the high school."

"Ah. I've heard you have a job. Are you planning on staying in town permanently?"

His stomach was in knots. He wanted to tell her he'd move here in a heartbeat to be with her, but he didn't want to scare her away.

But what would he do for a living if he did move here? The police station in Fisher Springs only employed three people, and their detective position was filled.

Maybe Davenport has openings.

Hell, maybe he could still work for Summit County. All he would have to do is convince his boss to let him work the eastern part of the county.

"It's something I'd consider," he said finally.

There, that left things open.

Kate fidgeted with her hands, and he could sense she was growing impatient.

He needed to get to the point before she kicked him out.

"Anyway, the guys on the crew decided to get me a massage, since I've been so sore this week. But when I went to the appointment, I discovered it was at an apartment building."

Kate stood up and walked across the room. "I don't know why you are telling me this. It really isn't my business."

Wilder stood and stepped closer to her. "It *is*. I told you I want to try again, and I meant it. And the reason I'm telling you this is because when the masseuse came to the front door to let me up into the building, I told her I'd changed my mind. She began to rub my shoulders and try to talk me into staying, and

Mr. Finley walked by at that moment and jumped to conclusions."

She walked back to the couch, grabbed a pillow, and hugged it as she sat down. "He must have seen something suspicious, to make you feel so hard-pressed as to warn me."

"What?" His brows shot up. "No! Bridgette was only massaging my back and neck."

"Wait, Bridgette?"

Thank god, Mr. Finley hadn't said anything.

"You remember her?"

Kate gripped the pillow tighter. "She went after your brother knowing he was with Holly. She's known for collecting conquests."

Wilder cocked his head, and his lips quirked up. "Do I detect a touch of jealousy?"

She frowned. "No. And I don't need to know what kind of massage you got. Is that why you're here?"

This was not going how he'd hoped.

"I didn't get any massage, I left. But yeah, I was worried Mr. Finley would give you the wrong impression."

"What does that matter?"

"I told you, I want to try again."

She opened her mouth to speak, but Wilder held up his hand.

"I know you said no, but before you say it again, hold on."

Shit. He had nothing to say. If she wouldn't give him another chance… Well, he deserved that, but…

No, it can't go this way.

"Let's be friends." He couldn't believe the words even as they left his mouth, but there they were.

"Friends?" she asked skeptically.

Shit. He didn't want to be friend zoned. But maybe if they spent time together as friends, she'd remember how it was when they were a couple.

"Yeah, we have a lot of friends in common, so we'll likely see each other a lot."

She arched a brow. "We'll see each other a lot? It sounds like you aren't considering staying here but have already decided to."

He raked his hand through his hair. He didn't want to lie to her, but he couldn't tell her the truth.

"No, I'm still thinking about it."

There, that was noncommittal.

Kate laughed.

"What?" he grunted.

"You're still a shitty liar."

God, he'd missed how matter of fact she could be.

"I want to stay long enough to make amends with my folks if I can. But that's not why I'm in Fisher Springs."

"I know, you're here for your brother's wedding. Don't worry about whether we're friends. We will work together on the party and anything else that comes up for the wedding. Then you'll leave, and everything will go back to normal."

No, it can't!

God, he was screwing this up. He wished he was one of those eloquent guys who always said the right thing.

"I know you don't want to hear me apologize again, but, Kate, believing Scott over you is my biggest regret in life. I'm so sorry. And I will spend every day making sure you know that. My head was a mess back then, with my parents. But now—"

"Now, what? You're in a better place?"

"Yes, I am. And I want us to try again."

"I've thought a lot about what you said on the phone last week. And the answer is still no. I spent *years* trying to get over you. I'm not about to let you do that to me again."

Shit. Why did he have to keep pushing? It was only pushing her away.

She stood up. "I finished everything that was needed for the bachelor/bachelorette party Saturday. So, we don't need to talk again. Now, I need you to please leave."

He stood. "Okay, I'll go, but this conversation isn't over."

He made his way out the door and to his car.

Leaving was the last thing he wanted to do, but he knew Kate; once she made up her mind, it was hard to change it. But he would see her at the party in a few days. Maybe he could convince her then.

His phone rang as he got into his car. He grinned, hoping it was Kate with a change of heart, but no such luck. Simpson.

"Coleman here," he answered.

"Glad I caught you. We might have a new lead. I'm meeting Joey tonight. He said there's been a new threat."

"Another one? The threat of a bomb isn't enough?"

"Apparently not."

Wilder sighed. "When you see him, can you pin him down on where the drugs are? because I'm doubting it is at Martin's development."

"Will do. Be ready to move on this threat if it checks out."

"Will do."

He tossed his phone in the passenger seat. Why would there be another threat? Shit. If he knew who was in charge, then maybe he'd know the answer to that question.

Chapter Sixteen

Five days had passed since Kate had turned down Wilder. Again. Watching him walk away that night, she had felt physically ill. And she hadn't felt much better since. She kept wondering if she was making a mistake not giving Wilder another chance.

"I can't wait for tonight!" Harmony singsonged as she walked past Kate carrying two plates of Logan's special meatloaf.

"Yeah. I'm not really looking forward to it, but I'll try to have fun."

Harmony frowned at her. "Try to have fun? Hold that thought. I'll be right back."

Kate watched as Harmony delivered the food to a table near the front. Her friend was glowing as she chatted up the customers.

Lauren, another one of her good friends, was sitting at the counter on her lunch break. Lauren used to work in the diner, but she'd left last year to start her own accounting business. It was doing really well, and

Kate hoped she would have the same luck with her own business.

"If you're worried about Wilder being there, pretend to be concerned about the decorations or something and use that to get away from wherever he is. Since you two planned it, I'm sure he'll be preoccupied too," Lauren suggested, then took a bite of her salad.

"I wish that were the case. Holly's bridesmaids took over all the decorating, and after that, there really wasn't much to the planning. I told Wilder I took care of everything so I'm sure he won't be preoccupied with anything."

Harmony returned and cornered Kate. "It's a bachelor/bachelorette party. You shouldn't have to *try* to have fun!"

"But I do have to try. Wilder will be there. And what if Martin shows up?"

"What's going on with you and Martin, anyway?" Lauren asked.

Harmony leaned against the counter. "I'm curious about that too, actually. He stormed out of here the other day looking pissed."

He *was* pissed, and at this point, Kate had no idea if she still had a contract with him or if he was going to try to pull out of their agreement.

"He was pissed because I confronted him," she admitted.

"About what?" Lauren asked.

"Martin paid Scott to make it look like I slept with him that night."

Lauren frowned in confusion.

"I'll fill you in later," Harmony told her.

Lauren had moved to town long after Wilder had left and didn't know the story. It wasn't one Kate ever talked about.

Harmony turned back to Kate. "That asshat Martin is the reason you and Wilder aren't together?"

She nodded.

"Does Wilder know?"

"Yes. Scott filled him in and then he told me."

"Wow. I'm sorry, but... *wow*. And it really sucks that his company is doing all of the new developments around here. I don't think I could work with him without killing him," Harmony shook her head.

Kate wasn't sure she could either.

"But you know what?" Harmony continued. "Even if he cancels that contract, or you decide you can't work with him, there are plenty of people in this town that would love your services."

Kate rolled her eyes. "I know you're trying to be helpful, but I've already asked around and most people here don't use a landscape designer. If they did then I wouldn't need Martin."

"Have you approached any other developers? Any businesses?" Lauren asked.

Kate grabbed a towel and began wiping down the counter. "Not exactly, no."

"Why the hell not?"

"Honestly, I'm not sure how to approach them. What do I say? 'Here, look at my great designs'?"

"Yes! That's exactly what you say!" Harmony threw her hands in the air. "How the hell do you think I sell myself as a wedding photographer? I shove my photos in people's faces and say 'Look'!"

Kate turned to her and gave her a hug. "Thank you. But we both know your business is growing because of referrals."

"True. But that's not how it started. It will happen for you too."

"You know, I started with only one account—Zach's," Lauren reminded her. "But look at me now."

She was known as the town accountant, and Kate knew she kept quite busy. Although, after inheriting the Chanler mansion and, based on the rumors, a *lot* of money, she didn't have to work at all.

Maybe that's why Kate liked her so much: because of her great work ethic.

"I hear what you're saying," she told her friends. "I'll have to focus on new options after the wedding. After Wilder leaves."

If he leaves.

Harmony smiled. "Ah. You're still fighting? Maybe you two can smooth things over tonight." She stuck her tongue out between her teeth and bumped her with her hip.

Kate took a step back and leaned against the back counter, staring at the nearly empty dining room.

She usually enjoyed the conversation during these lulls, but not so much today. Today, she needed to think.

She let out a sigh. "We're not fighting. He actually asked me on a date. I said no."

Lauren and Harmony shared a look.

"Why would you say *no*?" Harmony demanded.

Well, it was clear what her opinion was.

"You think I should say yes?"

"Yes!" both Harmony and Lauren said together.

"Why?"

"Look," Harmony put her arm around Kate's shoulders. "I knew you two back then. No one was better suited for each other."

Kate laughed. "I guess you never heard us argue. I was getting too wild, according to him. He wanted to save up and have kids right away, but I wanted to enjoy my twenties, do some traveling. We argued every weekend when I wanted to go out."

"And in between, when you didn't argue?" the redhead pressed.

The memories of her and Wilder at their apartment flooded back to her. Wilder had started on a construction crew in town, and Kate was working at the diner, so they didn't have a lot of time together during the day. At night, they would take turns cooking for each other. She always thought those dinners were so romantic.

"The middle stuff was good," she said quietly with a smile.

"And now, maybe you can get past your other concerns."

Harmony had a point. Kate had at least had the opportunity to travel these last ten years. But one major issue remained.

"Wilder believed Scott over me. I'm struggling to deal with that."

Harmony let out a breath and went to lean against the back counter next to Kate. "I understand why you're angry. Like I said when you first told me, I'd be pissed too. But one thing I've learned is that how we reacted ten years ago isn't the same as how we would now. We were all stupid kids back then."

"You really think two people can change that much?"

"*Pfft.* Look at me and Chase. We never would have worked out if we'd gotten together when we were younger. We needed time to mature."

What Harmony said made sense. But she and Chase hadn't hurt each other the way Kate and Wilder had.

Lauren spoke up around another bite of her salad. "This party would be a great chance for you two to talk. It won't feel like a date, and you can walk away any time you want."

"You know, that's not a bad idea. I'm not sure I can get past my anger, though."

"It's still fresh. Give it time." Harmony gave her a squeeze then let go.

Kate nodded. Based on the fact Wilder now had an apartment and a job, it appeared she had time.

Maybe her friends had a point; for now, she could talk to him, see what he'd been up to all these years. She knew for a fact the spark that had always been between them was still there... and it reminded her she'd never had that with anyone else. That didn't count for nothing.

After work, she went home to shower — she always smelled like greasy fries after a shift at the diner — then she tried on most of the contents of her closet, unsure what to wear. Half her wardrobe was too casual, and the other half seemed like she was trying too hard. Finally, she settled on a simple, purple dress and her tan heels that everyone said made her legs look longer.

Why the hell am I getting dressed up for Wilder? She sighed as she looked in the mirror.

Her anger toward him was fading. Harmony was right; they were different now, more mature. Maybe she should give him a chance.

Once upon a time, I vowed to spend my life with him.

By the time she left to go to the bar, her mind was spinning, both with anticipation at seeing Wilder, and with nerves as she hoped that everything would go right with the party.

When she walked into Brannigan's Pub, she barely recognized the place. Holly's bridesmaids had long ago relieved her of decorating duty, telling her they had it covered — and they did. Penis and boob balloons floated in the air and bobbed on the tables and floor, and penis confetti had been sprinkled on most of the surfaces.

Zach came up beside her and whispered, "I love you guys, but I swear to god, if there are any feckin' mini penises left here tomorrow, I might kill you."

She laughed out loud. "Zach Brannigan, your accent is out. Does this mean you are afraid of a little confetti?"

He growled. "You only just got here. You haven't seen the ice cubes, the jello mold, or face painter."

"Face painter? Isn't that for little kids?"

He shook his head. "Not these designs."

"Hey, check out what Bridgette did!" Chase said gleefully as he ran up to them. Painted across his cheek was a naked woman... with red hair.

Kate balked. "Is that supposed to be Harmony?"

"Yeah. Pretty cool, huh?"

She closed her eyes and shook her head. She loved Chase, but sometimes he didn't think things through. "Your ex-hookup painted a naked woman on your face? Harmony might not be happy."

At one point, Bridgette had been a big issue for Harmony. Fortunately, she and Chase had worked past it.

Still, he paled. "You think she'll hate it?"

"Hate what?" Harmony asked as she looped her arm through Chase's.

"His face paint," Kate supplied.

The real redhead turned to Chase, and her eyebrows went up. "Is that supposed to be me?"

He nodded.

Harmony glanced over at Bridgette, who gave her a smile and wave.

Harmony gave her a fake smile, then turned back and examined Chase's face more closely. "I guess she could have done worse. Maybe we can be civil after all." She pulled on Chase's arm. "Let's dance."

Kate watched them step away, surprised.

"That's not how I saw that goin'," Zach admitted, echoing her thoughts.

"Yeah, I guess our Harmony is growing up."

"Hey, if you need to escape at any point tonight, my office is available to you, okay?"

She was touched by his offer. Zach was such a dear friend. Last year, he'd asked her why she had a different last name than her parents, she'd broken down crying and told him what happened with Wilder and how she kept her married name. Now, she was glad she had.

"Thank you. I might take you up on that."

"Well, enjoy yourself. I know you've been workin' extra hard for Holly, but don't forget to have some fun. I need to get back to the bar."

She nodded. "Thank you for letting us rent the place out."

"Of course. Besides, I like havin' my friends here instead of some of the obnoxious townsfolk."

Kate gave him a grin before he walked away.

When he was gone, she made the rounds, acting like she was making sure everything was going well. In truth, she was looking for Wilder, but she hadn't spotted him yet.

Instead, she found Holly sitting at a booth next to Lauren and Tabitha, taking a shot.

"How's the party?" Kate asked.

"Good!" Holly shouted.

Kate's eyes traveled to Bridgette as she painted another guest's face, knowing very well that she and Holly were not friends. "How did she get invited?"

The bride-to-be shrugged. "My sister booked a face painter and had no idea who Bridgette was. But once she got here, I wasn't going to make a scene. Besides, she's doing a great job avoiding William. Here, try this." Holly handed her a jello shot.

Kate was about to guzzle it down when she noticed something catch Bridgette's attention. She followed the blonde woman's line of vision and found... Wilder.

He was standing at the door, wearing fitted jeans and a blue Henley that stretched over his broad chest.

"Wilder really filled out, didn't he?" Holly said appreciatively.

"Yeah, he really did," Kate agreed quietly. She couldn't take her eyes off him.

The feeling appeared to be mutual; he was staring at her, smiling.

But then movement in the corner of her eye caught Kate's attention. Bridgette was sashaying—yes, *sashaying*—over to Wilder. But Wilder was so fixated on Kate, he didn't notice Bridgette until she'd wrapped herself around his arm and was whispering something in his ear.

He shook his head, frowning.

"What do you think that's about?" Kate asked Holly.

The bachelorette snorted. "It's exactly what you think. Wilder is fresh meat in this town, and Bridgette is always hungry."

Kate ground her teeth.

Holly covered her mouth with her hands. "Oh shit, Kate, I'm sorry!"

"What?"

"I thought you were done with Wilder. I wouldn't have said that if I'd known."

"Known what?"

"That you still have feelings for him."

Kate glanced at Holly, who was smiling at her—as were Lauren and Tabitha. "I don't have feelings for him," she insisted.

That was a lie, but it came out naturally.

Tabitha shook her head. "Oh, Kate... if that's true, then why did you destroy that poor jello shot?"

Kate looked down, and sure enough, her hands were now a red, gooey mess. "Shit. I need to go wash up."

She glanced at Wilder as she passed him on the way to the ladies' room. Big mistake: Bridgette was all over him. That bothered her more than she wanted to admit.

Darting into the bathroom, she washed her hands and stared at herself in the mirror as her eyes welled with tears. What the hell was she going to do? Clearly, she still had strong feelings for the man, but the idea of opening her heart to him scared her senseless.

The door opened, and she turned away to grab a paper towel, pretending to dry her hands.

Then she heard the lock click.

She spun back around and braced herself against the sink. "Wilder? What are you doing? This is the women's bathroom."

"We need to talk."

Up close, he was even hotter than he had been across the room. The blue Henley brought out his eyes. His dark hair was combed back, and his stubble was trimmed close. The man was sex on a stick. He always had been, but the years had been kind to him.

"In the bathroom?" she asked. Then she ducked down and looked under the stall doors.

No one else was in there.

He nodded. "We need privacy for this conversation."

"Wilder, I didn't mean to glare at Bridgette. You can do whatever you want."

What the hell am I saying? I don't mean that.

She shook her head rapidly. "No, I take that back. I *did* mean to glare at her, and I *don't* want you to do anything with her."

Wilder grinned. "You're jealous?"

She stepped back. "What? No. That's not—"

Wilder sighed. "I really wish we could delve deeper into this right now, but there's something else I need to tell you."

The way he pinned her with his stare had her stomach doing flip-flops. Was he going to tell her he still loved her? If he did, how would she respond?

Sweat beaded on the back of her neck, and she flipped her hair over her shoulder to provide some relief.

"Everyone here might be in danger."

Okay, this was not where she'd expected this to go.

She laughed to relieve some of the tension. "Yes, in danger of drinking too much and finding confetti penises stuck to their faces in the morning."

Wilder barked a laugh. "God, I've missed you."

Those four words were all it took to crack her heart open a little, and all she could think was, *I missed you too.*

He visibly swallowed. "Look, can you stay where I can see you the rest of the night?"

She narrowed her eyes. That was an odd instruction. "Why?"

"I can't say. Please, trust me on this one."

Normally, she would do the opposite if a man made a request like this, but there was something in his tone... She knew she needed to take him seriously. Hell, or maybe she just wanted to.

"Okay," she agreed. "Should I be scared?"

He stepped closer to her and tucked some of her hair behind her ear. "No. Not as long as you're with me." He moved to her side. "Ready to go back to the party?"

She nodded, ignoring the fluttering in her belly.

The moment he opened the door, the loud beat of music blasted them.

"About time!" some drunk girl yelled as she ran into the bathroom.

"And what were you two doing in there?" Holly grinned and waggled her eyebrows as they walked past her in the line that had formed for the bathroom.

"None of your business," Wilder retorted, then he grabbed Kate's hand and led her the rest of the way down the hallway.

When they got to the main room, she jerked her hand from his grip. "Why did you say that? Now the whole town will think we're back together."

He leaned down and whispered in her ear, "Might as well get them used to the idea. It's inevitable."

Then he stepped back and winked.

Chapter Seventeen

The last thing Wilder wanted to do was walk away from Kate. But he had to stay alert. There was a threat at this party, and he needed to find it. And when he was near Kate, he was only focused on her.

Fuck, why did Joey wait so long to give Simpson this information?

Joey didn't show up for his meeting with Simpson earlier this week. Simpson finally tracked him down earlier today which means Wilder had only had a couple of hours to digest the tip—not that there was much to it. Simpson told him that someone from Idaho, Joey didn't know who, would be at a pub party tonight in Fisher Springs, and looking for the guy in charge. It was the vaguest fucking tip he'd ever heard. But the only pub in town was Brannigan's, and the only event planned at the pub was his brother's fucking bachelor party.

So much for keeping his work and personal life separate. At every turn, they insisted on colliding. He meant what he'd said to Kate: he wanted her back. But tonight, he had to focus on the case.

He hoped he'd see Joey here. That man had to know more, and Wilder would do whatever it took to get it out of him. He didn't care anymore if Joey knew he was there undercover. Not when this threat was hitting so close to his friends and family. And Kate.

But he hadn't seen Joey in the fifteen minutes he'd spent driving around town, or in the ten minutes he'd been inside this pub.

He scanned the crowd, looking for someone that looked out of place. Unfortunately, the crowd was a mix of ages and dress. Anyone would fit in here tonight.

"So, you and Kate are finally back together, then?"

Wilder spun around to find Martin sipping on a beer.

Shit. He didn't have time for this. Martin's glassy eyes told him he'd already had a few drinks. The man was clearly enjoying himself.

But then he remembered this was his brother's bachelor/bachelorette party, and neither William nor Holly were friends with Martin. Or at least, that he knew of.

He scowled. "Why are you here?"

It came off ruder than he meant, but dammit, it was hard not saying anything.

Martin smiled. "I've been waiting to see your anger. What amazes me is that you've known what I did for an entire week, and not done anything about it."

Shit. Why was the man trying to provoke him? Martin was here to have a confrontation?

Wait, maybe Martin was the 'guy in charge'. He was in charge of the housing development, and even though Wilder hadn't seen anything there, that had been Joey's first tip.

Is Martin trying to use me to create some distraction because the other man is already here?

Wilder shook his head. No, that was too far-fetched, even for him.

Seeming disappointed that Wilder didn't respond to his goading, the man continued. "I'm here to wish the happy couple a lifetime of happiness."

"I didn't think you knew them that well."

Martin finished his beer and motioned for another one. A woman behind the counter who Wilder didn't recognize gave him a refill.

"I know Holly. I dated her older sister a few years back."

Wilder bit back the first thought to come to him, which was that he was surprised anyone from Fisher Springs would date Martin, knowing who he was.

He was saved by Martin's phone lighting up on the bar in front of him, but Wilder didn't catch the name on the screen before Martin pocketed the phone.

"It looks like I have some business to take care of tonight." Martin chugged his new beer then nodded at Wilder as he walked toward the door.

Well, shit. Either Martin wasn't the guy in charge, or he was meeting the guy outside. Or Joey's tip was worthless, which was very possible. But why the hell had he chugged his beer? This wasn't college.

He wanted to see what Martin was up to, but he couldn't very well get up and follow him out the door. Wilder scanned the space, and his eyes landed on a pack of cigarettes and lighter by the elbow of a man who was engrossed in a conversation with a brunette at the bar.

Wilder palmed both items as he walked by, then he stepped outside, grateful to at least have an excuse if he needed it.

Martin was nowhere to be seen on the sidewalk, but his car was still parked across the street, identifiable by the large decal on the driver's door advertising *Fisher Springs Development*. Assured the man was still near, Wilder glanced around as he walked a few steps away from the pub's front door.

When he heard voices, he took a step closer to the edge of the pub. They sounded like they were coming from the alleyway between the pub and the next building.

"We'll follow through on July Fourth. I'm not going to warn you again."

He didn't recognize the voice, and as he peered around the corner, he only saw two shadows on the wall. One shadowy figure's hands moved, indicating. He must be speaking but it was too quiet to hear.

"I'll tell my boss. He won't be happy." The first voice said.

The sound of footsteps walked away from Wilder. He had to know if that was Martin. But by the time he made his way down the alley, all he saw was the shadow as it made its way to the street behind the pub.

As he was cursing his near miss, a car door slammed behind him. He spun on his heel.

"Wilder? What are you doing out here?"

Wilder held up the pack of cigarettes to show Martin, who'd apparently just exited his car. "Was thinking about a smoke. Were you in there this whole time?" he gestured to the vehicle.

Martin was holding his phone. "Yeah, that business I had to see to was a call. It went better than I'd hoped, so I was going to go back into the pub. You smoke now?"

Wilder nodded, his hope sinking as he realized the man in the alley could not have been Martin. *Who the hell is the guy in charge, then?* "Sometimes."

It was a lame answer, but he didn't have to explain himself to this guy.

Martin bobbed his head.

Once Martin went inside, Wilder leaned against the building. Maybe whoever had been in the alley would make their way back to the pub's entrance.

After ten minutes of fruitless waiting, with no one coming around the other side of the building, he decided to rejoin the party.

"Seriously, my cigarettes and lighter were right here! Someone stole them!" the guy at the bar was yelling.

"Hey, man..." Wilder bent down to the floor next to the barstool, trusting the dim lighting of the pub to conceal the fact he was already holding the items in question. Then he stood up, holding out the cigarettes and lighter. "Is this what you're looking for?"

The guy's face lit up. "Oh, thank you, yes." He turned to the bartender. "I'm sorry I was yelling. Just a little nicotine withdrawal."

Wilder stepped away, right into the path of Chase, who was grinning. "What?" he asked.

"I knew it was a matter of time for you and Kate. Way to announce it too. The entire town knows you two were going at it in the bathroom."

"What? That's not—"

"Wilder!"

"Oh shit. Good luck," Chase ducked his head and shuffled off.

Wilder spun around and came face to face with Kate's father.

*When the hell did he get here? And **why** the hell is he here?*

Apparently, renting the pub wasn't stopping anyone from just walking in.

Before Wilder could say a word, Frank's fist connected with Wilder's face. Wilder hadn't seen it coming and hadn't braced for it, so he went down with a thud. Chase was at his side in an instant.

As he glanced up, he saw Zach holding the mayor back.

"I heard what you did in the bathroom with my daughter!" He was glaring at Wilder, red-faced.

Wilder rubbed his temple, which now hurt like hell. "I can assure you that's not what happened."

"Stay away from my daughter! I'm not going to warn you again."

What the hell?

That's what he'd heard outside. But that had been the other guy... hadn't it?

If Frank is the guy in charge, and was out in the alley, how the hell did he get inside the pub without me seeing him go through the front door?

His mind was racing as Chase helped him up and over to a booth, where he sat in a daze. Gradually, he realized the music had stopped, and when he glanced around, the guests were all staring at him.

Zach brought over a bar towel full of ice. "Here."

Wilder put it to his temple and winced in pain. "When did the mayor get here?"

"No idea. But he's gone now," Chase said.

Wilder grunted in acknowledgment. "Please tell them to turn the music back on. I don't want to ruin my brother's party."

Chase nodded to someone, and a moment later, the music came back on.

Wilder sat amidst the din, trying to make sense of it all, but his head was pounding, making it harder to think.

His friend grimaced. "You've been away awhile, but as you can see, rumors still spread faster than wildfire around here."

Shit. Rumors. "Where's Kate?" He could only imagine the hell she was catching just then.

Chase glanced around. "Probably wherever Holly is."

Wilder pushed to his feet and looked around as he made his way to the bar, still holding the makeshift icepack to his temple, but he couldn't find her.

Zach approached him, arms crossed. "You lookin' for Kate? She went home. She was upset."

Dammit. Although, it shouldn't surprise him that he'd asked her to stay where he could see her, and she'd done the opposite.

"Wilder! I'm glad you're still here. I'm so excited about this party!"

He cringed, recognizing the voice, then lowered the ice as he turned to find his mother and father standing behind him, grinning. Why the hell were they here?

His mother leaned in and gave him a hug.

He hadn't said more than a few words to this woman in ten years, and suddenly, she was *hugging* him?

"I'm so sorry we haven't spoken all these years. Please forgive me," his mom said.

He pulled away and stared into her glassy eyes.

"Sure." While he had been pissed about their reaction, he was done being angry and hurt. They had all made mistakes and he wanted to move past them.

She gave him another quick hug.

"I would have met you at the house. I'm not sure you want to be here. It's your son's bachelor party."

Please take the hint. And don't look too close at the confetti.

Now he really needed to identify the potential bomber if he was here. And the guy in charge. There was no way he would let his parents get caught in the middle of what was going on.

She crossed her arms. "And it is Holly's bachelorette party. But don't worry, I only stopped by to say hi. Plus, I wanted to see how the decor turned out. Aren't these the cutest confetti you've seen?"

Zach coughed from behind the bar to get their attention. "Can I get you two anything?" he asked.

"A beer would be great," his mother replied.

A beer? Sounded like they were sticking around longer than just saying hi.

She grabbed some of the confetti and tossed it in the air to land on Wilder.

Wilder's gaze met Zach's who was trying not to laugh as he poured a beer from the tap.

"Mom, you do realize the *cute* confetti are all penises, right?"

She shrugged, then asked, "Where's Kate?"

"Why do you want to know?" he asked with a frown.

Zach handed her the beer, then turned to her husband.

"Nothing for me, thanks."

His mom took a drink then shouted, "Dad mentioned you wanted to get her back. I'm just helping you, son."

Wilder scrubbed a hand down his face. "Please don't. Let me handle everything."

Zach continued to stand there listening to their conversation. He was glaring at Wilder, his arms now crossed.

"You want to get Kate back?" Zach asked.

The man was all muscle and tattoos. Frankly, he was intimidating.

"Yes, he does," his mother trilled. "Isn't that wonderful?"

Zach raised a brow. "Yeah. Wonderful." It didn't take a refined ear to hear his sarcasm. "We'll talk about this after the party," he promised, jabbing a finger at Wilder.

Great. Something to look forward to.

"Hello, Mr. And Mrs. Loprete!" Chase said from behind him. "Welcome to the party."

Wilder turned to face Chase at the same time the pub door thudded open across the room. Melia

Fisher walked in. Just like the last time Wilder saw her, she was wearing a very fitted dress. Tonight, her hair was down, and she was wearing a lot of makeup.

She beelined across the pub, straight to her cousin Martin.

"Excuse me," Wilder said to his parents, then he made his way over toward the Fishers.

He leaned up against a post near them and pulled out his phone. He began typing hoping he appeared to be really into texting someone.

"Martin, what did you do?" Melia demanded as Wilder came within earshot.

"I called Nick," Martin shrugged.

"Why the hell would you do that?!"

"You said your ex was coming here. He has a restraining order, Melia. If he shows up, Nick will be able to arrest him on the spot."

"Martin! It's bad enough that Officer Chase Harvey is here, but now you invited *Nick*? Fuck! I know you're trying to be helpful, but you're failing."

Martin shoved his hands in his pockets. "Turns out Nick was on his way here anyway, so it's no big deal."

"Yes, it is!"

"You don't want the police here?" he asked her. "*No.*"

Well, that was interesting. Maybe there was more to Melia than Wilder had given her credit for.

Martin huffed. "What's going on, Melia? You told me your ex was coming here tonight, and a man does not drive seven hours for nothing."

Seven hours? He could be the guy from Idaho that Joey told Simpson about.

Melia lowered her voice. "Martin, please leave it alone. I've got it handled."

"Fine. But I'm staying here and keeping an eye on you."

She rolled her eyes and growled, "Yes, Father."

When she moved to head to the bar, Wilder stepped away from the post but continued to stare at his phone. He bumped into her, then spun around to face her.

"Oh, I'm so sorry."

She was looking down, checking her phone. "No worries. This place is getting crowded."

"Melia?"

She glanced up. "Wilder?" She smiled and put her phone away. "I shouldn't be surprised to see you. This is your brother's party after all."

"Yes, it is. I still can't get over how you've changed. No more pigtails." He lightly tugged on her hair.

Hell, he may be flirting a little, but he had to know what was going on, and he knew she used to have a crush on him. He was the one person she wouldn't spit on when he walked by. Instead, she'd turn bright red and say hi.

It was cute at the time.

She grinned. "No more pigtails. You've really filled out yourself." She reached out and gave his bicep a squeeze.

"Thank you. How are you doing this evening?" he asked.

"Better now." She winked at him.

Now he had to figure out how to ask about this ex.

Her smile fell as she reached for his temple. "You're bruised. What happened?"

He winced at her touch. "Frank Waters still doesn't like me."

"Frank did this?" Her hand went to her mouth. Wilder nodded.

"You need to ice it. It will help. I'll get you some."

She began to step away but Wilder grabbed her wrist.

"I already did." He leaned down so only she could hear him. "I overheard what Martin said. You have a restraining order with your ex. Did he hit you? Is he coming here tonight?"

Melia pulled her wrist out of Wilder's grasp and stepped back. "You ask a lot of questions, don't you?"

He shrugged. "Just worried about you."

Narrowed eyes looked at him suspiciously. "Why?"

"Men shouldn't hit women. Period. If he's a threat, I want to know."

Melia smiled and stepped closer, placing her hand on Wilder's chest. "He's not. And I don't want to talk about my ex. This is a party after all. We should be having fun."

Her hand snaked up around his neck and she stepped closer. He swallowed unsure how to keep his distance while still getting her to open up.

"Why are they having this party two weeks before the wedding? I thought bachelor parties were the night before." Her free hand moved to his chest.

Wilder laughed as he stepped them back to avoid a conga line that danced by. In doing so, he was able to extract himself from her wandering hands.

"Not if they don't want to be hung over at their wedding."

Melia stared at the dancers. "Good point."

"William said the pub wasn't available next weekend, so they grabbed tonight."

The music seemed louder than it had moments ago and Wilder found himself shouting.

"So, you're a realtor?"

She nodded.

Wilder glanced at the crowd. It had grown considerably since he first arrived, and the conga line had made its way to the dance floor. He turned to ask her more about her job but before he could, she grabbed his hand.

"I like what you're thinking. Let's dance!" Melia said as she drug him toward the dance floor.

What the hell? The last thing he wanted was to be spotted dancing with Melia. He glanced back at the bar to see his parents laughing with Holly. Then he spotted Zach, who arched a brow at him.

Wilder stopped before they reached the dance floor. "Sorry, I can't dance. I need to talk to my parents."

He spun around, leaving Melia as he beelined to the bar. Who knew, having his parents at a bachelor party was actually a good thing?

Chapter Eighteen

The next day, Kate was thankful she had the day off from the diner. And despite the fact the wedding was in two weeks, she had no appointments with Holly so she could stay home. Since Wilder returned, Holly had been leaning on her bridesmaids more and Kate wasn't going to complain about that. All she wanted to do was stay in her house — preferably under the covers.

After she'd come out of the bathroom with Wilder, the rumors spread faster than the 'Iced Tea Escapade.' She knew it was just a matter of time before her mother showed up to give her a lecture about her choices and how they reflected on the family.

She was thirty-one years old, and her mother still tried to control her. Well, she wasn't going to answer the door, so her mother could stew all she wanted.

Maybe it wouldn't be so bad if the bathroom rumor was actually *true*. Since he'd come back to town, Wilder had been all she could think about.

But now, something was going on, and he was keeping it from her.

'Everyone is in danger.'

Danger from what? Nothing had happened after she left — she'd asked Harmony, and her friend had filled her in on every detail. Including that, after Kate had left, Wilder spent a considerable amount of time talking to Melia Fisher.

Something wasn't right. And why did he come back so early for the wedding? Part of her thought it was to win her back, but she told him no when he'd asked for another try, and clearly, he took her answer seriously, since he'd moved on to laughing and having fun with Melia.

That last part, she had gotten out of Tabitha. Because yes, as soon as she'd heard about Melia, she asked *all* her friends.

Dammit. If she'd stayed, would he have talked to her all night? She would never know. After their encounter in the bathroom, she'd gotten out of the pub as soon as she could.

Part of her wondered if Wilder had lied about the danger. If he had truly been concerned, why was he so focused on Melia?

Shit. What was she doing? This wasn't high school. *If he wants to spend time with someone else, he has every right to.*

But even as she thought the words, her stomach turned. It felt wrong; the idea of Wilder with anyone else felt *wrong*.

Kate bolted upright. As much as she wanted to stay in bed all day, that last thought had her heart racing.

She grabbed her phone. It was one in the afternoon, and there were ten missed texts. All from Wilder.

Wilder: *Zach said you went home. Please text me that you're okay.*

Wilder: *Okay, so maybe you're mad at me. Sorry about the bathroom rumors.*

Wilder: *If I could, I'd go to your place now, but I have to stay here.*

Why did he have to stay? He never said, but as she kept reading through the messages, she smiled. He may have been talking to Melia, but he was clearly thinking about her.

A new message came in while she was reading them.

Wilder: *I need to see you.*

This was immediately followed by a knock on the front door.

She jumped up and looked in the mirror. Her hair was in every direction, and her eyes were red, swollen, and had streaks of black makeup underneath them. Cursing, she ran to the bathroom and washed her face. When she was done, she dashed back to her bedroom, grabbed her yoga pants, and put them on.

A sudden tap on her bedroom window made her jump. She was grateful the drapes were closed so whoever was out there couldn't see her.

"Kate? Are you in there?"

She exhaled at Wilder's voice, releasing some of the adrenaline pounding through her blood. But it was quickly replaced with dread. Oh god, maybe the rumors were worse than she thought, if he was circling her house trying to find her.

She took a deep breath to steel herself and made her way to the front door as Wilder was walking around the side of the house.

"You're bordering on stalking when you're trying to get in my bedroom window," she told him.

He flashed a smile. "Not stalking. Just worried about you." He stepped up onto her porch.

It was warm for late June, and he was wearing jeans and yet another shirt—this one a short-sleeve T— that was straining over his chest.

"You know, they make T-shirts in larger sizes."

He glanced down at his chest then back up at her, and grinned. "You don't say?"

She nodded. "They do. Then your poor shirts wouldn't have to try so hard to hold it together over your muscles."

He leaned against a post and crossed his arms, making the shirt strain even more. "You know, they make shirts that are less see-through." He winked.

She glanced down and realized her nipples were showing through her thin, white tank top. "Shit." She crossed her arms.

"I really don't mind," he winked. "But maybe instead of giving all your neighbors a show, we should go inside." Then he turned and waved.

Kate glanced in the direction of his gesture to find Mr. Finley standing on his front porch.

"Shit!" She jumped back into her house, but left the door open for Wilder.

He chuckled and followed her inside, closing the door behind him. Meanwhile, she raced to the bedroom and tossed on a sweatshirt.

When she returned, he shook his head.

"I can't deny I'm disappointed. I really enjoyed the view."

Ignoring his comment, she sat on the couch. "Why are you here?"

He sat down on the other end facing her. "I was worried about you after last night. I know firsthand how crazy this town gets when it comes to gossip."

She rolled her eyes. "Well, you coming here, and me standing on my porch in this," she pointed to her chest, "isn't going to help."

"True. The entire town thinks we're together now."

She groaned.

His voice softened. "Aw, you're killing me. It wouldn't be that bad. Maybe we should make it official." He scooted closer to her on the couch.

She didn't like the turn the conversation was taking. With his tone, and his cologne wafting in the air, she knew it wouldn't take much for her to get sucked back into his orbit.

She crossed her legs and folded her arms over her chest. "What were you talking about last night? You said we were in danger."

He sighed as he ran his hand through his hair. "There's something I need to tell you… about why I'm here in town."

She grabbed a throw pillow and hugged it to her chest. "What do you mean? I thought you were here for your brother's wedding." *And maybe to try to win me back.*

"I am, but there's another reason." He pulled something out of his back pocket and handed it to her.

A badge.

"Detective Coleman," she read. She glanced up at him. "Coleman?"

"It's my mother's last name."

"You changed your name? Why?"

He winced. "That's not what's important right now."

Her fingers moved over the letters on his badge as a breeze from the open window blew the curtains aside. The snap and rustle of the fabric caught Wilder's attention, and as his eyes were on the drapes, she took a moment to stare at his profile.

All this time he'd been gone, this was what he'd been doing?

"You're a cop?" As the shock of it sunk in, she was glad she was sitting down. If anyone had asked her what Wilder would be doing now, she would never have guessed he was a cop. All these years, how many dangerous situations had he been in?

"I'm a detective with the Summit County Sheriff's Office," he answered, turning his attention back to her.

"Have you been shot?" She asked as she returned her gaze to his badge.

"Fortunately, no."

She sighed with relief. "How long have you worked for them?" She extended her arm, holding out his badge.

He gently took it from her, tucked it back in his pocket, then leaned forward on the couch. "After I left Fisher Springs, I got a job working construction with a friend. But I knew I didn't want to do that for the rest of my life. So, I joined the police academy."

Kate went through her memories. Never once had she heard Wilder even mention any interest in becoming a cop. Had he hidden that from her?

"I was a different person when I left Fisher Springs," he explained. "I was broken, Kate. To put myself back together, I decided to make major changes in my life. Joining the police academy was one of them."

She nodded, looking down at the floor. "Major changes. Your job and your last name."

"I didn't want you to find me," he admitted, speaking barely above a whisper.

Tears trickled down her cheeks as she met his gaze. "You hated me that much?"

She could see the pain in his eyes as he reached for her hand, but still she pulled away and stood up. Walking to the window, she let the breeze wash over her.

"I kept your name," she whispered. "I'm still Kate Loprete."

"I'm sorry, Kate. I was so raw that I had to put as much distance between us as possible. Looking back, I realize I acted rashly, about everything."

She spun back to face him when his voice became muffled, and she saw him cupping his face in his hands.

"I ruined us." His voice broke. "I'm so sorry. I was young and I let my pride get in the way."

There it was. Another crack in the armor she wore to protect herself from Wilder. Slowly, he was getting past her defenses.

He sat up, rubbing his face, and taking a deep breath to collect himself. "I didn't come here to lay that on you. I needed to tell you why I'm here and what's going on. But, Kate, you can't tell anyone else about this. No one can know. It could endanger my life."

She turned to him. "You're here as a detective?"

"Yes, I'm undercover."

"But... you have a job working construction, and an apartment."

None of this made sense.

"It's part of the cover," he told her gently.

So, he wasn't moving back? He wasn't here for her? He was here for a *job*?

She stepped toward her kitchen, needing space. She felt so stupid. Deep down, she'd hoped he'd really come back to town for her.

Although, if he had ever intended to do that, he wouldn't have waited ten years. Tears welled in her eyes.

Wilder jumped up and followed her. "Shit. No, Kate. Listen to me. Everything I've said about wanting to take you out, wanting to be with you again, that's all real."

"But you lied about why you're here."

"I had to."

Shaking her head, she grabbed a glass from the cupboard and filled it with water from the sink. Giving her eyes time to dry, she drank it with her back to him.

Once finished, she placed the glass in the sink. "And now we're all in danger? That's what you said last night."

"I can't get into all the details, but that's what my source told me."

She scoffed. "Your source." She turned to face him. "If everyone is in danger, why did you spend the night talking to Melia?"

His eyebrows shot up. "Because I thought she might have information. All I knew last night was that someone outside the party might want to hurt someone who was there and that someone was the guy in charge."

"Who?"

"At first, I thought Martin Fisher might be the one in charge, but I figured out last night it's not him, but then I heard Martin talking to Melia and it sounded like she might be in danger."

"You think Melia is in danger?"

He shrugged. "That's the problem, I don't know. I was trying to find out more about her ex last night, and what exactly she sells as a realtor, but she wasn't into those topics."

Kate would bet she wasn't. Melia was known for dressing provocatively and being quite the flirt.

"I can tell you what she sells," she said. "She sells whatever Martin is building."

Wilder crossed his arms. "He does enough of that in Fisher Springs to keep her in business?"

She shrugged. "You'd have to ask her, but lately, Martin's company has been building a lot, especially north of Davenport."

He pulled his phone out of his pocket and typed something out. "I'll have someone look into her."

Why was he being so cryptic?

"What kind of danger are we in?" she asked as Wilder pocketed his phone. "Why are you here exactly?"

He let out a heavy sigh. "Look, you can't say anything to anyone about this, okay?"

She nodded.

"There are drugs moving through Fisher Springs. And another group wants to take over the business — by force."

She lifted a brow. "Drugs in Fisher Springs? Although... I guess I can't say I'm surprised. Not after Joey."

He stepped forward. "Yeah, what exactly happened with Joey?"

She stepped back, leaning against the counter. *What **didn't** happen with Joey?* She felt so bad for the guy, but he had dug himself into a hole that he couldn't get out of.

"His mom died," she began, "and he's never been the same. He started using, and then he lost his job as a detective, even though the police chief is his dad. He's been in and out of rehab a few times... It's been hard to watch."

Wilder nodded in silent contemplation. "Who does Joey hang out with?"

Kate cocked her head. "I have no idea anymore. Once he started using, he kind of dropped out of the public eye. I haven't actually spoken to the man in years, we don't exactly hang in the same circles."

"No, of course not. Sorry. I'm trying to get a feel for how rampant the drug problem is here."

"I really don't know." She stared at him for a beat. "I'm still trying to wrap my head around the fact you're a cop."

"Detective." He grinned.

When she only rolled her eyes, his gaze wandered toward his left. He stepped closer to her refrigerator and examined her collection of magnets.

She frowned. "How did you go from construction to being a detective?"

He sighed as he pulled off one magnet. "It's a long story. But you know what? I'll have plenty of time to tell you when we go on our date."

Their date? He still wanted that.

But she had too many questions.

"Timmy's is still around?" he asked, holding up the magnet menu from what used to be their favorite pizza place.

"Yeah. Wilder, why are you telling me all this? Isn't that blowing your cover?"

He smiled. "How could I not tell you? I'd do anything to keep you safe."

Memories flooded her of all the times he'd walked her home, which he would do anytime they went out in high school. Even then, he said he wanted to make sure she got home safely. He'd always put her first and worried about her safety.

She supposed it really wasn't a far stretch that it was his job to serve and protect now.

"A cop." She shook her head as she stared at him, trying to imagine it. "Wait. Do you have a uniform?"

His eyes darkened. "Do you want to see me in a uniform, Kate?"

His voice had gone low and suggestive, and it sent need vibrating through her.

He stepped closer until he stood right in front of her. Then he ran his thumb along her jaw.

One moment, she'd wanted this man to leave town, and now, all she wanted was for him to kiss her.

She squeezed her eyes shut. No, she couldn't go there.

He stepped back, frowning. "I should go."

He took another step back. "Call me when you're ready for a date." He winked, then retreated from her kitchen. A moment later, she heard her door close.

The more time she spent with him, the more she was warming up to giving him another chance. But at the same time, she wasn't sure she could risk her heart on him again.

Chapter Nineteen

"*Fuck!*" Wilder pounded on the steering wheel.

It was Monday morning, and he'd just parked his car on Main Street after leaving the housing development—upon getting fired.

Martin fucking Fisher was behind this, he knew it. There was no other reason to let him go. Topher had wanted to tell him the real reason, Wilder could see it in his eyes. But all he could say was that Wilder's services were no longer needed.

What if Joey was right, and that housing development was at the heart of the drug operation? How the hell was he going to get more information?

Although, he hadn't seen or heard anything to indicate that crimes of any kind were taking place there. But he had less than two weeks until his town was supposed to get bombed, and he was no closer to figuring out who was involved than when he'd shown up Memorial Day weekend.

To make matters worse, as Wilder was leaving the job site, Billy said he'd heard that Wilder had a wild time in the pub bathroom. This damn town was going to ruin him and Kate before they ever got a chance to start.

He had wanted to stay at Kate's longer the day before, but he could tell she was uncomfortable. Not only that, but he'd hit her with a lot of information, and she needed time to process.

She mentioned she'd be with Holly doing something wedding-related this afternoon, so he figured he'd grab lunch from the diner while she wasn't working, then head home and go over Simpson's notes again. There was something he was missing; he could feel it.

He was eager to check out the diner. William had gone on and on about Logan's meatloaf and insisted Wilder had to try it. Logan hadn't owned Lucky's when Wilder had left town, so this meatloaf would be a new experience.

The moment he stepped inside the diner, he smiled. Logan hadn't changed a thing. It was like stepping into a time warp. The booths were all red, and the floor reminded him of a checkerboard, with its white and black tiles. This place screamed nineteen-fifties. Even the photos on the wall were all of musicians from that era.

He was still staring at the decor as he sat on a stool at the counter next to a dark-haired man.

Another man popped out from the back. Looking at the guy next to him, he said, "Cody, I forgot to ask. Did you want white or wheat toast with that?"

"Wheat."

The man laughed. "I should have known." Then he popped back through the door, disappearing into the kitchen.

Wilder glanced at the menu in front of him but pushed it aside. He already knew what he wanted.

"Hey, Wilder. What can I get you?"

He glanced up to find Harmony smiling at him. "Meatloaf, please. William raves about it."

"Sure." Harmony continued to grin at him.

"What?" he asked.

"I'm so happy for you and Kate."

He groaned. "Harmony, nothing happened in the bathroom. We aren't back together."

She leaned forward. "Live in denial all you want, but you two are destined to be together."

He sighed. "Yeah, well, I hope you're right."

"I always am." She spun around and went back to the kitchen.

The man at his side laughed. "I'd forgotten how everyone is in everyone else's business here."

Wilder grunted, then took the man in. He had dark, wavy hair, was dressed casually, and Wilder could tell he was built under those clothes. If he had to guess, he'd say the man was military.

"I'm Cody." The man stuck out his hand.

"Wilder." He grasped it with his own, and they shook.

"I was here a while back, helping out a friend. Great town you have here."

"Yeah, it is. I've been gone for ten years, though. Didn't realize how much I missed it until I came back."

Cody nodded. "I know how that goes."

The man from the kitchen came back out, carrying a large plate of food.

"Logan, have you thought about my offer?" Cody asked as the man set the platter down in front of him.

So, this was Logan? He wasn't anything like Wilder had envisioned. By contrast, Logan was much younger—closer to his age and attractive.

Did Kate ever date this guy?

Shaking his head, he grabbed his glass of water and drank it down. The last thing he needed to do was let his mind wander there. That was something he did *not* need to know.

Logan smiled at Cody as he leaned on the other side of the counter. "I've thought about it a bit. I'll keep it in mind. But I can't leave town, my mom needs me. Although... I would be lying if I said that getting back out there didn't sound exciting."

Harmony came back out from the kitchen and placed a second plate of food in front of Cody. "It's good to see you back in town. You staying a while?" she asked.

"No. Just long enough to try to recruit this guy, and then I'll swing by to see Zach and Jessie." Cody shoved a forkful of food in his mouth.

Harmony glanced between the two men. "You want to recruit Logan? For what?"

Her boss shook his head. "It doesn't matter."

Cody took a sip of water. "I work for a security team, and since Logan is former military, I thought it would be something he'd enjoy."

Harmony crossed her arms. "You know, I don't know too much about your history, Logan. What branch did you serve?"

"Navy."

Cody grinned. "He's being modest. Tell her."

Logan sighed. "Navy SEALs."

Harmony's eyes widened. "You were a SEAL? Damn, Logan, that's impressive! Why'd you leave?"

"Mom needed me." He shrugged. "Anyway, I've got to get back before the pies burn."

"Hey," Cody stopped him, then pulled out his wallet. "Here's my card. Call me if you change your mind." He set it on the counter.

Wilder glanced at it. *Morgan Thompson Security.* Huh. He'd actually worked with a guy from that company on a case a while back.

Cody continued to eat while Wilder waited until Harmony and Logan had retreated into the back, then asked, "How's Stormy doing?"

Cody glanced up, grinning. "You know Stormy?"

Wilder looked around. No one was close. He nodded, then murmured, "Worked with him. I'm a detective in the next county over, but no one here can know that."

Cody arched a brow.

Wilder realized how crazy he sounded, so he pulled out his badge.

Cody nodded. "More trouble in this town? That's too bad. It's a nice place." He shoveled another forkful of food in his mouth.

"Yeah, it is," Wilder agreed. "Hopefully after I solve this case, there won't be any more trouble."

"What's going on? If you don't mind me asking."

Wilder wasn't normally one to trust others quickly, but he knew Stormy only hired guys he trusted.

"Drugs," he finally answered. "Some guy from Idaho is coming to meet with a contact here. I have to figure out who the contact is."

Cody dropped his fork. "Did you say Idaho?"

"Yeah."

"It's not related to the Bannon family, is it?"

Wilder's eyes widened. "You know about the Bannons? "

Cody nodded. "I dealt with those assholes the last time I was here."

"Do you think they'd come back?"

Cody shook his head. "Not the guys I dealt with. They're dead. But I figure someone else in that family probably stepped up."

Wilder turned to Cody and opened his mouth but closed it. He wasn't sure how to ask.

Cody chuckled. "No, I didn't kill them, I promise. The whole thing was pretty fucked up. You should ask Jessie Doyle about it. Do you know her?"

Wilder shook his head.

"She's with Zach Brannigan."

"I know who he is."

Cody nodded. "Good guy. He can tell you what happened."

He finished off his food, then rose from his stool. As he placed some money on the counter, he turned to Wilder. "It was nice to meet you. Maybe I'll see you again, if I'm ever back up this way."

"Good to meet you too."

Cody left as Harmony brought out Wilder's meatloaf.

"Thank you," he said before taking a bite.

Damn, it *was* good.

As he ate, he thought over the conversation he'd just had. He was curious about what had happened to the Bannons. He wanted to ask Chase but how could he without blowing his cover? It was bad enough he was keeping the truth from his friend, but Simpson was worried that someone in the local police department might be involved.

"I heard Cody mention Jessie. She's a hoot."

Wilder was so deep in thought, he hadn't realized Harmony was still standing there.

He swallowed his bite. "Oh yeah?"

"Yeah. I love her. And she's perfect for Zach. Did you know she gave up her job with the FBI to move here?"

What? "Jessie was with the FBI?"

"Uh huh. That's how she and Zach met. But now she's a badass private investigator."

Wilder set his fork down. "Does she have an office in town?"

Harmony laughed. "She does. You looking to have someone investigated?" Then her smile fell. "It had better not be Kate. You should know, I'll totally snitch on you."

He shook his head. "No, just curious. The town has changed a lot in the last ten years."

"It has. Hopefully, you'll stick around and get to know everyone again." She gave him a wink then walked over to another customer.

Stay in Fisher Springs...

He wanted Kate; there was no doubt about that. But he hadn't really thought about whether she'd move with him to Summit County, or if he'd come back here.

Maybe it was about time he did.

But in the meantime, he was on the hunt for a private investigator named Jessie.

Chapter Twenty

"Kate, thank you for coming with me on such short notice," Holly said as she sniffed the lilies on display on the counter.

They were at the flower shop. Again. Though not much had changed since they'd been in yesterday except the place wasn't as busy on a Monday afternoon.

Kate took a deep breath, enjoying the floral, earthy scent in the air. Flowering plants were on display in the front window and on a few tables near the entrance.

"I'm still not sure what was wrong with the hydrangeas you originally picked out," she said.

"They didn't go with my color scheme."

"But weren't they blue?"

Holly shook her head as she walked toward the back of the shop, where coolers held several bouquets of flowers. "There was no guarantee they could get the blue ones, and what if the ones we ended up with were pink? No, I couldn't do it."

As they approached, Becca set three vases of new flower arrangements on the counter.

Two weeks ago, Kate had never met Becca, Fisher Spring's new florist. But now, she felt like they were becoming fast friends while commiserating over Holly's indecisiveness about the *'right'* flowers for her wedding.

"And what was wrong with the white flowers you picked last time?"

Kate couldn't remember the name of them, but she'd read it on an invoice somewhere.

"My mother picked those out. Carnations! Can you believe it?" Holly scoffed and shook her head as she walked to the counter.

"What's wrong with carnations?" Kate asked as she followed.

Holly's hand went to her chest. "Are you serious? Everyone knows carnations are for funerals. Well, everyone except my mom and, apparently, you."

"She's right," Becca confirmed. "I tried to talk her into something else, Holly, but she was set on carnations."

Holly nodded. "Trust me. I know how stubborn she can be. I'm happy you're being so flexible about this."

"There's still time to get the order in," Becca said as she motioned to the flowers on the counter. "The first vase contains a sample table arrangement.

The second, a bridesmaid bouquet. And the third holds the bride's bouquet."

Kate couldn't deny that all three were stunning, but the bride's bouquet was by far the best. It was a mix of white and pink lilies with greenery throughout. But she knew Holly would reject it because of the pink.

"I love it!" Holly squealed. "Thank you so much!" She ran around the counter and gave Becca a hug. Then she turned to Kate. "Okay, let's go."

What the hell?

Kate frowned. "I'm happy you love them, but I don't understand. You didn't want pink."

Holly laughed. "I didn't want *pure* pink. This is different."

Kate had to let it go. She'd struggled to understand Holly's thought process time and time again.

"Okay," she said. "But I'm not sure why you dragged me here, saying it was urgent."

"Thank you, Becca," Holly called as she tossed an arm over Kate's shoulders and led her out of the shop. "The flowers aren't the urgent matter," the bride-to-be said knowingly.

Kate groaned, realizing where this was going.

The other woman steamrolled right over her. "Tell me what really happened in that bathroom at my bachelorette party. I know it wasn't what everyone is saying, because if you and Wilder were back together, you wouldn't have left the party early. Alone."

Kate glanced around, hoping no one could hear them. They were in the clear, but still... "I think I need a beer for this conversation."

"Understood."

They walked the few blocks to Brannigan's Pub and stepped inside. Thankfully, it was still early enough that it wasn't crowded.

"Go grab a booth. I'll get us a couple of beers," Holly said.

Kate nodded.

She went to the back booth and sat down. A few minutes later, Holly plopped a pitcher of beer and two glasses on the table and joined her.

What the hell? How did one drink turn into a pitcher?

"I can see the protest forming on your lips," Holly held up a hand to forestall her. "I anticipate you have a lot going on, so I'm just thinking ahead." She poured a glass of beer for each of them then leaned back and stared at Kate.

Kate shifted in her seat, trying to figure out where to start. She couldn't share what Wilder had said in the bathroom, as he'd sworn her to secrecy, but she could tell Holly the rest.

"A couple of weeks ago, Wilder said he wanted me back."

Holly's eyebrows shot up. "Really?"

"Yes, he learned the truth about what happened with Scott and realized he'd made a huge mistake."

"I heard about Scott from William. Tell me more about Wilder wanting you back." She leaned in.

Kate opened her mouth, but then stopped. Something niggled at her brain. "You're being weird. Why?"

Holly was staring at her and trying really hard not to grin.

Kate sighed. "You already knew."

Holly nodded. "Sorry, but Wilder came over to ask William for advice. He didn't realize I was sitting in the next room and could hear everything. Seriously, though... that man wants you back."

Kate shifted uncomfortably. That was something she knew. What she should do about it? Well, that was another thing.

"I'm scared to give him another chance," she admitted.

Holly took her hands. "Sweetie, I know the idea of opening your heart to him again has got to be absolutely terrifying... but look at the alternative."

"You mean not opening up?"

Holly nodded. "I know we didn't really know each other back then, but from what I've heard and seen for myself in the time I've known you, you've been closed off since he left town. Do you want to live like that forever?"

Kate was about to object; she had opened herself up when she'd dated Mitchell. But then she realized, no, she really hadn't. They had always had an expiration date, and simply agreeing to see someone more than a couple of times wasn't 'opening up'.

Thinking back over the past ten years, she discovered Holly was right. Kate had kept herself closed off.

Could she open herself now, after all this time? The idea of getting hurt again was too much. But no matter what she decided when it came to Wilder, she could get hurt. Hell, she was already hurting.

Kate took a sip of her beer. "Maybe you're right."

Holly sat up straighter. "I am? Does this mean you're going to give Wilder a chance?"

Kate grinned. "I want to."

Holly jumped up and shouted, "*Yes!*"

Across the pub, the door opened, and Holly's smile grew bigger as her eyes gazed past Kate, tracking someone walking in.

"What are you smiling about?"

"It's like he heard you." Holly clapped. "This is perfect!"

That means —

Kate turned to find herself staring into Wilder's blue eyes as he approached their table.

"Good afternoon," he said.

"Same to you," Holly replied. "Hey, I need to go. Can you help Kate finish off this pitcher?"

She didn't wait for an answer; she was out the door before anyone could object.

Kate glanced across the table and realized the woman hadn't even taken a sip of her beer.

"Are you celebrating or trying to get drunk?" Wilder asked as he slid into the vacated seat.

"Neither. I came in for a beer, and Holly bought a pitcher."

That woman had never bought a pitcher in all the years Kate had known her.

Kate scowled. "Holly asked you to come here, didn't she? This was a setup." She shook her head. She was tired of everyone interfering in her life.

"No, she didn't. I had lunch at the diner and met a guy who told me about Jessie, the private investigator. After walking around town and not finding her office, I came in here to ask Zach. I understand they're a couple."

"So, this isn't a setup?"

Wilder smiled. "Nope."

Now she felt embarrassed. "You don't have to stay. I don't want to keep you from what you're doing."

Wilder reached across the table and took her hand in his. "Kate, any chance I have to spend time with you, I will take."

Instead of pulling away, she kept her hand where it was and enjoyed the moment they were having.

"Speaking of time together..." Kate swallowed as heat crept up the back of her neck.

Why was this so hard to say?

"Yes?" Wilder asked, grinning.

She took a deep breath and met his gaze. "Any chance that offer for a date is still on the table?"

His eyebrows shot up. "Kate, are you saying you want to go on a date with me?"

She nodded.

He squeezed her hand. "It is taking everything in me not to get up and pull you into my arms." He glanced around the pub. "But I think we've started enough rumors in this place, don't you?"

She couldn't help but laugh. It was true. "Yeah, maybe we should learn to be a little more private. At least until we know if..."

She couldn't say the words.

It was very possible things between them might not work out. They weren't the same people they had been when they were kids; maybe they were being naive and simply acting on an old attraction.

"Hey," he said gently.

She glanced up and met his eyes, noticing his had bags under them.

Has he been sleeping?

"What's going on?" he asked. "You were with me one minute, and the next, you're in your head. Are you already having second thoughts?" He absently rubbed his thumb over her hand the way he used to whenever he held it.

The memory was strong, and before she could stop it, tears sprang from her eyes.

That only seemed to concern Wilder more. "Kate?"

She shook her head. "You being back, and here… it's a lot."

"I know." He took her other hand in his.

"I'm scared. I was devastated when you left me. I don't think I could survive that again."

He stood and swung around to her side of the booth, sliding in beside her, then pulled her into his arms. "Screw the rumors. I need you to know I'm so sorry about all of that. If I could take any of it back, I would. I was such an idiot."

Her hands were against his chest and despite her fears, she enjoyed touching him again.

"Kate." He pulled back to look her in the eyes. "We were kids then. I'd like to think we're more mature now. If anything comes up, we will talk it out. Okay?"

She nodded, and he pulled her close again.

"I really want to kiss you right now," he murmured, "but I'm not going to when we have an audience."

She grinned. "Well, when are you taking me on this date? Play your cards right and you might get that kiss."

"Oh really? Well, let's go. The date has begun." He stood up and helped her out of the booth.

"Where are we going?" she asked.

"It's a surprise." He held her hand as he led her outside.

It was a beautiful late June afternoon, and her gaze was drawn to the flower baskets that hung every few feet on Main Street. It was her favorite part of this area.

As they walked further down the road, she noticed that Holly's shop, Through the Needle, had a very bright red, white, and blue quilt in the window. It was beautiful, and perfect for the July Fourth holiday coming up.

Kate really didn't care where Wilder took her on this date. She only wanted to spend time with him, get to know him again.

"How's the investigation going?" she asked.

"Slowly. I do have to come back here and talk to Jessie in a couple of hours."

"We'll have you back in time. Are you getting enough sleep?" She was worried he wasn't taking care of himself.

Wilder stopped and turned to her. "I'm fine. But listen, this case is really important, and I have to put it first. That means I might not be able to spend much time with you until after the wedding. But once this is wrapped up, I'm all yours."

Hers. She really liked the sound of that.

She gave him a smile and a nod. "So… you still owe me the story about why you joined the police force."

He barked a laugh. "I do."

He led her toward the apartments at the end of town and began to speak.

"After I left Fisher Springs, I got a job on a construction crew about an hour or so drive from here. A friend let me sleep on his couch until I could get my own place, and I ended up staying with him for a couple of months. During that time, someone was breaking into the cars in the apartment building's lot at least twice a week. One resident set up a video camera, but it never caught anything."

"Was the thief a ghost?"

Wilder chuckled. "No, just skilled. I figured if he was never caught on video, then he must know the camera was there."

Kate stopped. "Another resident?"

"That was my first thought. I left my friend's place one night, parked two blocks away, then walked back and hid behind a tree at the edge of the parking lot. I was determined to figure out who it was."

"Did you?"

Wilder nodded. "I did. It turns out it *was* a resident, and he was looking for money, spare change, and anything he could easily sell. The cops came and arrested him."

He stopped speaking as two kids riding bikes approached them on the sidewalk. Wilder stepped behind her, and they stayed to the right to let the kids pass. Then he stepped up beside her again.

"So that was your turning moment?" she asked.

He shrugged. "One of them. I was always interested in joining the force, but I didn't think you'd be okay with it."

He didn't pursue his dream because of her?

He must have seen the confusion on her face, because he said, "Remember that time I joked about enlisting in the Army, and you freaked out?"

The memory came back, and she snorted. "Yes. I freaked out because we spent nearly every day together, and if you enlisted, I wouldn't see you for months at a time."

He laughed. "*That* was it? I thought it was because you thought it was too dangerous."

She bumped him with her shoulder. "We really were horrible at communication, weren't we?"

They stopped on the next corner, then crossed the street to the apartment building's parking lot. These were the same apartments where Harmony had lived before she'd moved in with Chase, so Kate was very familiar with them.

"Yeah," Wilder huffed. "Good thing we are older and wiser now. Let's go, my car is parked over there." He nodded to a row of cars parked in the shade.

"And where are we going?"

He grinned. "You'll have to come along to see."

Chapter Twenty-One

She'd said yes. Wilder couldn't believe it as he lay in bed the next morning, reliving the previous night.

Yesterday when Kate had finally agreed to go on a date with him. He hadn't wanted to wait another minute, even if that meant postponing his search for Jessie.

It had been worth it. They had driven to a few spots where they used to hang out in high school, and they'd talked and shared what they've been doing the past ten years.

Learning Kate was a homeowner had surprised the hell out of him; it wasn't that he didn't think she could do it, but he didn't think she'd *want* to. And when she spoke about her landscaping design business, she lit up.

When they were together, they had been so busy trying to pay the bills that they'd never really thought of pursuing careers they'd enjoy. But he should have seen her interest, the way she'd sketch out gardens and claim they would be a part of their future home.

They had both taken unexpected paths over the years, but he felt certain they could make their way back to each other. They were *supposed* to. He had no doubt they were meant to be together, so he was going to do whatever was necessary to convince her.

After they had returned from their nostalgic tour and pulled into the apartment parking lot, he had leaned in to kiss her. Haughtily, she'd turned her head, so he kissed her cheek instead. Then she told him he hadn't earned the kiss yet.

He laughed at the memory. There was no doubt in his mind he was going to earn that kiss very soon.

But he needed to put those thoughts on hold. He had lost track of time talking with Kate yesterday, and by the time he'd gotten home, it had been too late to try to find Jessie.

Today, he would find her and see if she had any idea who might be involved in a drug ring in Fisher Springs.

Fortunately, Kate had finally fessed up that she knew where Jessie's office was. Technically it wasn't an office but when she had to meet anyone, she did it at the pub, right there in public. It was brilliant, really. And why he couldn't find her the day before. She met by appointment only.

And Jessie had agreed to meet with him this morning.

When he entered Brannigan's, the lights were all on and bright. That was a first. But then, the place wasn't open for business yet. Zach was behind the bar with a woman Wilder didn't recognize, restocking the shelves.

As he took in the pub in full light, he noticed framed photographs of various Washington state locations hanging on the walls. A beautiful shot of Mount Rainier during a sunrise was to the right of the bar. How had he never noticed that before?

"They're beautiful, aren't they?" a voice spoke up behind him. "The photographer's based in Seattle. Zach took me to one of her exhibitions, and I have to say I was impressed."

"They are," he agreed, turning around to see a dark-haired woman with ice blue eyes staring back at him.

"You must be Wilder," she said.

"Yes. Jessie?"

"Yes. Let's have a seat."

He followed her to the back booth, where they each slid into a side. Jessie had a small frame and he wondered how she fared when investigating people who didn't want to be investigated.

When she was settled, she looked up at him, and he was again struck by her eyes. They were so light.

"What can I do for you?" she asked.

Wilder took a breath and explained honestly why he was in Fisher Springs. He'd already discussed it with Detective Simpson and received permission to include Jessie.

"Wait a minute. Have you communicated any of this with the Fisher Springs Police Department?"

Wilder shook his head. "My superiors know the chief's son had a drug problem. They felt he might not be objective, so they didn't want him involved."

Jessie stared at him. "Then they don't know the chief. The man fired his son due to his drug use. His own son. Trust me, he's not in on any of this."

"Be that as it may, I don't think I can get my superior on board."

"What's his name? I'll take care of it."

Okay, maybe she was used to working for the FBI and being in charge, but that wasn't going to fly here.

Wilder leaned back and crossed his arms. "No."

She arched a brow. "You want me to help you and *not* alert the police chief that someone has threatened to bomb his town?"

"That's correct."

Jessie blew out a breath and muttered, "Unbelievable."

Wilder could feel his temper rising. "Look, we don't know who is involved. I'm friends with Chase and trust him implicitly but my superiors won't budge on this. It's not our call."

Jessie stood up. "Then I don't know if I can help you."

Wilder stood. "Jessie, I need you. I'll work on trying to get permission to bring the Chief in on this, okay? And if it makes you feel any better, the King County Sheriff's department is bringing in a bomb sniffing dog July third."

When Jessie sat back down, Wilder followed suit. Then he watched as she thought it all through. He could tell she knew how thorough those dogs could be — as long as you had them in the right area to start with.

Their heavy silence was interrupted by the sound of breaking glass, and they both jumped.

"Dammit!" Zach yelled.

Wilder turned his way.

"All good. Just broke a glass," Zach informed them.

Wilder returned his attention back to Jessie, whose arms were now crossed.

"Fine. I'll help. But if anything goes sideways, we're calling in Nick and Chase."

He knew he had to give her something or he'd lose her entirely.

"Fair enough," he relented.

Jessie stood up again. "I'll do some digging and call you if I find anything."

He nodded. "I hope you have more luck than I did. I suspect the tip about the housing development was a false lead."

She pursed her lips. "Maybe. I'm no fan of Martin's, but it wouldn't surprise me if he had his hand in something like this."

"If he does, he hides it well."

"Hopefully not too well." Jessie cracked a smile then walked past the bar and down the hall.

Apparently, our meeting is over. Wilder chuckled to himself.

That was for the best. He had someone else he wanted to track down today anyway.

"Before you go," Zach said as Wilder was almost to the door.

Wilder spun around.

"If you hurt her, I will hunt you down."

"I won't hurt her. I'm all in when it comes to Kate."

To Wilder's shock, Zach smiled. "As long as that's true, we're good." But then he dropped his smile. "The moment it's not true, I'll find you."

Wilder gave the man a nod and left.

Wilder was in his car, his hand on the door handle. He was about to step out, when he spied Melia Fisher walk into the unmarked, two-story, nondescript office building with a man in a suit. Squinting to see better, he realized that man was Joey Dunin.

Dammit, he was trying to run into Melia 'accidentally', but he wasn't ready to deal with Joey. Lying to Joey about why he was back in town would not be easy, and he planned to put it off as long as he could.

He had been hoping to track Melia down, though, so when he'd seen her driving down Main Street, he had followed her. Now they were here— likely Melia's office, but there were no signs out front.

If he didn't go in now, he still needed to find some way to run into her. But the woman had flirted with him at the bar, so he couldn't call and ask her to meet him for a drink; she might take it the wrong way. And he couldn't very well explain that no, it wasn't a date, he simply wanted to grill her about her cousin Martin.

Deciding to wait for her to emerge from the building, he ran his hand over his scruff. His beard was growing in, and he'd spent five minutes this morning staring at himself in the mirror, debating whether to shave. All he wanted to know was what Kate liked. She used to like his scruff, but that was a long time ago.

He pulled out his phone and sent Kate a text.

Wilder: *Beard or smooth?*

He hadn't even had a chance to set his phone down before it buzzed.

Kate: *Depends on what we're doing.*

He frowned in confusion. Then it hit him what she meant.

Damn. As each other's firsts, they had been shy around each other. Maybe this would be a perk of having been apart all these years: they now knew what they wanted and how to ask for it.

But his smile fell when he realized Kate has had ten years to ask for what she wants — from other men. That thought didn't sit well with him.

But it wasn't like he'd waited for her all these years; no, he was being a hypocrite.

Maybe we can agree to not talk about anyone else we've been with.

A black SUV pulled up in front of the building, tearing him from his thoughts. Two men got out, both wearing torn jeans and sweatshirts, and entered the building.

His phone buzzed, recapturing his attention.

Kate: *Not going to bite? All right. I prefer some facial hair.*

He smiled; glad he hadn't shaved.

Wilder: *I'm saving the biting for later. ;)*

Five minutes later, the two men exited the building, got back in the SUV, and drove off.

Huh. They couldn't have been in there more than five minutes. Maybe they had the wrong address

Kate: *You are making it really hard to not take this down a path we shouldn't go down just yet.*

Wilder: *Things are really hard all right.*

Kate: *You did not say that.*

Wilder: *But I did. (Eggplant emoji)*

His phone buzzed again, and he couldn't wait to see Kate's reply. But it wasn't Kate.

Simpson: *We got the name of a possible suspect in Idaho. I'm working on finding more. Guy's name is Brogan Miller. He works with the Bannons.*

Melia walked out of the building alone and got into her car. Relieved he may get his opportunity after all; Wilder pocketed his phone then followed as she drove back into downtown Fisher Springs.

She finally parked on Main Street, and he drove past, parking a block over. Then he ran back to Main Street, rounding the corner in time to see the door to Cozy Croissant closing.

Now, this is a great spot to run into her.

Smiling, he went in.

Behind the counter was the same dark-haired girl from the last time he was here. "Melia! How are you?"

"I'm good." Melia was staring at the glass case full of croissants and sandwiches.

"Do you want your usual?"

"Yes please."

The smell of fresh baked bread wafted in the air and Wilder's stomach growled as he perused the fare.

Ahead of him, Melia paid for her items, and the girl handed her a coffee and a croissant.
When she turned, Wilder made sure to be staring hard at the croissants as if he hadn't noticed her.

"Wilder?"

He met her gaze. "Melia? Hi!"

"I'm so happy I ran into you again." She smiled.

"Do you want to share a table?" he asked.

"That would be great."

"I'll meet you there."

As Melia found a spot for them, he ordered a coffee and a croissant. At the rate he was eating these croissants, he wouldn't fit into his jeans much longer.

His phone buzzed in his pocket, and he smiled. He knew it was Kate, and he couldn't wait to get back to their conversation, but first, he had to talk to Melia. So, ignoring the device for now, he made his way over to the woman he hoped had some answers for him.

"Have you decided if you are back for good?" Melia asked as he sat down. "I'd love to sell you a house."

He shook his head. "I'm back for my brother's wedding. The rest, I'm unsure about."

She took a sip of her coffee. "I understand. If you need any incentive to stick around, I'm sure I could be persuasive." Melia rubbed her leg up Wilder's calf under the table. "I was hoping to make that clear at the bachelor party, but you ran off."

If he'd had any doubt what kind of *persuasion* she'd use, he had none now.

He scooted away. "Melia, I'm sorry if I gave you the wrong impression..."

She cocked her head. "You've been very clear. You don't want to say if you are sticking around. Look, I get it. I'm not looking for a relationship either. But while you're in town, we can keep each other company. You know?" She scooted closer.

Oh hell. He knew someone was going to see this and tell Kate, and the last thing he wanted was to screw up anything they had going.

Wilder scooted away one last time. "Melia, seriously. I'm still concerned about this ex of yours. Is he giving you a rough time?"

Her playful demeanor suddenly disappeared and was replaced by what he guessed was her business persona. The smile was gone, and her voice turned cold. "I don't see how my ex is any of your concern."

"He's not. But I'm worried about you."

"Why?"

"Why?" he echoed.

"Yeah. Why, Wilder? I haven't seen you in over ten years, and you come into town and say you're worried about me? Before you left, we weren't even really friends. So why don't you stop with the bullshit and tell me what's really going on."

Well, shit. If little Melia saw through all his lies, he clearly wasn't on his A-game. But he couldn't tell her the truth. So, what the hell was he going to say?

He settled on a different truth. "Yes, maybe we weren't the best of friends, but that's not going to stop me from trying to help you if you're in trouble."

Her smile returned. "You have a hero complex. Hey, if that's the reason you aren't taking me up on my proposal, you think I need saving, don't worry about it. I'm all grown up and I can take care of myself."

Trying to ignore her veiled offer again, he pressed, "Seriously, a restraining order? Can you at least tell me about him, so I can call and warn you if I see him around town?"

She leaned back and crossed her arms. "Tell you about him?"

Wilder shrugged. "Yeah, what he looks like. What he does for a living."

She narrowed her eyes at him. "Brogan's tall, blond, and works in sales."

Brogan? Shit.

He nodded, needing more, he asked, "What's his last name?"

She huffed a breath. "Look, you don't need to worry about me — or him. You take care of yourself, and if you change your mind, let me know." Melia winked then stood up, taking her coffee and croissant with her.

Wilder pulled his phone out to text Simpson.

Wilder: *Can you run a background check on the guy? I think there might be a restraining order filed against him by a local woman here in town.*

Simpson: *Already ran the check. I'll send it over. No restraining orders.*

Either there was more than one Brogan or Melia was lying. But why would she lie about something like that?

Chapter Twenty-Two

Wilder leaned back in his chair as he finished his croissant and scrolled through his text thread with Kate, a smile growing on his lips. She'd agreed to another date with him that night, and he couldn't wait.

Still, that gave him a few hours to try to find out more about Melia's ex. Despite the lack of restraining order, he suspected the man was their Idaho threat.

He sipped the last of his coffee and surveyed his surroundings. The shop was more crowded than it had been when he first came in. A group of women laughed together at a table behind him. A dark-haired man sat at a table to his left, typing away on his laptop, oblivious to anyone else. It wasn't so crowded that he felt the need to forfeit his seat, though.

Wilder turned his attention back to his phone and pulled up the background check Simpson had sent for Brogan Miller. While Simpson hadn't found up any restraining orders, how many Brogans from Idaho had interest in Fisher Springs?

Now the question was, what, if anything, did Melia know about his business. She'd said he was in sales; that he was, the selling of meth.

The woman was a successful real estate agent, from what Wilder could tell. He was doubtful she knew the truth. Or maybe she did and that was why she'd ended the relationship.

He needed more insight, but clearly Melia wasn't feeling chatty about the subject. That left him few options.

Dammit.

"I swear I'm not stalking you."

Wilder glanced up to see Scott standing in front of him. Scott was Melia's brother. Maybe he would know something.

"Have a seat. There's something I want to ask you," Wilder said.

Scott frowned then sat down. "Really? I told you everything I knew."

Wilder shook his head. "No, this is about your sister. Do you know about her ex?"

Scott laughed. "Wow, I thought the rumor was you and Kate were getting back together. If you're interested in my sister, you should know, she's not into relationships."

Shit. He was giving the guy the wrong impression.

"As for an ex, Melia doesn't share any of her dating life with me."

Scott's phone rang and he retrieved it from his pocket. "I got to take this. Nice chat."

The man put the phone to his ear as he stood up then he walked out of the coffee shop.

As much as he didn't want to see Martin right now — and he was sure the feeling was mutual — the man was the only other person who might have some answers for him. But hell. How would he get answers if Martin was involved?

"Wilder."

He didn't even have to look up; he knew who that voice belonged to. Kate's father didn't seem like he belonged in such a happy place as the Cozy Croissant.

The mayor sat down next to him, forcing Wilder to acknowledge him.

"I was just about to leave," Wilder said as he finished his coffee.

"Don't worry. This won't take long."

Great. Another threat from his ex-father-in-law. Just what he needed.

"I ran a background check on you," Frank said.

Oh shit. That, he hadn't anticipated.

" — and I found something very interesting."

Wilder had to play it cool.

He leaned back, looked the older man in the eyes. "What was that?"

"Well, first I ran into a wall, since everything in your life appeared to have stopped ten years ago. Then

I discovered you changed your last name. Curious thing to do. But the new search was fruitful. You're a detective with the Summit County Sheriff's Office."

Frank crossed his arms. "So why are you here, working construction? I asked Chief Dunin if his office was working with yours, and he had no idea what I was talking about."

This nosy motherfucker might have blown his case wide open. Hell, he was a suspect; maybe he was trying to out Wilder.

"Ex-detective."

The mayor's brows shot up. "Ex?"

"Yeah. I used to be a detective, now I'm not. That's why I'm back. And since I used to work construction, it made sense to give it a go again."

The lies just rolled out.

"Why aren't you a detective anymore?" Frank grilled.

"That's not something I want to talk about. Now, if you'll excuse me, I need to go." Wilder stood up.

"A dirty cop?" Frank said loudly.

A few heads turned.

Wilder had to suppress his temper. Of course, that's where the man's mind would go, and he probably loved the fact there were witnesses to this conversation. He had never thought Wilder was good enough for his daughter, and now, given the opportunity to think the worst of him, he did.

"Excuse me?" Wilder asked.

"I'm guessing you were a dirty cop. You were probably caught doing something disgusting and let go from your position."

Wilder grabbed his empty coffee cup and napkin. "That's quite an accusation." Then he walked away, tossing his garbage on the way out the door.

He wasn't going to argue with the man, especially not with an audience. Let him think whatever the hell he wanted, as long as it didn't interfere with his investigation.

Instead of going straight to see Martin, Wilder went home. He needed to tell Captain Nelson and Simpson that Frank Waters blew his cover to the Chief of police, and it was time to pull Chief Dunin into the investigation. Also, now he wasn't sure how to talk to Martin. Frank was friends with him, and if he'd mentioned any of this, it would look strange that Wilder was asking so many questions.

Hell, Martin will find it strange either way.

By that evening, everything was set up with his boss in case anyone called in asking whether Wilder worked for them. He'd also found out that Simpson was working with an Officer Bartlett in Idaho to gather more information on their suspect there.

As for him... he hated the idea of investigating Kate's dad, but he couldn't shake the idea that Frank was involved in all of this. Wilder hoped he was wrong, and that Frank was simply a nosy ex-father-in-law, but he was also the mayor and made it a point to say he knew everything that went on in his town.

Well, Wilder would know how true that was soon enough. Simpson had agreed to have his office run a full background on him.

There was nothing more Wilder could do until Simpson got back to him, so he was going to enjoy his date night with Kate.

The texts between them had been growing more and more sexually suggestive. By the time Kate opened her door for him, it took all his strength not to pull her into his arms and make it clear exactly how he felt about her.

"Hi," she said as her eyes took him in. He wasn't going to lie; he loved how she ogled him. "Come in."

He stepped in and immediately smelled something delicious. Familiar.

"Is that your chili?"

She smiled. "It is. It's been a long time since I cooked it for you."

"Damn I've missed it." Then he did pull her into his arms. "I've missed you even more."

She still fit perfectly against him. As he gazed down at her, her pink, full lips were calling to him and he yearned to feel them again.

"I've missed you too, Wilder."

"Are you going to make me wait until the end of this date to see if I've earned that kiss?"

She grinned then shook her head. "You've earned it."

Yes!

He bent down and pressed his lips to hers, and what was meant to be a soft kiss quickly turned hot and heavy.

Kate pulled him closer to her, and when she parted her lips, he was a goner. His entire body was on fire for this woman. How could he have forgotten their intense chemistry?

Right, because he'd forced himself to.

Never again.

He swept his tongue in, and their kiss deepened. He walked her backward until her back was up against a wall. Without breaking contact, she yanked his shirt up, and he stepped back, pulling it all the way off.

Her eyes widened. "You got tattoos." She traced the ink on his shoulder and chest with her fingertips.

The feel of her touch was electrifying, and he hoped like hell she wasn't going to stop and ask about those tattoos right now.

She didn't. Instead, she leapt into his arms, wrapping her legs around his waist, and he held her as she kissed him harder.

Interesting. His Kate liked tattoos.

He pushed her against the wall and ground into her, which caused her to moan. His lips moved to her neck, and she tilted her head, giving him access.

Using her legs, she pulled him closer, and he ground against her again.

"You like that?" he asked.

"So much," she rasped.

While keeping one hand on her ass, holding her up, he slid his other hand under her T-shirt. His thumb grazed over her nipple, and it pebbled under his touch.

"Let's go to my bedroom," she panted.

"You sure? I don't want to move too fast."

"I'm sure. We have ten years to make up for. I don't think we can go fast enough."

He let her legs down, and she took his hand, leading him down the hall.

Part of him was still worried they were moving too fast, but he also agreed with her and didn't want to waste another moment.

He stepped into her bedroom, and his eyes landed on the large queen bed in the middle with all white bedding. The walls were a dark blue and there were several white accents throughout the room. Her place looked a hell of a lot nicer than his.

"Do you want to check out my dresser or me?" Kate teased.

He chuckled. "Sorry. I like your color choices in here."

She smiled. "That's good. Maybe you'll like my color choices here too." She pulled her shirt up over her head, revealing a blue bra.

"Blue always was my favorite color," he rumbled. He pulled her close, and his hands slipped below the waistband of her pants to squeeze her ass—which was bare. "No panties?"

She shook her head.

He groaned and grabbed her ass harder as he pressed her against him.

There was no doubt she could feel what she was doing to him.

"Take your pants off," she demanded.

He grinned. "You too."

He slowly undid the button and zipper on his jeans while watching her peel off her jeans. The smell of her arousal made him dizzy. He wanted her more than he'd ever wanted anything in his life.

Once he'd stripped out of his pants, he pushed her back on the bed and kissed his way up her thigh until he was at the apex, then he licked up her center.

"I missed this so much," he growled, then dove back in.

"Me too," she said, fisting his hair.

The more she tugged, the harder he sucked, and after a minute, she strained, "Wilder, I'm close."

He kept his tongue concentrated on her clit but moved his hand up to pinch her nipple through her bra. She cried out, and her body clenched at her release. He savored the taste of her on his tongue again.

Gradually, she relaxed, and he kissed his way up her stomach as her breathing slowed.

"Are you on birth control?" he asked.

"I am. And I'm clean. It's been a while since I've been with anyone."

"Me too. And I'm clean."

She knew what he was asking. "I want to go bare with you, Wilder."

Grinning, he yanked off his boxer briefs, and Kate began to stroke him, but he stopped her. "I'm not going to last if you do that."

Then he laid her back down, hovering over her and staring into her eyes. In this moment, he was overwhelmed with emotion. He'd never thought he'd see her again, much less have another chance to love her.

"Ready?" he asked.

She nodded.

He leaned down and kissed her deeply as he slid inside her. They both moaned.

"You feel so fucking good," he said.

Sweat beaded on his back, and he knew he wouldn't last much longer. He moved in and out slowly, but when she raked her nails down his back, he lost control and started pounding harder and harder.

"Oh, fuck yes, Wilder. Right there."

Another thrust, and Kate's legs tightened around his back as he felt her pulsate around his cock.

He thrust one more time and he was done. His orgasm raced through him, intense, making him see stars, and he pushed in as far as he could as he released all he had.

Once his breathing slowed down, he lifted his head and looked into Kate's eyes. "Wow."

"I know."

He rested his forehead on hers. "We should probably eat before we try to catch up on all ten years."

She laughed. "You're probably right."

Chapter Twenty-Three

Kate woke up sore, and memories from the night before flooded back. After they'd eaten dinner, they'd ended up back in bed, where they'd remained for the rest of the night.

She stretched her arms to the sides, and her hand connected with something hard and warm. She turned to find Wilder on his side, watching her.

"Morning," he said, smiling.

Damn he was hot.

She traced his tattoos with her fingers. "Morning."

He pulled her into his arms, and she snuggled in, though her mind was racing.

What does this mean for us? Could we possibly have a future?

"You're thinking loudly," he said as he rubbed her back with one hand.

She leaned back so she could look him in the eyes. "What happens when your case ends?"

He smiled. "I've thought about that a lot. And the answer to that depends on you."

She frowned. "Me?"

He nodded. "My hope is that you're open to us trying again. If you are, I'll find a place here in Fisher Springs."

"But what about your job?"

"It's only about a thirty-minute drive to the station. The distance isn't a problem. I just have to convince my captain to keep me stationed on the east side."

Her heart burst with emotion. He'd already thought about this? She smiled.

"Kate, after ten years without you, I'd do anything to keep us together. You have to know that. And I would never have pursued you if I didn't think we could make it work."

"You wouldn't have?"

He shook his head. "We've already hurt so much. But one thing I'm certain of is you are my one. I'm so sorry I let Martin ruin us."

She sat up. "No more apologies. No more looking back. I only want to look forward with you."

"Okay."

She stared at his chest. "Except... when did you get the tattoos?"

He grinned. "You like them?"

She leaned forward and licked the one on his left shoulder. "Very much, yes."

He quickly sat up, and the next thing she knew, she was on her back, looking up at him.

"Good to know. I got them after I joined the police academy. The dragon on my shoulder extends down my back."

She realized she hadn't seen his back. "Let me see," she said, trying to crawl under his arm for a better look.

He sat up and swiveled around so she could get a better look. One wing of the dragon extended down its length.

"Wow, it's beautiful."

He glanced at her over his shoulder with a brow arched. "Beautiful?"

"Something wrong with that?"

He turned back around and pinned her arms above her head. "Yeah, it's powerful." He kissed her and crawled between her legs. "And manly," he said as he ground into her.

"Wilder," she moaned.

"And this other one," he motioned to the tattoo on his chest, "is an eagle."

"Why an eagle?"

He kissed her neck. "Because eagles are cool as fuck."

She laughed and traced the eagle, grazing his nipple.

He groaned. "Dammit, Kate."

She froze. "What's wrong?"

His eyes met hers. "I want nothing more than to plan a future with you. I really wanted to take this slow, but I can't seem to."

She laughed again, then wrapped her legs around his waist. "I think it's a little late to take it slow." She grabbed his ass, pushing him to grind into her.

Wilder moaned. "Okay, so we might not have gone slow physically... but we didn't the first time either."

He was right. They'd moved fast after they first started dating. They had a chemistry she'd never felt with anyone else.

"But we can go slow with rest," he assured her. "I won't pressure you to take the next steps until you're ready." He leaned down and kissed the spot below her ear that always got her going.

"The rest?" She really was trying to pay attention, but between his mouth on her neck and his cock grinding between her legs, she was struggling.

"Yeah, you know... saying the L-word, moving in together, getting remarried. And then babies."

She pushed him up.

He rolled off her and flopped onto his back. "Shit. I'm sorry. I don't mean to sound like I'm in a rush or pressuring you. I know having kids was an issue between us before."

She stared at the ceiling. That was an understatement; it had been a *huge* issue between them. "You wanted them right away."

Over the course of their reunion, they had talked about what they had been doing the last ten years, but one subject they had not yet discussed was the nature of their subsequent relationships.

"Wilder, do you have kids?"

He laughed beside her. "No."

Kate rolled onto her side to stare at him. "But you were so adamant about having them young."

"I was. But once we weren't together, it didn't matter. I didn't want kids for the sake of kids, Kate. I wanted *our* babies."

Her stomach fluttered, both with gratitude and uncertainty. Their babies?

His finger brushed between her brows, where she was sure there was a line. "I tried dating over the years, but nothing ever worked out. All I could think was they weren't you. I finally decided to stop trying."

She rolled onto her back and stared at the ceiling again. All these years, she'd figured he'd moved on, found someone, and started a family. But instead, they'd both spent all those years missing each other.

"What about you?" he asked quietly. "Did you get serious about anyone else?"

She couldn't help but laugh. "No. I couldn't. I wasn't willing to go through that kind of pain again."

He pulled her close. "I'm so sor—"

She put her finger over his lips.

He took a deep breath. "Okay, no more apologies. But I will say this: holding you in my arms right now makes me the happiest man. And I'll do whatever it takes to keep you here."

Kate snuggled in. "I'd like that. But right now, we both need to get to work."

He chuckled. "Unfortunately, you're right."

She nodded, then grinned. "But I think we could spare a few minutes."

She pushed him on his back and straddled him as she kissed his tattoos, then worked her way down to his stomach. His breathing sped up as she worked her way lower down his still naked body.

She ran her fingers down his length, enjoying how silky smooth his skin was there. Then she took him in her mouth, staring deep into his eyes as she ran her tongue along the underside

Pure hunger looked back at her.

"Kate, that feels so good," he huffed out.

His cock throbbed in her mouth, and she knew it wouldn't take long.

"Kate, come here," he motioned. "I want to come inside you. Ride me, baby."

His words caused her clit to pulsate. Wilder hadn't been much of a dirty talker back when they were young, but she loved that he was now.

She crawled up his body and positioned him at her entrance. She couldn't remember when she'd ever felt so turned on by a man.

"That's it. God, you're so wet," he purred as his fingers found her clit.

She pushed down, taking him to the hilt. Then she rose and dropped back down increasingly harder each time as her orgasm built.

"Kate, come now," he demanded.

It worked, and she came so hard, there were spots in her vision.

He grabbed her hips and pumped into her with a groan, chasing his own orgasm.

"Kate," he sighed after a moment, releasing her hips. "I don't want to leave your bed."

"You don't have to. I'll be right back."

She ran to the bathroom and cleaned up, catching herself in the mirror. Her hair was a mess, but she was smiling. She looked truly happy for the first time since... well, she couldn't remember when. It was a nice feeling.

When she came back to the bedroom, Wilder was sitting up, frowning at his phone.

"Uh oh. That doesn't look good," she said.

He turned his gaze to her. "It's not. Your father told Dunin I'm a detective, and now the chief wants to talk to me."

"What? How does my dad know you're a detective?"

"Apparently, he ran a background on me."

Kate closed her eyes. "I'm sorry my dad can be an asshole."

Wilder chuckled. "Yes, he can. But I'm afraid I have to go soon. But first, I want some more time with you."

Chapter Twenty-Four

Wilder tapped at his steering wheel as he drove to Kate's house.

Nine days.

That was all the time he had left to find out who was really in charge of selling drugs here in Fisher Springs and try to stop Brogan Miller, or whoever the hell the Bannons were sending, from bombing their town.

Thanks to Frank Waters, the Fisher Springs Police Department was involved in the investigation. That had been a fun conversation. Simpson was pissed they'd had to bring them in, Chief Dunin was pissed the county had an undercover investigation going on in his town, and Wilder was pissed that Kate's dad might have damaged the investigation.

Hopefully, Frank hadn't said anything to Martin. Wilder had plans to stalk Martin this weekend, and if that didn't pan out... well, he wasn't sure what he was going to do.

But it was Friday night, and he had a date with Kate. It had been a few days since he stayed overnight with her, and he couldn't wait for another. But it seemed they couldn't get their schedules to mesh. Kate had some landscape design contract that she said would keep her busy most evenings.

At first, he'd thought she was blowing him off. When he asked if that was the case, she swore she wasn't. So finally, they'd agreed to another date tonight. She'd mentioned she had some news to tell him tonight as well.

As he approached her house, he was stunned to see Martin's car parked out front. There was no missing it, with its obnoxious *Fisher Springs Development* decal.

Why would Martin Fisher be at Kate's house?

No answer that crossed his mind was good.

He parked in front of her house and quietly stepped up onto her porch. Then he peered in the living room window.

Kate was sitting down, looking at something on her kitchen table. Martin was beside her, his arm on her chair, practically touching her, and leaning in way too close.

What the fuck is going on?

He continued to watch. Kate was focused on whatever was on the table, while Martin was focused on her.

Wilder checked the time; he was fifteen minutes early. Damn, earlier than he'd thought. But he had been anxious to see her again.

He knocked on the door, then stepped back.

The door swung open, and Kate's eyes widened.

"Is it six already?" she asked.

"Almost," Wilder said, rocking back on his heels, not liking the reaction she gave to seeing him.

"Sorry, I lost track of time working on my designs. Come in."

Well, at least she was inviting him in. That was a good sign.

He stepped in while Martin stood next to the kitchen table, arms crossed glaring at him.

"Martin, what are you doing here?"

Martin grinned. "Oh, didn't Kate tell you?"

Wilder glanced at Kate, who walked to the table and started stacking papers.

"I hadn't had the chance yet," she said.

"Well, allow me. We're working together — every night this week, as a matter of fact. Lots of late nights." Martin grinned.

Kate's hands went to her hips. "What are you doing, Martin?"

The man had the nerve to try to look innocent.

Kate huffed. "We are working together on the landscape design of the new housing development, and he stopped by to approve a few changes I made. We have not been working together late every night."

"We could be."

Wilder fisted his hands. He wanted to punch this guy… but he couldn't. Not as long as he was working his case. But damn, as soon as he solved it, if Martin wasn't arrested, he would show him just how angry he was.

"Martin, I think we're done here," Kate said. "I have plans now."

Martin shoved his hands in his pockets. "With *him*? Really?"

"Are you seriously questioning her plans right now?" Wilder asked, stepping forward.

"I'm surprised she'd want to spend any time with a man that would take someone else's word over hers. That must have really stung." He turned back to Kate. "I'd never do that to you."

"No, you'd just ruin any other relationship she tried to have," Wilder snapped, moving closer.

"Martin, please leave," Kate said firmly.

The man grabbed his jacket off the back of a kitchen chair and put it on. Slowly.

If he was trying to irk Wilder further, it was working.

"Kate, call me with any changes, or if you need anything at all. You have my number." He winked at Wilder and then let himself out.

After he was gone, Wilder remained where he was, taking several deep breaths.

"Wilder, I can explain."

"You're working for Martin?" he growled.

Kate turned back to the table and resumed moving papers around. "Yes, I signed a contract with him before you came back to town, before I knew everything—"

"And you didn't try to get out of it once you knew?"

She stilled. "I hate what Martin did. Do I want to punish him for it? Yes. But this contract is the difference between me having a landscaping design business or not having one. So yes, I went forward with it."

"He's a client, then?"

"Yes."

"And after this project, what will you do?"

She flopped into the kitchen chair. "I don't know. My plan had been to try to get all of the business he had to offer. But now... I don't know what to do. This has turned my entire world upside down."

Wilder sat in the chair next to her and took her hand in his. "I'm sorry. It's just—"

She squeezed his hand. "I know." Her eyes welled with tears. "I know, Wilder."

He stood and pulled her up and into his arms, holding her as she wept.

"We'll figure something out for your business," he promised.

She leaned back. "We?"

He nodded. "Yes, we. I told you I want us back. I meant it. I want it all, Kate."

She stepped away from him. "What if we're moving too fast? We haven't gotten to know each other well enough as adults. What if we hate each other now?"

He chuckled. "That won't happen."

"How do you know?"

He took her hands in his. "I know. I know you are my one."

Damn... Being this close to her, all he wanted was to take her into the bedroom and show her how much he still cared. He couldn't blame her for doubting them—not after the way he'd ended things. He had to earn back her trust and love. Slowly.

He sighed. "We should go, otherwise we might find all of our get-to-know-each-other-again time being spent in the bedroom."

She smiled. "That wouldn't be so bad, would it?"

That sent a jolt to his cock.

Would it be so bad?

"Um."

Kate laughed. "It's good to know I can still throw you off."

He stepped toward her, and she stepped back. Repeating this, he backed her up until her back hit a wall. Then he leaned in and whispered in her ear, "You were kidding?"

When he pulled back, her smile was gone, and heat emanated from her eyes.

She squirmed the way she used to when she was turned on. "I was, but I might reconsider," she admitted.

Staring into her eyes, he leaned in until their lips were almost touching.

The chemistry between them had always been hot, but right now, it was a fucking inferno. He had to step back before he did something he'd regret.

As much as he wanted her, they needed to take time to get to know each other again, *outside* of the bedroom.

He moved a piece of hair behind her ear. "We will get to that. Promise. But right now, I want to take you somewhere."

"Oh yeah?"

"Mmhmm."

"Sounds mysterious."

"Maybe."

She studied his appearance for clues. "Shorts and a T-shirt. Shall I wear the same?"

Kate was currently wearing a pink dress that he loved.

"No. What you have on is perfect."

"Okay, I'll be right back. I left my purse in the bedroom."

After she left the room, he checked his phone.

Simpson: *Joey's got something new for us.*

Wilder was running out of patience. So far, Joey's tips hadn't been helpful.

Wilder: *Better be good.*

Simpson: *It is. I told him we needed to know who the guy in charge was.*

Wilder: *I hope he answered you.*

Simpson: *Well, what he said next was interesting.*

"Ready," Kate said, coming out from the hallway.

Wilder pocketed his phone.

He knew that he'd likely would be working all weekend, and this would be the only time he'd have with Kate. He'd check his messages in a couple of hours. Right now, he had somewhere special to take his woman.

Chapter Twenty-Five

An hour later, they were lying on a blanket at Tunes and Brews, a music event being held in the park every Friday evening in June. The band was playing country covers, and they were decent.

The sun was shining to their left and wouldn't be setting for another couple of hours. That's what made summer Wilder's favorite time of year; the long days, when it felt like anything was possible.

"When did they start doing this?" Wilder asked.

"Tunes and Brews? A couple of years ago. It's really popular and a great chance for locals and high schoolers to get to play for an audience."

Wilder nodded to the band onstage. "Do you think they're in high school?"

"I know they are. I saw them perform here last year. I think they're seniors now."

She was here last year? He watched as she enjoyed the music. *Was she here on a date?*

Did he even want to know?

"I came with Chase and Harmony," she filled in for him. "I really enjoyed it; I don't know why I haven't been back."

Wilder let his gaze wander to his right where several couples were dancing. He was about to ask Kate if she wanted to join them, when the sun was suddenly blocked by a tall figure.

He glanced up and saw Kate's father towering over them.

"Kate?"

Wilder turned in time to see Kate's smile fall.

"Father."

The mayor crossed his arms as he glared at her. "What are you doing here with him?"

Wilder chuckled. "I'm sitting right here, you know."

The man ignored him.

"I'm on a date. If you don't mind, I'll talk to you later."

Go Kate.

Her dad had always been a prick, but Kate had walked on eggshells around him back when they were younger. It was great to see her not giving a damn what the old man thought.

"A date? Are you kidding me? After what he did to you? Have you learned nothing?"

A few people nearby stared as the mayor's voice grew louder.

Kate stood up. "This is my life and my choice."

"Kate? What a lovely surprise." Her mom walked up, and her gaze went from Kate to Wilder. Her brow furrowed. "Oh, you two are here together?"

"Martha, they're on a date," Frank spit out.

His wife pursed her lips. "Really? That's disappointing, Kate."

"Again, I'm right here," Wilder said.

"Well, I guess now that the entire town has seen you together, we will have to show support," Martha said, smoothing her dress.

"Good god, Martha, you can't be serious. This boy destroyed our daughter."

Martha's hands went to her hips. "Yes, but that was years ago, and everyone in town is rooting for them to get back together. It wouldn't look proper if we fought them on it, now, would it?"

The mayor ground his teeth. "We are not in agreement on this. If you'll excuse me, I'm going to visit the beer garden."

As he walked away, Wilder noticed the look of sadness on Martha's face.

"Well, don't mind him," she said quietly. "He'll come around. I'll leave you two be."

After she left, several people continued to turn and glance back at Kate and Wilder. He wanted to tell them to mind their own fucking business, but if he was going to live in this town again, he needed to play nice.

"I'm sorry about that," Kate said.

Wilder pulled her into his arms. "Don't be. You can't control your parents."

"Oh shit. Don't look, but the Fisher clan has arrived."

Wilder glanced in the direction Kate was staring. Melia, Scott, Martin, and a woman Wilder didn't recognize were walking near the stage. Martin then laid down a large blanket, and they all slowly sat down.

He couldn't be surprised. There wasn't a lot to do in a small town on a Friday night.

Two men joined the Fishers, setting up short folding chairs. The group was smiling and joking around.

"Who's that talking to Martin?" Wilder asked.

Kate glanced over. "Another Fisher. You don't recognize him?"

He squinted.

"Is that Colt?"

"Yes, it is. And Justin's with him. I guess they're friends."

"Justin?"

Kate's cheeks flushed red. "He's a few years younger than us. He works at the grocery store."

He didn't have to ask; it was obvious by her reaction that they'd dated. Odds were she'd dated a few guys in town. That was something he'd have to get used to.

"Hey, I'm going to find the bathroom. I'll be back," Kate said as she stood.

"I'll be here."

While she was gone, Wilder checked his messages.

Simpson: *Joey said the guy in charge, or contact, isn't Martin. But if he doesn't know who it is, then how does he know that?*

Simpson: *Anyway, that's not the tip. Joey says a big deal is going down tonight. Can you get to the housing development and check it out?*

Wilder closed his eyes. Dammit. The last thing he wanted was to leave Kate. But it was for the case.

Abruptly, Melia stood, and the movement caught his attention. He watched as she walked toward the bathrooms, glanced back at her family, then turned toward the parking lot.

Interesting.

When Kate returned, Wilder jumped up.

"I need to go too. I'll be right back." He kissed her cheek then walked toward the bathrooms.

That was when he saw Frank walking in the same direction Melia had gone.

Are they meeting in the parking lot?

He turned and made his way into the trees that lined the park, then cut through until the parking lot came into view. Posting up behind a tree, he spotted Melia leaning against a car. The mayor stepped up to her, and a beat later, she shook her head.

Damn, he wished he could hear what they were saying.

The mayor's hands went to his hips, and he took a few steps away from her, shaking his head.

Then he turned back around and said something. Melia pushed off the car, and the mayor opened the same vehicle's trunk and grabbed a backpack.

To get closer, Wilder crouched down and moved forward to hide behind a car. The pair were a row over and down at least ten cars. How could he get even closer to hear what was going on without being seen?

He made his way to the front of the car and while remaining bent down, made his way by the next several cars, thanking whoever had made sure the parking lot was all dirt. If it had been gravel, they would have heard him creeping up.

He finally stopped when the next spot over was empty. If he kept going, he risked being seen.

Wilder spotted two men getting out of a van a few cars down from Frank. It was the same two men he'd seen go into the office building when he was watching Melia. One was even wearing the same torn jeans and sweatshirt.

The men stopped in front of Frank and Melia.

"Here. This is all of it," Frank said.

One man reached for the backpack, but Frank pulled it back.

"I want your assurance this matter is over," Kate's father snapped.

The other man jerked the bag from Frank's grip. "It is."

Then the two men turned and walked back to the van.

Wilder memorized the license plate and texted it to Simpson. Maybe he'd get a hit and find their next lead.

Once the men were gone, Frank nodded to Melia. "You go back first."

She gave a nod and then walked back toward the music. After she left, Kate's father surveyed the parking lot, forcing Wilder to duck back to avoid detection.

"Son of a bitch," Frank muttered. He continued to curse under his breath as he made his way back to the music festival.

What the hell was that? Was that related to the drugs being sold in this town?

No, the mayor would never be involved in something like that. Would he? Maybe Melia and the mayor are the contact people? But why the hell would they take such a risk?

The answer was obvious.

Money. Of course. It's always for money. And probably power, in the mayor's case.

His mind was getting out of control. He had to not jump to conclusions and find out what was in the bag.

But there was nothing he could do until Simpson ran those plates, and Kate would be wondering where he was. So, he got up and jogged across the lot—until he heard a car turn in.

Panicked, he bent down, pretending to tie his shoe. His gut told him it wouldn't be good to be caught out here, especially if the owners of the van came back.

The car pulled into the empty spot, right next to where he crouched.

Crap.

He stayed crouched. Odds were, whoever it was would walk the other way through the lot, and on to the festival, and he'd be able to go on his way with no one the wiser.

Two car doors opened and closed. Wilder counted to himself to allow time for whoever it was to leave the area.

"Wilder?"

Wilder looked up to see Chase and Harmony.

Seriously? He'd forgotten how small this town really was.

After pretending to finish tying his shoe, he stood up. "Good to see you guys."

"You too," Chase replied. "I love live music. I wish they did this year-round."

"Maybe you should suggest it to the mayor," Harmony told him.

"Well, I don't mean to keep you," Wilder interjected. "I should be getting back too." He stepped to the side, moving slowly, and watched from the corner of his eye as the two walked toward the beer garden.

Without a look back, Wilder stepped back into the trees and made his way back to Kate.

As much as he hated cutting their date short so he could go to the housing development, he would be happy to put some distance between himself and her dad.

Although, he had to wonder what he'd witnessed. Maybe that was why he hadn't seen anything while working on the construction crew; maybe the money exchanges and product drop-offs were happening a little at a time instead of in one big delivery.

But if that's true, why the hell would the mayor get involved?

Chapter Twenty-Six

Kate poured herself a glass of wine and flopped down on her couch. While she understood Wilder had to cut their date short because of his case, something had felt off as he'd driven her home.

She thought back over their conversation before they left for the park. *Maybe he's acting funny because he said he wanted it all with me, and I hesitated?*

No, something else was going on. He had mentioned talking to Jessie, so maybe she'd know.

Kate grabbed her phone, but before she could type out a text to her friend, there was a knock at her door.

Smiling, she stood up. *Maybe Wilder came back.* But when she peered out, she saw her dad on the porch.

She opened the door. "Dad?"

"Sweetheart. I'm glad I found you."

"I thought you were at the park with Mom."

"I was. But something came up and I had to talk to you right away."

"Is Mom all right? And Lily?"

Her dad reached out and rubbed her shoulders. "They're fine. Let's sit." He nodded toward the couch.

She let him guide her and then took a healthy drink of wine. If her family was all fine, then there was only one other reason he would be here. "I know you don't like Wilder, but I really don't want to discuss him with you."

Her dad let out a sigh. "I'm sorry to be the one to tell you this, but I hired someone to look into him."

"I don't want to hear about this." She jumped up. Wilder had mentioned the background report and while she was pissed off, she knew it wouldn't do any good to yell at her dad about it.

"Kate, you two haven't talked in ten years. From what I understand, *no one* has talked to him in ten years."

She paced the room. "I'm sure William has."

"But we don't know. We don't know anything about where he's been, what he's done."

She couldn't believe her dad would do this. But then, why wouldn't he? He was looking for anything, any reason at all to keep them apart. And if he was here, he must have found something.

"Kate, Wilder used to be a detective in Summit County."

She stopped pacing and turned to him. "Used to be?"

He nodded. "He was fired a few months ago. Apparently, he was a dirty cop. A prosecutor might even be pressing charges."

What? No, Wilder said he was here on a case, that he was currently a detective. And how could he be dirty? He had always been one of the most honest people she'd known.

She shook her head. "No, you must be mistaken."

Her dad reached into his jacket pocket, pulled out a folded piece of paper, and handed it to her. "I verified everything."

She opened it to find a summary of a background check. Under 'employment' it stated he had been let go and was being investigated.

But her eye caught on another line: *spouse*. A name was listed, and it wasn't hers.

She dropped the paper. Wilder had lied to her? About everything? What did he want from her, then?

No. There was no way this could be right.

"Honey, I'm so sorry to be the one to tell y —"

"Please leave," she croaked. "I need to be alone."

He frowned in what she could be forgiven for mistaking for concern. "Are you sure? Maybe you should call Harmony to come over."

"I will." She knew she needed to placate her dad to get him to leave.

He bent down and grabbed the paper, returning it to his pocket. "I'm sorry," he repeated. "But it's better you know now."

Kate heard the door close as he left, but she felt nothing. Only numb.

This can't be true.

If she asked Wilder, would he tell her the truth? Could she really trust him?

Being with him had felt so right. Was it real, or was it just her fantasy?

Maybe she *should* call Harmony.

When she grabbed her phone, she saw the text she'd started to write to Jessie.

Wait… Jessie.

She was a private investigator. Maybe she could find out what was really going on.

She made the call.

"Kate?" Jessie answered right away. "Hi, how are you doing?"

"Not great. I got some bad news about Wilder. Are you free to meet me?"

"Sure. I can come over right now."

"Actually, can I come to you?"

Kate had no idea what Jessie might use in running checks on people, but she figured odds were better to talk her into helping her at her place. She had to know if any of this was true.

"Sure."

"I'll see you in five."

* * *

"I have to say I'm surprised," Jessie said, pacing in front of her couch. "I didn't get the impression he was lying. Do you have the paper? I'd like to see it."

Kate recalled the image of her dad grabbing it off the floor. "No, my dad took it with him when he left."

"Huh." Jessie stopped pacing. "Follow me."

Kate obeyed, following her friend to a home office.

Jessie sat down and pulled up a website. "What's Wilder's last name?"

"Loprete."

Jessie ran her search. After a moment, she muttered, "That's odd."

"What?"

"All the records on him ended about ten years ago."

Kate furrowed her brow, then remembered tracing the letters of his badge. "Oh, sorry. He changed it to Coleman."

Jessie's fingers flew over the keys. "He changed his last name? Do you know why?"

Her stomach sank. "To avoid me."

"Ouch. Sorry. Oh, I found him," Jessie said.

Kate couldn't look; she wasn't sure she wanted to see the truth.

When it became clear that Kate wasn't going to take the initiative to look at the screen herself, Jessie spoke.

"Well, based on my initial research, he hasn't remarried that I see. I guess he could have flown to Vegas or something. And as far as the job, I can't get into personnel records for police officers, but I did message a friend who works in that county."

"Thank you."

He may or may not be married. *Fuck.* And he may have been fired.

"Oh, Dane messaged back. He knows Wilder. Actually, he says they're good friends."

Kate perked up. "Really? What are the odds?"

Jessie shrugged. "They are similar age, same precinct. Not surprising. Anyway, he says that no, Wilder wasn't fired and isn't a dirty cop—and he wants to know who the son of a bitch is that's saying he was."

Jessie snorted, then her phone rang. "Dane, thanks for the information. Uh huh. I can't say. Wait."

She looked at Kate then handed her the phone. "Dane wants to talk to you."

Kate stared at the phone. The man on the other line knew Wilder... the version of him she didn't know.

She took the phone, her hand shaking. "Hello?"

"Hey, who's this?"

"Kate."

The other end was silent.

"Hello?"

"Kate? Like… Wilder's Kate?"

Her heart was pounding out of her chest. "Yes. You know about me?"

"Holy shit. Yeah, I do. But only because I got Wilder drunk once. And I do mean once. After that, he wouldn't ever drink more than two beers."

She wanted to ask more, but it felt wrong. Like she was invading his privacy. She decided to stick to the reason she was there. "I was told Wilder was fired for being a dirty cop, and that he's married. Is any of that true?"

Dane guffawed. "I'm sorry, I shouldn't laugh. It's just so opposite from the truth. And really, I do want to know who's spreading this shit."

Kate's eyes welled up with tears of relief. But then she realized how far her dad would go to keep them apart.

"My dad. He doesn't want us together."

"Together? Are you two back together?"

Were they? Wilder had made it clear that was what he wanted. And that's what she wanted too.

Dane chuckled softly at her silence. "Look, just so you know, Wilder is a great detective. As for having a wife, I've never even seen him with a girlfriend, and I've known him for eight years."

"Thank you."

"Hey, Kate? Don't hurt him. The one night he told me about you, he was a mess. Don't get back with him unless you're sure."

Dane ended the call, leaving Kate's mind racing.

"My dad lied," she choked out. "Not only did he lie, but he went to the effort to have a fake document created."

Jessie got up from her chair and hugged Kate. "I'm so sorry."

"Thank you," Kate said.

"But if you and Wilder are going to be together, you need to tell him about this—about all of it. You need to be on the same team. Trust me on that one. That's a lesson I learned the hard way."

Jessie was right. Kate had to tell Wilder that, instead of calling and asking him directly to refute her father's accusations, she had gone to Jessie and spoken to his friend.

Yeah, that would go over well.

Chapter Twenty-Seven

One week. That was all Wilder had until July fourth.

After dropping Kate off at home following the Tunes and Brews event, he had gone to the housing development... and seen nothing. He also saw nothing all day Saturday and for a few hours this morning.

Finally, he gave up and went into town. He needed to find Joey and get some answers, no more of these bullshit false tips.

But first, he needed more coffee.

Stepping into the Cozy Croissant always put a smile on his face. The smell of fresh coffee and baked bread would put anyone in a good mood. But as he got deeper into the shop, he heard Melia's voice.

Glancing over, he saw she was sitting with Joey. *Wow, finding him was easier than I thought it'd be.*

He needed to know what Joey knew but the man wasn't going to talk freely with Melia around.

Keeping his head down and moving quickly, he approached the counter.

"What can I get you?" the barista asked.

"Black coffee and a croissant."

As she gathered his items, he listened to Melia.

"Since that development is almost done, we're going to move distribution to this new development I'll be overseeing."

Wilder glanced over to see Joey frowning.

"What's the rush? We still have a couple of weeks before those condos will be finished."

Condos? Shit, was *that* the housing development he had been referring to? How many were there in this tiny town?

"There's already been too much interest in the units," Melia protested. "We have random people stopping by daily, trying to get a peek of one. We need to move things *today*."

Joey nodded. "Okay, you're right. The move will cause a delay in distribution, though."

Melia put her hand on his knee. "I know. But I know you can explain to him why this is necessary."

"Here's your coffee and croissant," the woman at the counter said from behind Wilder. "Can I get you anything else?"

He turned his attention back to her and gave a tight smile. "No thank you." Then he paid and took a seat not too far from the pair. He stared at his phone to appear busy hoping to catch their conversation.

Fortunately, Joey didn't notice him. Or hell, maybe he didn't recognize him; it had been ten years. Either way, Joey finished his coffee and left but Melia stayed seated.

Wilder continued to stare at his phone, pretending not to notice that Melia was now facing him. Damn, this woman was too observant. He was hoping she would simply leave so he could chase after Joey. He didn't want anyone around when he questioned that man and he suspected Melia might just follow him.

No such luck.

Instead of leaving, Melia sat down in the chair across from him at his little table. "Funny seeing you here again."

Wilder glanced up to see her smiling at him.

"What are you doing here, Wilder?"

He frowned and stared down at the table. "Just enjoying a cup of coffee."

She shook her head. "No, I mean why are you back in Fisher Springs?"

He let out an exasperated sigh. "I told you, I'm here for my brother's wedding."

She leaned forward and lowered her voice. "I don't believe you."

Of course, she wouldn't. He'd already gotten her suspicious by asking too many questions about her ex.

"A man who's only here for a wedding doesn't sneak around parking lots to listen in on conversations," she continued. "Nor does he interrogate someone about their ex."

Shit. She had seen him? Time to take a different angle.

He leaned back and gave her his best smile. "What can I say? I'm a curious guy."

"And what are you curious about?"

"You."

Melia laughed. "Now, see, if you had taken me up on my offer, I might buy that line." Her smile dropped. "But I heard you used to be a cop until you got your hands dirty."

Wilder shifted in his seat. The mayor wasn't one to gossip—or so he thought. But he'd told Melia. Why?

"Is that what you're looking for? Something dirty?" She smiled again.

He swallowed. Was she referring to drugs or sex? He couldn't tell. "What are you talking about, Melia?"

She leaned forward. "What exactly were you involved in when you got fired?"

He frowned. "That's personal."

She nodded. "Well, if you care to share, I might have an opportunity for you."

At that moment, a woman walked by, pulling a toddler behind her. The toddler smiled at Melia, who watched the child.

Wilder hoped the hunch he was feeling about her was wrong. Why would a young, beautiful, successful woman get caught up in drug trafficking?

But this was his ticket to the inside… which he desperately needed.

He shrugged, trying to play it cool. "I pocketed some money for looking the other way on a few drug deals."

Melia nodded, her eyes still on the child. "Do you carry a gun?"

"Now you're the one asking too many questions," he warned.

She laughed as she directed her attention back to him. "Like I said, I might have an opportunity for you."

With a frown, he asked, "What exactly do you want me to do?"

"Security. I have a side business, and it sounds like you'd be a perfect fit. There have been some threats recently, and who better to keep my operation safe than an ex-cop?"

A side business… threats… Could she really be the guy in charge?

"What kind of threats?" he asked.

She shrugged a shoulder. "Someone thinks I'm weak and can be pushed aside. I need to show them they're wrong."

Behind him, the toddler laughed. Wilder took a sip of his coffee while watching Melia, who was once again focused on the child.

"Is this related to your ex?" he asked. "The one you have a restraining order against?"

Melia met his gaze as she pointed a finger at him. "You're a smart one. It does. Sadly, I should never have gotten involved with him. Now he thinks he can come in and take over."

"And how does he plan to do that? Is he coming here?" Wilder glanced around.

"Are you saying you'll help me?"

Before Wilder could answer, his brother entered the shop. William noticed Wilder and saw how close he was sitting to Melia and arched a brow.

Wilder firmed his lips and subtly shook his head, conveying to his brother to let it go.

William must have gotten the message, because he went to the counter instead of joining them at the table.

Wilder directed his attention back to Melia. Cocking his head, he told her, "Of course I'll help you. I don't want some asshole pushing you around."

She smiled and reached for his hand. "Thank you, Wilder."

He wanted to pull away, but knew he needed to earn her trust.

Seemingly unaware of his discomfort, Melia went on. "He says he's coming this weekend, and if I don't hand over everything, I'll regret it." She rolled her eyes.

"Regret it?" Wilder leaned forward in a show of interest. "What do you think he means?"

The odds she would mention were low, but he had to try.

She snorted. "That he'd do something to harm me. The man has a bit of a history of doing that."

Knowing that a man had harmed her like that solidified Wilder's determination to keep him away from her.

"What exactly does he want you to hand over?"

She shrugged. "Just some items he bought me while we were together."

Wilder leaned back. "Expensive items?"

She nodded.

"What if he brings friends to help him retrieve these items?"

She snorted. "Brogan is a lone wolf. There's no way he's working with anyone."

"How can you be sure?"

She glanced at someone who walked in, then back to Wilder. "I dated him for six months. He never mentioned any friends. All he wanted was to spend time with me."

That was all she was basing this on?

He resisted the urge to call her out on her ignorance. "I'll help you, but you have to tell me about any communication you have with him. I know you don't think he'll bring anyone with him, but I'm not so sure."

Melia leaned back and crossed her arms. "Okay. But if you're protecting me, you'll have to stick with me. Will Kate be all right with that?"

Wilder shrugged and took another sip of his coffee. Kate would understand, wouldn't she?

Melia leaned forward. "Start tomorrow. That will give you time to tell her today."

"Tell her what exactly?"

"That you'll be staying at my house. I'll need 'round-the-clock protection." Then she winked.

Fuck. What had he gotten himself into?

Chapter Twenty-Eight

After checking the time, Kate realized she only had a couple of hours to get ready for her date with Wilder and prepare their dinner. One of his favorite meals had been her meatloaf, back when they'd take turns cooking for each other. God, she missed his carne asada. Maybe she would talk him into making some soon.

After getting the meatloaf prepared and into the oven, she went to her closet. They had agreed that since it felt like the entire town was watching them, it would be easier to get to know each other if they stayed in, rather than going out and being interrogated. And a date in called for a more casual outfit.

But not too casual.

Memories of her previous weekend with Wilder had her in the mood for a repeat, so she chose a short, blue, summer dress.

At seven o'clock, there was a knock on her door. She grinned. He'd always been punctual.

She swung open the door to find Wilder in a black suit jacket, a light blue button-up with the top button undone, and dark wash jeans. But she hadn't been expecting the smoldering look in his eyes.

"Hi," she said, then stepped back so he could come in.

As he entered, his eyes trailed from her legs slowly up her body. By the time they locked with hers, she couldn't take anymore. She grabbed the lapels of his jacket and pulled him close, crashing her lips to his.

She was about ready to crawl up his form when the oven timer went off.

Wilder jumped back. His lips were swollen from their kiss, and he stared at her with hooded eyes.

No one could hold a candle to this man. He was right; they were meant to be together. She knew it. And tonight, she was going to tell him how she felt.

She was so mesmerized, returning his heated gaze with her own, she blocked out everything else.

"What's that sound?" he asked.

Finally, Kate focused. Then she laughed. "The oven timer. Dinner's ready."

"Why does it sound like a dying duck?"

That actually wasn't a bad description.

She smirked. "Old oven. Old timer."

Wilder followed her into the kitchen and watched as she pulled the dish out of the oven and set it on top of the stove. He bent down, trying to peer around it. "This thing looks like a fire hazard. How did

I not notice it before?" He stood back up and stared at the stovetop burners.

She shrugged. "It works. That's all I need for now."

"How often do you cook?"

"A few nights a week."

He shook his head.

"Hey, are you going to brood over my oven, or can we have a nice meal?" Her tone turned more serious. "Or did you want to talk first?"

He kissed her forehead. "Let's eat. Is there anything I can grab?"

"Yes, there's a salad in the fridge."

Using the potholders, she carried the meatloaf to her kitchen table. Wilder set the salad next to it. Then she retrieved plates and utensils while he grabbed napkins off the counter. They moved in unison, like they used to right after they were married.

Once everything was on the table, they plated their food and sat down.

"This is very familiar," she said.

He took her hand in his. "It is."

"I've been thinking, and… you're right."

He squeezed her hand. "I'm always right. But what are you talking about specifically?"

She rolled her eyes, but answered, "About us. We are right together, and I want it all with you, too, Wilder."

"Really?"

"Yes."

"Woohoo!" He jumped up, pulled her out of her chair into a hug, and twirled her around.

She laughed at his enthusiasm. "Should we discuss details, then?"

His smile fell. "We should eat first." He set her down and returned to his chair.

Kate sat down and watched him. Something was on his mind. She didn't want to push, but she hoped like hell he'd discuss it with her after their meal.

Wilder took a bite. "Damn, Kate. I forgot how good this was."

"Thank you."

As they ate in uncomfortable silence, she kicked herself for not putting on some music — anything to take the pressure off of them.

When they were done, Wilder held out his hand. "Come sit with me? We can clean up later."

"Sure." She took his hand and let him lead her to the couch, trying hard not to let her nerves get the best of her.

He sat down and pulled her onto his lap, holding her close while his thumb rubbed small circles on her back.

She leaned her head on his chest. "What's going on?"

He let out a sigh. "My case. I got a break today."

She pulled back and tried to catch his gaze. "That's great."

But he didn't look happy.

"Isn't it?" she pressed.

He glanced up. Worry etched his eyes. "Yeah, but that break involves me providing security for Melia Fisher."

A weight settled in her chest. "Melia? Why would she need security?" She tried to push down the jealousy she felt, knowing this was the same woman he'd talked to at the bachelor party.

He tucked a piece of her hair behind her ear. "I can't say. But starting tomorrow, I'll have to be by her side twenty-four-seven until this case is solved."

Twenty-four… "Wait. Are you going to be staying at her house?"

He nodded.

The idea alone made her sick.

She stood up, trying to breathe through her panic. She wasn't normally a jealous person, but Melia was a beautiful, successful woman who was not known for respecting boundaries.

"Kate." Wilder came up behind her and put his arms around her waist. "I want to be clear. I'll only be there as part of this case, to provide security. She thinks I'm an ex-dirty-cop—I can't say any more about that. But I will tell you that the only woman I want is you, and I won't do anything to screw that up."

Ex-dirty cop? That was the second time she'd heard that story. And the first… had her dad stumbled upon Wilder's cover in his search for answers?

"Wilder, I trust you. It's her I don't trust."

She turned to face Wilder, and he took her face into his hands.

"I never stopped loving you, Kate. I can't tell you how sorry I am that I don't have more time to show you. Because, after the wedding and the festival next weekend, I'll probably have to go back to my apartment in Summit County."

Her breath caught in her throat. "So, this is our last night together?"

She believed the pain she saw in his eyes.

He grimaced. "For now. I already told you I can commute from here in the future, but I don't want to rush you. We will move forward when you're ready."

She frowned. "How far away do you live?"

"About an hour. But like I said, I can move closer when we are ready."

Still, she wondered how often they would see each other until then.

"Is this why you acted weird during dinner?" she asked.

He nodded. "I wasn't sure how I was going to tell you. Trust me, I want nothing more than to spend my last week here with you."

"I know."

He tilted her chin up and stared into her eyes. "Do you?"

She nodded, wanting to believe him. She really did.

"I love you, Kate. I've realized these past few weeks that I never stopped, and I'm so damn thankful to have this second chance with you."

And there went the final crack in her armor.

Tears welled in her eyes. "I love you too, Wilder. I love you so much it scares me."

"I know." He pulled her close and kissed her hair. "I know."

She inhaled his scent as she snuggled into him. This next week without him would suck, but if tonight was all they had, she wanted to make the most of it.

She tilted her head back and snaked her arms around his neck. He bowed his head, meeting her halfway in a tender kiss, and she poured all of her emotion into it.

He broke their connection only to bend down and sweep his arm under her legs. The next thing she knew, he was carrying her to the bedroom. After he set her on her feet, he unzipped the back of her dress. It slid down and pooled at her feet.

She pushed his jacket off his shoulders, and he shrugged out of it and pulled his shirt over his head before stepping closer and resuming their kiss.

Her hands found his belt and unhooked it. With a dirty grin, he took over removing the rest of his clothes while she took off her bra and panties.

She sat on the end of the bed and scooted backward, and he followed her up on hands and knees, then stretched out and positioned himself between her legs. Maintaining eye contact the entire time, he entered her in one smooth glide.

"Damn, you're so wet for me," he murmured.

Then they moved together differently than they had in the past. And all the while, he kept his eyes locked on hers, making sure she knew how he felt.

That depth of love was too much, and a tear fell from her eye. He leaned down and kissed it away. Then he brought his lips to hers.

This was what she needed. She would hold on to this feeling until she saw him again.

Chapter Twenty-Nine

Wilder picked up the usual from the Cozy Croissant for the third morning in a row: two coffees and two croissants. Before he rushed it back to Melia, he sat in his car, taking a moment to think through everything that had happened the last few days.

While Melia had claimed to need protection from an abusive ex-boyfriend, Wilder had already overheard enough to confirm his suspicions of the truth. Melia was allowing drugs to be sold at the condo construction site outside Davenport—although, she was careful to never use the words *drugs* or *meth*. She always talked about 'moving the product'.

Joey hadn't been wrong when he'd tipped them off about a housing site. But either he hadn't realized Simpson believed the development to be in Fisher Springs, not the neighboring town, or he'd been vague on purpose.

Wilder honestly didn't know which was more likely.

Still in his car outside the coffee shop, he called Simpson to check in.

"Simpson here."

"It's Coleman."

"Got anything?"

Wilder quickly informed the other detective that he believed Melia was in charge of the drug operation, despite the fact she'd referred to a 'him' when he'd overheard her talking to Joey. He also told Simpson that Joey was much more involved than they'd realized.

"Is that so? Because Joey finally admitted the person in charge is Melia Fisher."

"Did he say what happened to Jerry Blight?" Wilder suspected the original name given by Joey had been bogus all along.

"I asked, and he said that was the name Melia kept saying, but Joey says he doesn't believe it's real anymore."

Wilder was silent for a beat, then asked, "Why tell you about Melia now? He must have suspected before this."

Simpson made a sound in the back of his throat. "That's a good question. Unfortunately, I don't have the answer."

Wilder ran his hand through his hair. Thinking back on the previous tips, he concluded that, although Joey hadn't tried to mislead them, he certainly hadn't given as much detail as he should have.

So why start giving us what we want now? Because we only have four days to stop the town from being bombed? Or is he in partnership with Melia? Or...

Oh shit.

"Does Joey know there's an undercover cop in town?"

Simpson laughed. "Son, this isn't my first rodeo. No, he doesn't know. When I first spoke with him, he said he would only give information if we didn't involve his dad."

"The chief."

"That's the one. I told him there was no need to do that, since I have a contact in Idaho trying to stop it from that end. Then I said if that doesn't work, my men will come in this weekend."

"But when the chief first found out I was here from Frank, he might have said something in passing about an unauthorized undercover investigation being carried out under his nose."

"I don't think so," Simpson said confidently. "Joey would have asked me about it."

Wilder blew out a breath. *Good.* The idea that Joey might know why he was really there was concerning. He didn't know Joey well enough anymore to know what he'd do.

"As long as he believes that we're good," he said finally. "I need to get back."

"Okay, good luck. Check in again tonight."

"Will do." Wilder ended the call and stared through his windshield, taking another moment before he had to return to Melia.

His brother and Holly walked down the sidewalk toward him, hand in hand. They were smiling as they spoke to each other. Then they stopped outside the Cozy Croissant, and William held the door open for his fiancée.

Even though Wilder talked to William now and again, he hadn't seen him much over the years. He realized now how much he regretted that.

A move back to Fisher Springs will be good for my family too.

Unable to put off his return any longer, he drove back to the condo development where he'd been spending his days.

It was better than where he'd been spending his nights; unfortunately, Melia hadn't been lying about him staying at her place. He'd been able to dodge her advances by explaining he wouldn't mix personal with business. That had seemed to work because so far, she had left him in peace on her pull-out couch.

When he walked into Melia's office a few minutes later, he abruptly stuttered to a stop. Joey was sitting in her chair, and Melia was nowhere to be seen.

Wilder set the coffees down on the desk. "Joey?"

This was the first time they'd been alone since he'd been back.

Joey smiled, which enhanced the wrinkles around his eyes.

Jesus. He looked ten years older than he really was.

"Wilder. I'd hoped to have a chance to talk with you." Joey stood up and walked around the desk. "Come here."

Sweat broke out on Wilder's neck as he was unsure of Joey's intentions.

But then the man pulled him in for a hug. "Remember that time I busted you and Kate behind Conway's barn?" he laughed. "That was one of the funniest calls I ever got. Conway was certain someone was there to steal his cows."

Wilder and Kate had been seniors in high school at the time, and Joey had joined the Fisher Springs Police Department a couple of years before. They had been very grateful when he let them go without reporting anything to their parents.

Wilder let out the breath he was holding. "I remember."

"I was sad to see you leave town. Never had a chance to say goodbye. My mom worried about you too."

A well of emotion hit Wilder as he thought about Mrs. Dunin, but since he wasn't supposed to know, he was forced to swallow the lump in his throat and ask, "How are your parents doing?"

Joey let out a loud sigh and leaned against the desk. "My mom passed away a few years ago. Cancer."

"Shit. Joey. I'm so sorry."

"Yeah. It sucked. My dad's the same as he ever was. Threw himself into work after that, though. We don't talk much anymore."

"You don't? Is he still the chief of police here?" Wilder picked up his coffee and took a sip as he watched for a reaction.

Joey laughed. "Yes, he is. But I quit the force."

Hm. No sign that his dad had mentioned Wilder.

"You working in another town now?" he asked.

Joey shook his head. "No. I decided being a cop wasn't for me."

"Wilder, you're here." Melia entered, walked behind her desk to her now empty chair, and sat down. "Do you remember Joey?"

"I do. We were just catching up."

She opened a desk drawer and tossed her purse inside, then she pointed to one of the cups in front of her. "Is this mine?"

"It is."

She took a sip. "Mmn. Thanks. I needed that." She glanced between Joey and Wilder as she set her cup back down. "I bet you two have a lot to talk about, since you were both detectives who got fired."

Joey's gaze jerked to Wilder. "You were fired?"

"Yes, he was," Melia answered for him.

"What about you? I thought you said you quit," Wilder said to Joey. Better to get him on the defensive before he asked too many questions.

The other man stared at his shoes. "I did. It sounds better than 'I used drugs on the job and got caught'." He shrugged.

"Drugs? But you were always so rulebound."

Joey looked up. "I was. Until my mom died. Then all the rules seemed stupid. I admit, I made some poor choices. But you, Wilder... you became a detective, really?"

Wilder took another sip of his coffee. "After things ended with Kate, I needed a new beginning, you know?" Then he turned to Melia. "I forgot to ask you how you knew about my career."

Melia smiled. "Must have heard it through the grapevine."

Wilder had asked a few people if they'd heard anything about what he'd been up to, and they hadn't. The only person that knew his story was the mayor — who Melia had been with in the parking lot on the night of the music festival.

What else has he shared with her?

"Why did you get fired?" Joey asked, pulling Wilder from his thoughts on the mayor.

His gaze met Melia's, and she smiled.

"Wilder took payouts to look the other way on some deals. Got caught."

Joey frowned.

Wilder needed to get on a new subject before the man could ask any questions.

"What do you do now, Joey?" he asked, even though he'd heard enough to have an idea.

Joey grinned. "Well, Melia here was kind enough to let me help out here. I oversee the materials. You know, ordering and purchasing."

"Speaking of that. Joey, you're needed on our *other* project. They're expecting the order within the hour."

He pushed off the desk. "I'll be there." He stopped in front of Wilder and held out his hand. "Great seeing you again."

Wilder shook his hand. "You too."

Joey whistled as he walked out the door.

"Now, I need you to follow me," Melia said as she stood up.

"Sure thing. Where are we going?"

"I'm meeting someone in the E building."

The E building? He hadn't been in that one yet but based on the state of the others he'd visited, he figured it was probably getting appliances delivered or installed.

"Sure."

He walked beside her, taking in the property. He'd been told that, by the time it was all done, there would be fifty condos on this site.

"Have you sold any of these yet?" he asked.

He couldn't imagine this many people moving out this way. At least this development was on the far side of Davenport, and not near Fisher Springs. Although, it wasn't too far a drive, if someone wanted to visit his town.

"A few," she said. Then she fell silent and pulled out her phone, tapping away on the screen.

She wasn't the most talkative person when he was the one asking questions.

Once they arrived at the E building, he held the door open for her.

"Thanks," she said, never looking up.

Just inside the building, the door to the first unit was open. The inside appeared finished and already furnished.

It must be a model.

"Oh shoot. I forgot something. Can you wait here? I'll be right back."

"Sure."

Wilder flashed her a smile as she left. But he wasn't stupid. If she were really worried about her safety, she would have asked him to come with her. No, she didn't need to meet anyone here; she wanted him out of her office for some reason.

He gave her a ten-second head start, then started back that way. He had made it to building B when he saw a car pull up and park in front of A, which housed her office.

Ducking back against the wall, he kept himself out of sight. When he heard a car door, he glanced around the building — and saw the mayor.

"Thanks for meeting me on short notice," Frank said.

"No problem," Melia said.

"Here. The details are inside."

The mayor handed Melia an envelope, which she immediately went about opening. As she worked, the man glanced around as if worried someone would see him.

"Looks good," she said.

Frank smiled.

Wilder was pretty sure that was the first time he'd seen a real smile on Frank's face.

Kate's father got back into his car, and Wilder realized Melia was going to be returning to building E—where he was not—any moment.

Cursing under his breath, he jogged back to the apartment, making it with enough time to settle on the couch and stare out the window into the greenbelt that backed up to the condos.

"Sorry about that," Melia said, returning a moment later. "I had to take care of something—Oh no."

Wilder turned to see her frowning at her phone.

"Something wrong?" he asked.

"My meeting has been postponed. Guess we can go back to my office." She shrugged.

Wilder bit his lip to hide his smile. Melia had to be the worst liar he'd ever seen. Now that he knew her tell of avoiding eye contract, it was easy to keep tabs on her lies.

They walked back to her office in silence as she tapped on her phone.

As soon as they got back, she sat in the chair behind her desk and told him, "Something has happened."

Wilder sat down in the other chair. "What?"

"As you know, I have a restraining order against my ex. Well, he's made it clear he's coming here this weekend to get some things back he believes are his."

"Are they?"

"No."

"What are these things?"

Melia shrugged again. "You know, the usual... like furniture, jewelry, stuff."

It was the 'stuff' Wilder wanted to know more about, but she obviously didn't want to elaborate. He tried a different question.

"Is it all at your house?"

She shook her head. "No, I don't keep it there."

He waited for her to say where she did keep it, but she didn't continue.

Holding back a sigh, he asked, "And how do you envision me protecting these items?"

Her lips curved up in the biggest smile he'd seen on her since he'd been back.

Melia was a beautiful woman... but she knew it and tried to use it to get what she wanted.

As opposed to Kate, who is effortlessly gorgeous.

He wished it was her smiling at him instead of Melia Fisher.

Dammit, man, focus.

"I don't need you protecting my stuff, I've got that covered," she said. "I need you to protect *me*. When my ex can't find what he's looking for, he'll come after me."

Wilder ran his hand through his hair. "I have to say, wouldn't it be easier to just give him the stuff? I don't know the value of it all, but some furniture and jewelry can't be worth the stress of looking over your shoulder all the time."

Melia leaned back in her chair. "I understand what you're saying, but if I give in to him on this, he'll keep demanding more. Guys like him keep taking until there is nothing left to take. I need to end this now."

"Okay, tell me where you need me, and I'll be there."

"I know you have your brother's wedding coming up, so how about I go wherever you need to be?"

She wanted his protection, but she wanted to lure her danger where his family would be? Why the hell would she think he'd take that risk?

"I don't think that's a good idea."

Melia leaned forward and clasped her hands under her chin. "Why not?"

"You said he's threatened you. Why would I want to bring that around my family? Besides, I don't want them to know I'm protecting you."

She leaned back. "Why not?"

Wilder blew out a breath. "My parents never knew I was a cop, much less a failed one. I'd rather they not learn how I'm qualified to act as security detail."

She nodded. "I get that. We can stick around my place—except on July Fourth. I can't miss the festival. I've gone every year since I was a kid."

She wanted to go to the festival—a public event where there would likely be a bomb? What the hell was he missing, here?

"That seems a bit public, don't you think?" he hedged.

"Yes, that's why it's perfect. What can he do with so many witnesses around?"

He studied her. Was she testing him to see if he and Joey had talked? She gave no indication of her true motives. He had no choice but to play along.

"Good point. Sounds like a plan."

Melia smiled. "Great."

Chapter Thirty

The next day, three days before the festival, Wilder was feeling better about everything. First, Simpson had assured him that he had a guy in Idaho following Brogan. Second, the weather forecast called for rain on the fourth. That was great news because it had forced William and Holly to come up with an alternative plan to keep their guests occupied for the holiday that would be indoors — and away from the festival.

Unfortunately, Simpson said he'd spoken to Chief Dunin and gotten no further insight. Though the chief did plan to cancel the festival if this bomb threat wasn't resolved soon, which brought Wilder some peace of mind.

And he needed all the peace he could get. He'd finally managed to get a few minutes away from Melia by telling her he needed to walk the condo property to make sure no one was lurking around.

While he understood he needed to stay by her side to protect her, his patience was wearing thin, and he needed a moment to himself. The woman vacillated from hardly talking at all to talking about nothing but her clothes. Apparently, she was doing a lot of online shopping and was excited about every shirt and skirt she bought. She talked to him like he had a clue who designers were or why it mattered she wore the 'right ones'.

Nope, he was happy in jeans and T-shirts. Sure, he would wear a button-up or a suit when the occasion called for it, but those items would be whatever he found at the local department store, with no care for what name was on the label.

He hadn't completely lied to Melia, though; it was important for him to get outside the condos every once in a while and check out the grounds. Even though Simpson had someone watching Brogan, Wilder was still certain the guy wasn't working alone.

Taking advantage of the little time he had to himself, he called Simpson.

"Any news?" he asked as soon as the man answered.

"Actually, yes. I'm glad you called. Our guy, Brogan, has been on the move. He's currently stopped at a house in Yakima. I'll send you a text when he leaves, but you might only have a couple of hours before he hits Fisher Springs."

Damn. He'd hoped Brogan wouldn't show until the fourth, but he was already in Yakima? That was too close.

"How many guys is he with?"

"He drove by himself."

He wasn't with anyone else?

Aw shit. "He knows you're following him," Wilder said.

He wasn't the one they should be watching; the bomb was likely with someone else.

"My guy says he's been very careful," Simpson insisted.

Wilder scoffed. "This dude isn't going to come alone to try to take over a substantial drug-trafficking business."

Simpson sighed in resignation. "Which means someone else is coming."

"Or already here," Wilder countered.

"I'll check with the police department in Idaho and see if they have eyes on the other gang members."

"Okay, let me know what you find out."

"Will do. Be careful, Wilder."

"Yeah." He ended the call and took a few breaths. The calm he'd managed to find earlier was gone.

Shit. He needed more eyes in this town. It actually wouldn't be so bad if the chief had told Nick and Chase about what was going on. Maybe he could convince Jessie to help too.

At least with the rain, the festival won't be so crowded.

His phone rang: Dane. He had been calling for the past several days, but Wilder had never been alone to take his friend's call. He was relieved that was not the case now.

"Dane, sorry I've missed your calls."

"No worries. I'm glad I finally reached you."

"Something wrong?"

Dane laughed. "I hope not. I spoke to your girl the other day. Did she mention that?"

What the hell? "Who?"

"Kate. Are you two back together?"

Wilder stared at his phone, then brought it back up to his ear. "You talked to Kate? Where are you?"

"I haven't gone anywhere; we spoke on the phone. An old friend, Jessie, called with some questions about you. I found out Kate was there, and I put two and two together, figured out she was your Kate."

Wilder took a deep breath. "Back up. Why was Jessie calling you?"

"Oh shit. I'm sorry. I figured Kate would have told you. It's all good. Jessie was calling to ask if you'd been fired or were married. Apparently, Kate's dad gave her some bad information. Don't worry, I set them straight."

What the hell? Why the fuck was someone always trying to interfere with him and Kate?

Although, he shouldn't be surprised Frank would try something.

"Thanks for letting me know."

There wasn't anything he could do now, but he'd be talking to Kate about this. What would happen if her dad made up more lies? Would she believe them? Why hadn't she come directly to him?

"No problem. Good luck there."

Wilder snorted. "Thanks." He ended the call and pocketed his phone.

Yeah, he needed to talk to Kate. But right now, he needed to figure out how to reach out to Nick, Chase, and Jessie when he was with Melia twenty-four-seven.

"Hey, you get lost?"

Wilder spun around at Melia's voice to find her watching him with an eyebrow arched.

"No, dealing with some wedding issues for my brother. Sorry, didn't mean to take so long."

She nodded. "Yeah, sorry. I've been taking all your time. I bet your brother hates me."

Wilder shook his head. "No, he's fine."

And William *was* fine. Apparently, Kate had been helping out quite a bit, so between her and Holly's bridesmaids, there wasn't anything left for him to do.

"You sure? Because I was thinking you could take tonight off and spend some time with him." Melia shrugged.

Well, this was new. "Do you no longer feel threatened?"

She shook her head. "It's not that. But Joey said he'd stay with me tonight."

Wilder furrowed his brow. If she was okay with only Joey's protection, why hadn't she used him from the beginning? "Joey knows about your ex and his threats?"

She nodded toward her office. "Let's walk and talk. I have a meeting in a few."

They began walking, and as their silence stretched on, Wilder thought she wasn't going to answer his question. Then she spoke up.

"Joey does know. In fact, he thinks he can talk my ex out of driving all the way over here."

Wilder glanced over at her, but walking side by side, he couldn't read her to see if she was lying. Did she know the man was only a couple of hours away? "You think he's still in Idaho?"

Melia stopped walking and turned to him. "Where else would he be?"

"Here. Isn't that why I'm with you all the time?"

She smiled. "That last bit is another reason you can take the night off. But if it will make you feel better, I spoke with him earlier and heard his mother in the background, so I know he's still in Idaho."

"Maybe he brought his mother here with him," Wilder offered.

She frowned. "His mother won't leave Idaho. It's a long story but believe me, she's not here."

"What time was this?"

She shrugged then began walking again. Wilder fell in step next to her. "About an hour ago," she estimated.

Since Brogan was just seen in Yakima, he knew she was lying to him. Hell, she probably always was. But why? Why had she wanted him with her and now she didn't?

Shit. This had probably never been about protection. He'd bet she was trying to keep him away from something.

Does that mean she knows I'm undercover? Does Joey?

He had to know.

"Is Joey meeting you here, then? I didn't really get a chance to chat with him yesterday."

"What do you want to talk to him about?"

Yeah, she's suspicious.

"You know, catch up. I spent a lot of time at his house with his mom when I was a teenager. Joey was like an older brother to me."

They reached the office, and Wilder held the door open for her.

"I didn't know that," she said as they entered.

No shit.

Not many did, but there was especially no reason she would. Melia was younger than him, and he hadn't hung out with any of the Fishers in high school.

His question about where she was meeting Joey was answered five minutes later when the man walked into the office.

"Ready to go?" he asked Melia.

"Yes." Then she turned to Wilder. "Enjoy your night off. I'll call you tomorrow if I need you."

If she needed him?

"Wait, you don't want me coming here tomorrow morning?"

Melia grabbed her purse from the desk drawer. "I'll call you if I do. I guess it will depend on how annoyed with Joey I am by then."

Joey grinned. "You will be charmed, not annoyed."

Wilder walked out with them and watched as Melia locked up. "Okay, then. I'll see you guys later."

Then he got in his car and pulled out his phone, pretending to type a message. Melia would figure he was messaging his brother. Instead, he was buying time.

Joey drove out of the parking lot with Melia in the passenger seat, and Wilder followed them at a distance. There was only one highway back into Fisher Springs, so he was able to let them gain some distance on him. The curves in the road helped shield him as well. But instead of taking the Fisher Springs exit, they kept going.

So did he.

He knew Melia's house was in town, so they had to be going somewhere else.

Joey took the next exit, and Wilder's heart was beating out of his chest as he followed. There were only a couple of properties out this way.

Maybe there's a new condo development I don't know about?

Although, deep down, he knew that wasn't likely.

When they turned down Waters Road, Wilder did not follow. It was a dead-end road, and he knew where they were going: Kate's parents' house.

For some reason, Melia didn't want Wilder with her when she went to see the mayor.

Chapter Thirty-One

Kate danced around her house as the music played loudly. She was downright giddy. Wilder called and said he had been given the night off and hoped to spend it with her. She hadn't counted on seeing him for a few more days, at the festival. She'd immediately said yes and then began dancing around her living room.

The last few days, she'd been wondering how often she'd see him once he returned to his regular job and life. Yes, he had said it wouldn't change anything, but she felt it would. She was happy to have one more night before he had to move back to his apartment.

When he knocked on the door, butterflies took over her stomach. He was there sooner than she'd expected.

She turned the music down and opened the door. Wilder stood on the other side, wearing his usual T-shirt and jeans. The T-shirt was a deep blue that really brought out his eyes — but it was the look in his eyes that had her attention.

"I've missed you," he said.

"I missed you too." She jumped into his arms. "Do you have to go back in the morning?" She pushed his hair back, loving how soft it was.

"I don't know." He kissed her neck.

"How did you get time off?"

He pulled back to look at her. "Joey is protecting her tonight."

She frowned. "Joey? Well, why wasn't he doing that the entire time?" She lowered her legs and found the ground again.

"Exactly. It's been bugging me too. I feel like she was toying with me."

Kate nodded. "Or it could have been that she was trying to get you into bed."

He laughed. "She tried that before she hired me."

Kate growled.

"Down, girl. I told her no every time."

She arched a brow. "*Every* time?"

His eyes lit up. "You know, I don't recall you being the jealous type. I hate to say this, but I kind of like it." The man looked a little pleased with himself.

She smacked him in the stomach. "Stop. I'm not that hung up on you."

"No?"

"Nope."

He grinned. "Huh. Well, I got a call from my friend Dane that says otherwise."

Her cheeks warmed, and she knew they were reddening. She turned away, hoping he wouldn't notice.

"Kate." His smile was gone.

Dammit. He was probably angry. She should have gone to him with her questions.

"Want something to drink?" she asked brightly as she made her way to the kitchen. Maybe she could take a few sips of wine before she had to deal with an interrogation.

God, he's a detective, so he'll be good at it, too.

"Kate." He was right behind her.

She pulled a glass out of the cupboard, ignoring him, then filled it with the wine she had open on the counter.

His hands went to either side of her, boxing her in. "Kate."

She spun around.

He leaned in. "Did you call Dane?"

Damn, she hadn't even gotten a sip of wine.

"No, Jessie did. But it was only because my dad showed me this document he claimed was a background check on you. It said you had been fired and you were married. I didn't want to believe it, so I went to Jessie to see what she could find."

She took a breath.

He arched a brow. He didn't look mad, but she wasn't sure if he'd hate her for this.

I should have told him.

"Anyway, Jessie couldn't find anything about any of it online, but when she saw that you worked in Summit County, she said she knew someone there. Next thing I know, I'm on the phone, talking to some guy who says he's your good friend."

She stopped to take another breath.

"He is." Wilder nodded. "I've known him a long time."

"Well, he confirmed that everything my dad claimed was a lie. I was going to tell you about this, but then we had only that one night until you were going to stay with Melia, and I didn't want to bring up anything negative. I'm sorry."

She braced herself for his reaction.

"Kate, I'm not mad."

He wasn't?

She blinked in surprise. "You're not?"

He shook his head.

Relief filled her. She'd been so worried he would accuse her of believing her dad over him. And really, she didn't, but so much time had gone by that she did question how well she knew him. She had to protect her heart and find out for herself.

"I really fucking missed you," he said as he dipped his head down and kissed her.

She wrapped her arms around his neck and leaned in to kiss him.

Their kiss started soft but heated quickly. Her hands found their way under his T-shirt as he pulled her closer, and she inched it up until he pulled back and yanked it off, tossing it on the floor. Then he pulled her shirt up and off.

Their lips crushed together as his hand moved down into her pants to grip her ass and pull her against his cock. He was hard and knowing she had that effect on him thrilled her.

His other hand was on her breast as he caressed her nipple. She moaned, and that was all it took.

They raced to get all their clothes off, then she kissed him, hard. He lifted her up to sit on the counter, and his fingers moved up her thigh until they found her clit. She pressed into his hand.

A beat later, Wilder moved his fingers down. "You're so wet."

He inserted a finger into her. Then another.

She tried to ride them, but lacked the ability to gain traction, sitting on the edge of the counter.

He grinned. "You want to ride my fingers, don't you?"

"Yes," she panted.

He pumped his fingers inside her as he kissed the skin behind her ear, down to her neck. His thumb found her clit, and he moved it in circles as his lips and tongue found her nipple.

"Wilder," she whimpered.

"That's it, baby."

He then bent down and took her clit in his mouth, sucking on it while staring into her eyes. He continued to pump his fingers, and it sent her over the edge. She grabbed his hair and pulled as her orgasm hit hard.

When she finished quivering, he stood up.

"Fuck that was hot. But so is this."

He spread her legs with his hands, lined up at her entrance, then plunged in. The counter put her at the perfect height, and he started slow but quickly built up speed. She reached her hands back behind her to gain traction.

His eyes were fixed on their connection as he pumped in and out. "I could stare at that perfect pussy all night long."

"Yes." She wanted more of his dirty talk.

But Wilder had other plans.

He leaned in and kissed her as he pumped harder. "Kate," he grunted out.

Her orgasm built, and the moment he touched her clit again, it set her off. Her entire body quaked with her release. Gripping her tight, Wilder buried himself to the hilt as his release came right after.

They stayed like that for a moment as their breathing calmed down.

"Come on." He picked her up and walked them through her bedroom to the master bathroom.

He found a washcloth in her bathroom closet and cleaned her up, then himself. Then he carried her to the bed, wrapping the covers — and himself — around her.

She settled into him.

"I love you," he whispered.

"I love you, too."

That was the last thing she remembered until the distant buzzing of Wilder's phone woke her. It was dark outside, and rain pelted the window. They must have fallen asleep and missed dinner.

She tried to go back to sleep, but Wilder's phone wouldn't stop.

She nudged him.

"Hmm?"

"I think you should check on that."

"What?"

"Your phone keeps buzzing."

He pulled her in tighter. "Yeah, let me enjoy this for one more minute."

They were lying naked in her bed, her head resting on his chest. She wanted to enjoy this for more than a minute. But...

"It might be Melia asking you to come back tonight."

Even as she said it, she hoped she was wrong. She didn't want Wilder to leave.

"I doubt it. I'm sure Joey is doing fine."

But when the phone vibrated again, Wilder got up in search of the device. Once he found it in the pocket of his discarded pants, he read through the messages.

She wanted to kiss away the line that formed between his brows. "What's wrong?"

"Nothing that can't wait." He tossed his phone on the nightstand. Then he settled back into bed and pulled her to his chest.

However, as she lay there with her hand on his chest, his heart rate sped up.

"What are you thinking about?" she asked.

"I can't stop thinking about it. Joey's been around here the entire time, from what I can tell. And he knows what Melia has going on. So why didn't she ask him to protect her earlier?"

"Did Melia figure out you weren't an *ex*-cop?"

"Detective," Wilder corrected with a grin. "And no, not that I know of. Why do you ask?"

Kate traced the tattoo on his chest. "Well, if she thought you were investigating her, hiring you as her bodyguard would be a good way to keep you where she could see you and away from anything incriminating." She snuggled closer.

She loved cuddling with this man. *Is it too soon to think about living together?*

"That's what I was thinking too. Shit." Wilder sat up. "I'm sorry, but I have to go."

"Why? I thought you were staying the night."

He leaned over and kissed her. "I want to, Kate. I really do. But if Melia knew I was here undercover, she might have been leading me down the wrong path all this time."

He hopped out of bed and got dressed while Kate watched.

"How can you find out?"

"I'm going to find Joey and Melia. I have a strong feeling they are doing something they don't want me to know about."

Chapter Thirty-Two

Wilder drove to Melia's neighborhood, cursing her all the way.

If she'd used him... Worse, if he'd *fallen* for it...

He parked two blocks down and walked toward her house. Her car was in the driveway. It was still dark out, but all the lights in the house were on, meaning he saw very clearly when someone walked past the front window.

He made his way into the neighbor's backyard and then hopped the short fence into Melia's. A window was open at the back of her house, and he heard voices.

"I don't agree with this." He recognized Joey's voice.

"Well, it doesn't matter, does it? This is my plan, not yours," Melia responded.

Wilder slowly stepped forward on the grass.

"But the mayor is innocent! What if your games cause him to be charged with all of this? At the very least, he'll likely lose his job."

The mayor is innocent? Then what was in the envelope and the backpack?

He really had no idea.

And why did Melia ditch me to go see the mayor with Joey?

Dammit. He had more questions than answers.

"Serves him right. He promised me that he and his wife were separating, but it was all a lie."

"Shit, Melia. That's what guys like him say to get women like you. Of course, he isn't leaving his wife."

Wait. Melia… and Frank? No. Frank was an asshole, but he wouldn't have an affair — especially not with Melia. Would he? She was younger than his daughters.

If Melia wanted to get revenge on the mayor, all she had to do was tell the town rumor mill. His reputation would be ruined. Why go to all this trouble?

Wilder stepped closer to the house.

"You already blackmailed the guy, probably almost giving him a heart attack. Isn't that enough?" Joey asked.

"No," Melia snapped.

Wilder heard the back door open, and he quickly moved to the side of the house and out of sight.

"Fucking Frank," Melia said under her breath.

The back door closed, and Wilder listened as footsteps moved on the back patio.

"Here. Thought you could use a drink," Joey said.

"Thanks."

Wilder peeked around the corner. He saw Melia holding a glass, but Joey didn't have one.

Maybe the guy was completely clean now; but if he was, why the hell would he be caught up in some drug-dealing business? The temptation would be too much. Or at least, Wilder thought it would be. He hadn't experienced addiction himself, though, so really, what the hell did he know?

"I'm sorry about that guy. But, Melia, you're putting the business at risk. What were you thinking, hiring Wilder?"

Melia drank her beverage down, then set the glass on a table beside her.

"He's perfect. Former detective. He can't help but try to put pieces together if there is a puzzle in front of him. Plus, it's no secret how much Frank dislikes Wilder and doesn't want him anywhere near his daughter. What better solution for Wilder than to put his father-in-law in jail?"

Wilder leaned against the house. She'd been playing him the whole time. He knew something hadn't been right, but he never would have considered this.

"Shit. Remind me to never date you," Joey said. "You're vindictive as hell."

"Not vindictive. Smart. Even Brogan thinks Frank is in charge."

"Why the hell would you want him to think that?" Joey asked.

"You know, you ask a lot of questions. Why do you care?"

Shit. Joey is going to get himself outted. Wilder looked around for any way to make a distraction and a getaway.

"Just curious is all. I'm supposed to be protecting you, but if you have Brogan thinking Frank is in charge, you're really not in danger, are you?"

"I wish it were that simple. Sadly, I am in danger. Just not from Brogan."

Not from Brogan?

Maybe she was referring to his team.

Wilder's phone buzzed in his pocket. He checked it.

Simpson: *Brogan just pulled into town. He's staying at some motel a block off Main Street. He's still alone.*

Yeah, Wilder knew the motel. It was the only one in town. But the guy was still alone? Why?

There was no way anyone would try to take over someone else's drug-dealing business alone. So, either Brogan wasn't really alone… or he wasn't the one who wanted to take it over.

"Not Brogan?" Joey yelled. "What the hell? You want me to protect you, but you lied about who from?"

"Jesus, Joey. What's the big deal?"

"The big deal, Melia, is that I need to know the threat I'm dealing with."

Wilder: *Overheard Melia admit Brogan isn't the threat.*

He pocketed his phone and strained to listen, hoping to hear who the real threat was.

"It doesn't matter. I've dealt with it. I'm tired, I'm going to shower," Melia said.

The back door shut again.

Wilder waited a couple of minutes but didn't hear Joey move. Though he did hear water turn on inside.

"Wilder. I know you're there. She just got in the shower."

Shit.

"Remember, I was once a detective too."

Wilder stepped into the light where Joey could see him. "What gave me away?"

"Your phone buzzed."

"You heard that?"

Joey shrugged. "I got skills."

"Who's the real threat?" Wilder asked.

Joey sighed. "I don't know. I tried to find out, but Melia is holding that close to her chest."

"Do you have any idea how she got involved in this? I thought she was a realtor. It doesn't make sense."

"It's all my fault." Joey shook his head. "She tried to help me. I don't know why; we weren't really friends. One time, I was struggling with sobriety. I called her and my dealer at the same time... she got there first."

"Why did you call Melia?"

Joey grinned. "I had a thing for her. It was stupid. But anyway, my dealer showed up shortly after, but when I told him I wasn't buying after all, he got mad about losing a sale. Melia asked how much he was out and paid him to make him go away. I guess she started to do the math in her head."

"That's all it took?"

Joey shrugged. "I didn't see her for a month after that. I kept to myself; other than the narcotics anonymous meetings I was attending. When I ran into her again, she told me she was dealing and would love for me to join her."

Joey laughed. "I pointed out that having an addict hold the stash wasn't a smart idea. But I really liked her, so I agreed to help. This was before I found out about her and Frank."

Joey's smile was gone. "That's when she hatched her plan. She bought on a large scale, I set up the deals, and we got a few guys working on the construction crews at various jobsites to do the small, local deals."

So, he was telling the truth about the housing development.

"Martin's sites?"

Joey nodded.

"Does Martin know?"

The shower turned off.

Joey whispered, "You'd better go."

Wilder nodded then spun around and walked to the sidewalk in front of the house and back to his car. Once in his car, he took a moment to process what Joey had told him.

The man had been pretty free with the information he was giving to who he believed was an ex-cop loyal to Melia.

He pulled out his phone.

Wilder: *When did you tell Joey about me?*

His phone rang.

"Yeah?" he answered.

"A couple of hours ago," Simpson admitted. "I was going to call you tonight to tell you. But listen, Joey said something isn't right—Melia's not acting nervous or afraid."

"She's not."

"Oh? How do you know, I thought you had the night off? And how did you overhear her earlier?"

"I felt that something wasn't right, so I came by her place and listened in on their conversation."

"Listened in? Wait, no, I don't want to know."

"Her window was open, and I could hear."

"From the street?"

"Not quite."

Simpson groaned.

Wilder pressed on, "She's setting up the mayor, Frank Waters."

"Wow, ballsy. Any idea why?"

"Sounds like a scorned lover situation."

Simpson sighed. "Let me see if I get this. Melia is running the operation. She claims she's been threatened to give up her business, but we don't know by whom. In the meantime, she's trying to set up the mayor to take the fall for something because... why exactly?"

"He wouldn't leave his wife."

"This reads more like a soap opera than a case. Tell me what you do know."

"Joey isn't using, I'm pretty sure of it... And he's deep inside Melia's operation, but even he doesn't know what's really going on."

Wilder noticed movement from the front of Melia's house. The porch light was off, so it was hard to make out, but someone was walking toward the car in the driveway. Based on how the figure moved, it was Melia.

She got into her car and backed up.

Wait, where's Joey?

"Melia is leaving her house alone," Wilder told Simpson urgently.

"Follow her."

"On it."

"Call me back with a report."

"Will do." Wilder ended the call and waited for Melia to pull out onto the road before starting his car.

He didn't have to follow her long; moments later, she pulled into the parking lot of the Fisher Springs Motel.

Wilder drove past the motel and parked up the road, then made his way back on foot, taking cover when he could see the lot. He spotted Melia walking toward a room.

The door opened as she approached. A blond man Wilder recognized from photographs appeared, smiling. Brogan Miller.

"Baby. It's so good to see you," Wilder heard the man say.

Melia jumped into his arms and wrapped her legs around his waist, and they kissed. He walked her inside and shut the door.

Well, so much for Brogan really being a threat. He looked more like a partner in crime.

Chapter Thirty-Three

"Are you sure this is really necessary?" Kate's dad asked.

"Frank, this is for your family's protection," Nick said.

Kate tried to relax on the couch at the Chanler mansion, but she couldn't.

Chase had picked up her and her sister Lily a couple of hours ago. Nick had arrived shortly after with her parents in tow. Then they'd all congregated in the living room.

She normally loved this room; this is where she would meet Lauren and her other friends for their book club. Lauren had furnished it with a comfortable couch and two chairs. It had a fireplace that she had tiled, and the biggest mantel Kate had ever seen. Now, she hoped that whatever the hell her dad had gotten them involved in wouldn't taint her memories of this space.

Apparently, a threat had been levied against her dad, and the authorities were concerned the entire family could be at risk. Nick and Lauren had thoughtfully offered to bring them to the Chanler mansion, since it could accommodate them all.

Lauren walked into the room with a tray of drinks. "I whipped up a few cocktails for those that might need one."

Both of her parents grabbed one, as did Lily.

Kate went ahead and grabbed one too. *What a night.*

It had started off great, when Wilder came over... but it all went to hell after he jumped out of bed and left.

Chase arrived a half hour ago and she kept looking toward the foyer hoping to see Wilder. No such luck.

Then there was a knock at the front door, and she jumped up.

Chase held his hand up to stop her. "I'll get it," he said.

A moment later, Ryker, Lily's fiancé, walked into the room. Lily launched herself at him.

"You okay?" he asked.

"Much better now."

Her dad rolled his eyes. He wasn't a fan of Ryker's. In fact, he wasn't a fan of any man either of his daughters dated. "How long do I have to be here? I have a meeting tonight."

"Oh, for God's sake, Frank. Really?" her mother asked.

Kate checked the time. It was after eight — a little late for a meeting, in her opinion.

"I'm afraid we will all be staying here this evening," Nick said.

Her dad downed the drink and grabbed another one. "What is this so-called threat, anyway?"

There was another knock on the door.

"I'll get it," Nick said.

Kate rested her head on the back of the couch and closed her eyes. Being in close quarters with her parents was not her first choice of how to spend the evening. Poor Holly still had things she needed for her wedding, which was in four days. But Holly had assured Kate that her bridesmaids had it covered.

Someone took her hand, and her eyes popped open.

"Hey," Wilder said as he sat down beside her.

She wrapped her arms around him and leaned into him.

"I'm so glad you're here. I think my family is going to drive me insane."

He chuckled. "I get that. But you need to stay here where it's safe."

"What's going on?" she asked.

He ran his hand up and down her back. It soothed her. "Some bad men think your dad has stolen something of theirs and they want it back."

She frowned. While her dad wasn't the greatest guy, he wasn't a thief. "What do they think he stole?"

"Unfortunately, I can't say," Wilder said.

Kate longed to be back in her own home. With Wilder.

"You know, I get threatened on occasion," her dad said. "It's part of the job. I'm sure I'll be fine if you let me go."

Wilder stood up and walked across the room until he stood in front of her dad. "You've been set up. The men looking for you believe you have stolen something very valuable from them."

"What? That's insane. I wouldn't steal anything. Who set me up?"

Nick stepped up before Wilder could answer. "Melia Fisher."

Her dad's face paled.

"How well do you know Ms. Fisher?" Nick asked.

Based on the flush of red now coloring her dad's cheeks, Kate would guess *very* well.

"Seriously?!" her mother shouted. "*Melia Fisher*? She's just a kid!" She crossed the room to where Lauren stood. "Lauren, I'm sorry but I think I need another drink."

The tray was already empty.

"Sure, follow me."

Lauren led Kate's mother out of the room, which was for the best. Did her dad really have an affair? And with Melia?

She glanced up at Wilder. News of her being found in bed with Scott had spread through the town faster than she ever understood. She figured Scott must have told everyone... or, knowing what she knew now, maybe it had been Martin. But now, seeing it firsthand, she understood why Wilder left town so fast. The truth alone was too much to face, but to have to do it with the whole town as an audience...

Maybe this was why her mom was so focused on keeping up appearances, on controlling how things looked. If she could keep the town gossip off of their family, maybe it would be easier to handle.

Once her mom was out of the room, her dad quietly answered Nick's question.

"We had an affair."

Damn it! She clutched the pillow next to her and tried not to cry. The woman was younger than she was. Ugh, *Melia* — who had also hit on Wilder, according to him.

Kate wasn't one to hate someone, but what she felt for that woman certainly came close.

Remembering her dad's disgust at Wilder's parents' open marriage, she clenched her jaw. How dare he judge? At least they were open about their inability to commit to each other. She knew there was no way her mom was okay with anything her dad had done.

"When did it end?" Nick asked.

Her dad shook his head. "It hasn't. At least, not that I know about. Dammit. I paid money to keep Martha from finding out. A lot of good that did me."

Nick narrowed his eyes. "What do you mean you paid money?"

"Two guys were blackmailing me and demanded five hundred thousand to keep quiet."

Chase crossed his arms. "I don't mean this to sound rude, but Frank... people in town already know you haven't been faithful. Why would you pay money in this case?"

People knew? How did she not know?

Her dad shifted in his seat. "Melia's pregnant. Or she was. And somehow, these guys found out."

Kate felt nauseous. He had gotten Melia *pregnant*? He'd probably insisted she get an abortion too; she wouldn't put it past him. She put her head between her knees.

"Melia was the one who blackmailed you," Wilder told him.

Kate looked up. Wilder knew?

"What the hell are you talking about?" her dad asked.

"Those two guys you paid money to were using a van that Melia rented."

Dad shook his head. "No, that's not right. She was scared people in town would find out about us and her reputation would be ruined."

"And when was the last time you saw Ms. Fisher?"

"Earlier this week. I met her at the condo construction site outside of Davenport."

"And what was the purpose of the meeting?" Wilder asked.

Her dad glared at him. "Not that it's any of your business, but I was there to give her a key and a note."

Nick arched a brow. "A key to what?"

Her dad sighed. "A hotel room. For tonight. I'm supposed to meet her there in thirty minutes."

Kate balked. The entire family was being held for their safety, and his 'meeting' was to go have sex with some other woman?

The more she thought about it, the more she realized she was wrong; she *could* hate someone, because right now, she *hated* her dad and what he'd done to her mom. Tears trickled down her cheeks and she didn't bother to wipe them away. No, her dad should see what he's done to this family.

"I need you to write down the hotel and room number," Nick said, handing him a piece of paper and pen.

"I'll go check it out," Wilder offered. He stepped toward Kate, to say goodbye, she assumed, but then turned back. "Frank, why did you give Martin Fisher an envelope of money at his housing development?"

Her dad paled. "How did you—" Then he closed his eyes. "I was paying him back."

"For what?"

"He took Melia to the clinic, since I couldn't."

"You made her get an *abortion*?" Lily screeched.

He shook his head. "No, it was her choice. I never asked her to do that."

Wilder went to Kate and wrapped his arms around her. "I'm sorry I have to go. I know the timing is shitty."

Kate nodded.

"Stay here," he told her. "Nick and Chase will keep you safe."

"But who will keep you safe?"

He pulled back and grinned. "I'm a pretty good detective, you know."

"Detective? You mean *ex*-detective, don't you?" her dad said. Then he turned to Nick. "This guy is a dirty cop, I wouldn't trust him to check out anything."

Kate stepped up to her dad. "He's not a dirty cop and he's not married. I know you lied about your background check, so you need to stop spreading lies about him."

He laughed. "Oh yeah? Or what? Are you threatening me now?"

She stared at him, mouth open in shock. Who the hell was this man? Did he ever even love her... or any of them?

"Kate, ignore him," Wilder murmured. "I'll be fine."

He moved her to the other side of the room, where she wrapped her arms around his neck and sank into him.

He rubbed her back. "I'll be back as soon as I can."

She hoped that meant tonight.

Chapter Thirty-Four

Wilder walked into the Fisher Springs Police Department the next morning. He did make it back to Kate last night, but only for a few hours. When his alarm went off this morning, he wanted to shut it off and stay in bed with her. But he was needed here.

The building was small. There were two desks in the main area, an office in the back, and what appeared to be the entrance to a small kitchen or breakroom off to the side.

It amazed him how different it was from the station he'd been working at. Of course, there were thirty employees at his station, while here, there were only three.

"Coleman. Glad you could make it," Chief Dunin said as he stepped out of the office.

Wilder had already met up with Dunin the night before, after the mayor had given them incorrect information about where he was meeting Melia. Wilder only figured it out after he had driven out there and discovered that hotel didn't have a ninth floor or any rooms that began with a nine. By the time he called Chase to tell him what he found, the mayor had snuck out the back door.

Wilder nearly shook his head in disgust at the memory. The man had left his daughters and wife in hiding to go meet his mistress. If he ended up dead by Martha's hand, Wilder would not blame her.

"I didn't say this before," he told the chief now, "but I'm sorry I didn't loop you in sooner. My boss and the other detective in charge insisted we not tell your department anything."

Dunin nodded. "I understand it was because my son Joey was the main informant. I don't like it, but I get it."

Nick and Chase walked in.

"Glad to see you're still in one piece," Chase said to Wilder.

After the wild goose chase to what he thought was Frank's hotel, Wilder had met up with Dunin to go have a chat with Brogan, who was still supposed to be at the motel on Main Street. The agent watching the guy never saw him leave the motel, yet he wasn't there by the time Wilder and the chief arrived.

Since no one else had eyes on any of the other 'gang members,' Wilder had simply driven around Fisher Springs, looking for anything suspicious.

All he'd gotten out of it was a lack of sleep and a deeper longing to spend time with Kate.

"Hey," Dunin greeted his officers. "I need you all to come into my office."

They all obliged, shuffling in.

"I got some information from Idaho, including photos of the men working with Brogan."

The chief pulled up the photos on his laptop, and the three men stared at each face. Not one looked familiar to Wilder.

"Can't say I've seen any of them," Chase said.

"Me neither," Nick said.

Dunin let out a sigh. "There's more. Apparently, these men drove over yesterday with three bombs."

"Drove over? They're already here in Fisher Springs?" Nick asked.

"We think so. Detective Simpson called me this morning. He's working with an agent at the FBI who is on the inside. He's in the car with them. Apparently, he's been undercover for the better part of a year."

Damn, and here Wilder was complaining about having to be undercover for a month.

"The agent called in when they were an hour away, making a bathroom stop," Dunin said. "Simpson made it very clear we are not to fuck up his case. He only told us about the bombs because if they step in, it could blow their agent's cover."

"The FBI is involved now?" Nick frowned.

"Not for this. It's us and the King County Sheriff's Office."

"And me. We had a tip that the bombs were going to be at the July Fourth festival," Wilder said.

"That's in two days. Why bring them to town early? What are these guys planning to do? Sight-see?" Chase asked.

"Simpson also told me the King County Sheriff's Department will be bringing their bomb-sniffing dog to town this morning," Dunin said. "Hopefully, we can find the bombs before these guys place them."

"Bomb-sniffing dog?" Chase asked. "That's pretty cool."

Wilder had gotten a chance to work with that team on a case the year before and had seen for himself that the dog was amazing. But today, it was anything but cool. Not when his town and his family were at risk.

He still thought of Fisher Springs as his town. And if he had his way, he'd be living here with Kate soon enough.

Dunin's phone rang.

"Dunin here."

They all watched as the chief frowned.

"Okay, thanks for the update. We'll meet you there."

He hung up the phone and stood up. "That was Detective Simpson. He arrived thirty minutes ago with the bomb unit. They walked through the motel parking lot, but their dog led them to the building next door."

"City Hall?" Nick asked.

Wilder glanced at his watch. It was after nine a.m. on a Friday. *Shit.* "It's full of employees, isn't it?"

"I'm afraid so." Dunin grabbed a jacket off a hook in his office and walked out the door.

The rest followed him.

"What are the odds they'll find all three bombs in one place?" Chase asked hopefully.

Slim to none was all Wilder could think.

They briskly walked the three blocks to City Hall and were met in the parking lot by Simpson.

"They only found one bomb," the detective reported.

"Where the hell would the others be?" Dunin asked.

"I don't know, but I do know the gang is pissed. Melia informed these guys that she couldn't turn over the business because the mayor caught her and confiscated her supply."

"Oh shit. And they believed her?" Nick asked.

"She sent some photos. Our agent on the inside says the mayor looks guilty, and that's all they needed to act."

"So that's why the bomb is at City Hall? They're going after the mayor?"

"Looks that way. I questioned Mr. Waters, and he swears up and down he has no idea what I'm talking about. He appears to be telling the truth, but that won't stop these guys from pursuing their missing two million dollars."

"Two million dollars?" Wilder choked. How the hell was Melia selling that much product and keeping it out of sight of everyone?

"Holy shit! That much meth is in our town?" Chase asked, shaking his head.

"I'm not sure it was solely out of Fisher Springs," Simpson said.

"Still, Melia walked away with two million dollars," Wilder said. "No, two-*point-five* million."

"Point-five?" Dunin asked.

He nodded. "From blackmailing Frank Waters. And we have no idea where she is."

Simpson put a hand in his pocket. "We do have a warrant for her arrest for blackmailing Frank Waters. We should be able to find her soon."

Pfft. Wilder didn't think any of them would be seeing her again. One thing he'd discovered in the time he'd spent with Melia was that she was smart and a planner. She likely had a plan B, C, D, and E.

"Where's Frank now?" he asked.

Simpson pointed.

Frank was standing at the end of the parking lot with his cellphone up to his ear. Several other employees were standing around in a group, looking shell-shocked.

"We're evacuating the building. And they have Bomber checking out other buildings nearby."

"Bomber?" Dunin asked.

Simpson smiled. "The bomb-sniffing dog. Fitting name."

"I'd bet that Brogan's guys will likely go after Melia, too. We should check out where she lives or maybe where her family lives," Wilder said.

Dunin pointed at Chase. "Chase, go with Wilder to check out the Fisher Farm. Nick, come with me and we'll go to her house."

They jogged back to the police station where their cars were parked, and then parted ways. Simpson stayed behind with the bomb unit as Bomber continued sniffing through the downtown area.

Fortunately, Fisher Farm wasn't too far out. Wilder was surprised to see several new houses where the old Johnson farm used to be.

"Johnson passed away a few years back, and his son sold off his property to Martin. Martin wants to turn this place into a suburb," Chase informed him.

Wilder frowned. "There's enough people that want to move out here? Are there more jobs locally now?"

"Nope. And to answer your question, over half of Martin's properties are sitting vacant. He believed in the 'build it, and they will come' theory." He snorted. "Hasn't panned out so far."

Over half were vacant? Well, if Melia couldn't sell the properties, it would make sense why she might look to another source of income.

The moment they arrived at the Fishers', Chase jumped out of the car. He got Scott and his parents out of the house and into the driveway, then Wilder and Chase swept the house, looking for bombs.

"We should probably have them stay out of here until Bomber can clear it," Chase said.

"You're right. They won't like it, but we can't take any chances."

Chase's phone rang while they were still inside the house.

"It's the chief," he told Wilder, then answered, "Hey, nothing here, but we got the Fishers outside… Mmhm… Okay… Will do."

Chase pocketed his phone. "We have to go. They found the second bomb at the bank."

They walked out of the house and over to the family, who was huddled together by a fencepost. Chase instructed them to remain outside until the bomb unit arrived, then the pair left, and Chase drove a little too fast, getting them to the bank in record time.

Once parked, they jumped out of the car and located Dunin.

"We found the third bomb," Dunin said, then looked to Wilder. "It's at the diner. It looks like Melia did a great job of framing the mayor. The bombs were meant for him and his two daughters."

His heartbeat quickened. "Shit! We should never have let them leave the mansion."

After Frank had ditched the protection of the mansion last night, and there was no evidence of a threat against Kate or Lily, they were allowed to return home and then today, to work. Dunin had said he would deal with Frank. But clearly, that didn't mean much since the man had been at City Hall.

"Kate's at the diner!"

Dunin nodded.

Ryker ran up to them wide-eyed and breathless. "Is Lily inside?"

Wilder frowned at Dunin.

"Lily works at the bank," the chief informed him.

Damn, he should have known that. He really should have asked Kate more about her family.

"I need to see her," Ryker insisted.

Wilder had met the man at the Chanler mansion the previous night. He didn't really know him, but he understood the protective instinct he seemed to be wrestling with — 'cause he was sure as hell feeling it toward Kate at the moment.

Wilder moved to step away, but Dunin grabbed his arm.

"There's nothing you can do. No one can go in or out until the bomb unit disarms it."

"Are they at the diner, then?"

Dunin shook his head. "They're having some trouble with this one," he nodded toward the bank.

Wilder spotted Simpson and ran to him. "What's going on?"

Simpson wiped his brow. "I don't have all the details, but apparently, there is some kind of failsafe on this bomb that the tech hasn't been able to work around yet."

All Wilder could think was that if the bomb at the diner was on a timer, they were wasting precious minutes.

"Can you get another bomb tech here? You knew there would be three bombs," he snapped.

Simpson nodded his head for Wilder to follow him away from the crowd.

"We have more techs, but someone called in a bomb threat in downtown Seattle. The King's County unit left. Bomber too since we knew the location of the bombs. They left us one technician."

Shit. "How do they know that threat was legitimate? Might be part of this plan."

Simpson shook his head. "Presence of a bomb has been confirmed by sight there."

Wilder ran his hand through his hair.

"Look, I know you have someone special inside the diner. The other officer told me." Simpson nodded behind Wilder. "We will get the tech over there as soon as possible. You have my word."

"Why aren't you evacuating the employees from the bank and the diner?"

Simpson clapped Wilder on the shoulder. "We don't know what triggers each bomb. Until the tech can get in and verify, everyone must remain where they are."

Wilder began to pace. *I can't stand around and do nothing.*

He tried to walk a few blocks to the diner, but Main Street was closed off, with officers from the county sheriff's department guarding it.

He held up his badge to the first officer he came to.

"Sorry," they shook their head. "No one gets through until the bomb has been defused."

His phone rang in his back pocket, and he pulled it out.

"Kate, are you all right?"

She sniffled, and his heart broke. "Do you know?" she asked.

"I do. There was a bomb at City Hall that the tech defused. Now he's working on one at the bank—"

"The bank? Oh no! Lily is there. And City Hall? Were we targeted? Is this because they thought my dad stole something?"

Wilder sighed. "I'm afraid so. Listen, Lily is fine, don't worry about her. And as soon as they get that bomb defused, the tech is headed your way."

Kate sniffled again. "I'm scared."

"I know. And if I could get to you, I would. But the sheriff's office has the area barricaded and they aren't letting anyone through."

"No, don't even try. Please. No one else needs to be hurt."

"You won't get hurt, either. You'll be out of there before you know it."

He needed to distract her.

"Can you tell me who else is in the diner?" he asked.

"Um. Harmony is here. She's talking to Chase on her phone. She's pretty upset. Logan is here, keeping everyone calm. And then we only had two customers, Mr. Finley and Martin."

"Martin is in there with you?"

"Yeah, Logan let me go to the back to avoid him."

"Remind me to thank Logan."

"Yeah, he's a great guy."

A woman tried to push past the police tape. "Please! My brother Logan is in there!" she yelled.

"No, ma'am, no one can get through. I'm sorry."

A dark-haired woman put her arm around the other woman's shoulders and led her away.

Wilder turned back to the diner. "Hey, Logan's sister is out here. Can he call her?"

"Sure, he's right here." He heard some shuffling then her voice was muffled. "Logan, you need to call your sister."

There was more shuffling. "He's doing it now."

"Where is the bomb located?"

Kate took a breath. "Under a table near the front door."

"Can you take a photo of it and send it to me? But don't get too close, don't touch it. I can zoom in on my phone."

"Okay. Just a minute."

Wilder listened as she pushed through the kitchen doors and walked out into the dining area. Then he heard a click—likely her taking the photo—and a muffled conversation he couldn't make out.

A moment later, she came back on. "I sent it to you and Chase. Harmony asked me to."

"Thanks. That's great. We are going to get you out."

"I hope so."

Wilder squeezed his eyes shut. "We will. I was serious about moving back here for us to be together. It's going to happen. Just focus on that, okay?"

"Okay."

Wilder's eyes caught on the business next door. Maybe he could distract her for a little bit.

"I keep forgetting to ask you, but is that a sex shop next door to the diner?"

Kate laughed. "It is."

"How the hell did that get approved in this town?"

"It's a long story. The owner's name is Sophie, and she and Logan argued about the shop the entire time she was setting it up. He thought it would hurt his business."

"Did it?"

"Not at all."

"Wilder! I need you," Dunin called from behind him.

He turned and nodded, then focused once more on his conversation. "I have to go, the chief needs me. I love you, Kate."

"I love you too."

Chapter Thirty-Five

Kate's hands were shaking as she pocketed her phone. As much as she wanted to stay on the line with Wilder until this was over, she understood he needed to do his job.

She pushed through the kitchen doors into the dining room and walked behind the counter, avoiding eye contact with everyone. After pouring herself a cup of coffee, she turned to find Martin at the counter. She jumped at his proximity, spilling coffee on herself.

"Shit, Martin. You snuck up on me."

"Sorry, I didn't mean to."

She dabbed at the coffee staining the T-shirt of her pink uniform, ignoring the man in front of her. Talking to Martin was the last thing she wanted to do right now.

He'd come to the diner this morning to give her some news: he had to cancel her landscape design contract. He claimed it was a budgetary issue, but she knew better.

"Look, I feel bad about what happened. I didn't want to cancel your contract, but since I haven't sold as many units as I wanted to, I couldn't justify the cost."

This man had sabotaged up her marriage and was now canceling the very contract keeping her in business, and he had yet to apologize for any of it. He wanted her to see things his way? Not going to happen.

Giving up on the stain, she took a drink of her coffee and tried to catch Harmony's eye, hoping her friend would come save her. But Harmony was sitting in a booth, staring out the window while talking on her phone to Chase.

Kate glanced out the window. Nothing had changed. Some officers she didn't recognize had put up police tape after they first discovered the bomb; now only a couple of officers stood inside the boundary. Everyone else was kept at a distance.

"Maybe if Wilder hadn't come to town, Melia would still be here and I would have sold more units," Martin growled.

What the fuck? She turned her attention back to the man. How did he manage to make this all about him? "Are you kidding me?"

"No, I'm not. Since Wilder came to town, everything has gone to shit. And now look at us! Sitting in a diner with a bomb." He pointed under the table. "Anyway, I guess it's for the best. Assuming we get out of here."

She didn't want to bite, but she had no idea what the hell he was talking about.

"What do you mean?"

"I mean if you end up with Wilder, I wouldn't have been able to work with you anyway."

It took all her self-control not to throw her coffee at him. Instead, she set the cup down on the counter and leaned forward. "You self-righteous asshole."

Her voice was calm, but the words got his attention. His eyes widened as she continued.

"You ruined my marriage and then ended the very contract that would get my business off the ground. But not once in your diatribe did you say you were sorry. No, you insulted me, and made it clear you only gave me the contract to get time with me."

"No, that's not true. I gave you the contract because you were the best!"

Everyone in the diner was staring at them now.

"Well, then, I guess you'll reinstate it."

What the hell was she saying? She didn't want to work with this asshole. But then again, it would help her build her portfolio and get other work.

Martin looked at her with a furrowed brow. "I told you, I had to make cuts."

Logan stepped up to the counter and glared at him. "Everything all right here, Kate?"

"Everything's fine, Logan," Martin sneered.

Still talking to Kate, Logan said, "I heard you say he ruined your marriage. What happened?"

Mr. Finley made his way to the counter. Kate knew that, if they survived all this, Mr. Finley would quickly tell the gossip mill all that he'd heard.

Martin must have realized that too, because he tried to explain, "It was a misunderstan—"

Kate cut him off. "No, it wasn't. He paid Scott to make it look like I slept with him. I didn't, but he did a great job of convincing Wilder. That's why he left town ten years ago. And do you know why Martin did that?"

"Why?" Mr. Finley asked dutifully.

"Because he thought that, with Wilder out of the picture, I'd actually date him. Fortunately, I already knew what an asshole he was from high school, so I didn't make that mistake again."

Martin's face flushed red, and he balled his fists. But Kate wasn't done.

"Then, when he realized I was really back with Wilder, he canceled my landscape design contract, claiming it was for budgetary reasons."

"Why would you want to work with him if he ruined your marriage?" Logan asked.

"Exactly," Martin said. "Maybe she was really out for revenge and would have sabotaged the developments or ripped me off out of spite."

Harmony got up from the booth and walked over with a scoff. "Kate isn't a vengeful person. We all know that."

Logan shook his head. "All this because you wanted to date Kate?"

Martin stood up and glared at Kate. "What the hell is your problem anyway? You've dated just about every guy in this town — or should I say *slept with* — yet you never give me the time of day."

Kate's mouth fell open. She'd had a few friends with benefits and a few one-night stands, but she certainly hadn't hooked up with 'every guy in this town'.

Logan got in Martin's face. "You need to apologize. She most certainly has not slept with all the guys in this town."

Martin laughed. "Okay, so not you or me."

Logan leapt at Martin and wrestled him to the ground, getting him on his stomach. Then he pulled something out of his back pocket.

He moved so quickly; Kate wasn't sure what was going on.

Finally, Logan hopped up, pulling Martin with him. Fisher's hands were tied behind his back.

Kate lifted a brow. "A wire tie?"

Logan nodded. "Before we found out about the bomb, I was in the back trying to organize all the cords in the office."

He deposited Martin on the bench Harmony had vacated. "Now sit here and keep your damn mouth shut or you'll end up much worse off than simply restrained."

He walked back to the counter, rejoining Kate.

"Those were some fast moves you had there," she said.

He shrugged. "Learned a few things in the service."

"He was a Navy SEAL, you know," Harmony added.

Before Kate could ask more, a voice boomed over a bullhorn.

"The bomb tech is here. Please step back from the door."

Logan went over to the booth and grabbed Martin, then shoved him behind the counter, where Mr. Finley also joined Harmony and Kate.

From there, the group watched a man dressed in some kind of large, helmeted, green bodysuit peer in at the bomb from the front door. He made no attempt to open it. Then he moved to the side of the building and peered in from a window.

A moment later, he placed a device on the window. Kate wasn't sure what to expect, but he pulled away a large, circular piece of glass and crawled through.

"Hello. I'm your friendly bomb tech," he said jovially. "Is this the only one you've seen in here?"

"The only bomb?" Kate asked.

"Yes," Logan replied. "I swept the back, and there are no others."

The man nodded. "I'll check the back exit. If there are no tripwires, you will all be free to leave." He went into the kitchen.

Five minutes later, he reappeared. "The back door is open. Please follow the officers once they come in."

As the man motioned to the back, Kate was struck by the fact he wasn't wearing gloves. His entire body was protected, but his hands weren't. She frowned as she studied his bare skin.

The tech must have noticed her gaze. "I don't wear gloves because they impede my hand movement. I need all my agility for this work."

Kate nodded, seeing the sense in that.

"Got to have balls of steel to do what you do, too," Logan added. "Thank you for your help."

An officer walked in from the kitchen. "Follow me," she said.

Kate practically ran to the door, following the officer's direction, until she was outside of the barricaded area, on the other side of Main Street.

"Kate!" Wilder shouted.

She turned to see him running toward her.

The moment he reached her, he pulled her into his arms. "I'm so happy you're out of that diner."

"Me too."

"The thought of losing you... it was too much. It made me sick."

"I know," she said into his shoulder.

She held him tightly for minutes, losing track of time.

"I don't want to let go," he murmured, echoing her thoughts.

"I'm sorry, Ms. Loprete," an officer interrupted, "but you'll need to come with me for questioning."

Wilder released her. "Find me when you're done, and I'll take you home."

Home...

Right now, that would be anywhere Wilder was. But she nodded and then followed the officer away from the crowd.

"I have to ask," the officer said as they walked away. "Why was Martin Fisher restrained with a wire tie?"

Kate smiled. "Because he's an asshole."

Chapter Thirty-Six

Wilder stared out at the crowd gathered at the Fisher Springs July Fourth festival. The rain hadn't come as expected, which meant there were quite a few people here; a crowd made larger due to William and Holly's guests sitting on blankets throughout the park.

There were no clouds in the sky, which made perfect conditions for watching the fireworks that would soar above the sky in a few hours.

While Wilder waited, he enjoyed hanging out with everyone under more relaxed circumstances. Plus, with the long summer days, it still remained light enough well into the evening to people-watch.

"I can't thank you guys enough for everything you did to ensure the town was safe for us. I thought for sure we would have to postpone the wedding," Holly said.

Wilder glanced at Nick then Chase. It had been a busy couple of days, but he felt certain his town was safe again.

"No problem. By the time the bombs were defused, the gang from Idaho figured out that Melia had double crossed them. They lost interest in the mayor pretty quickly at that point," Wilder said.

"Does this mean Melia is in danger?" William asked.

"Only if they find her."

Wilder had no idea where she'd gone, but he was sure she was with Brogan.

"I was so worried about you, Kate... and Lily. That must have been so traumatic. I'm sorry I haven't had a chance to really talk to you about it." Holly gave Kate's leg a squeeze.

"I'm fine. Yes, it was scary, but it's over and that's what matters."

Wilder watched as Kate smiled back at him. He'd been worried about her, after all that she'd gone through. Her sister was struggling with it; Wilder had gotten to know Ryker better over the last forty-eight hours, and the man had shared that Lily was having nightmares.

"Seriously, Wilder. I'm fine. I think having Martin there helped. I was able to focus my anger on him, and then when Logan tied him up... well, let's just say I really enjoyed that."

William laughed. "I wish I could have seen that."

"Here, you can. I took a video of Logan tying him up," Harmony said as she tapped on her phone.

Wilder wrapped an arm around Kate and pulled her in close, and their friends gathered around Harmony's phone to view the video.

"Thank you for that," William said after it was over.

"You two ready for tomorrow?" Wilder asked.

William beamed. "Very ready."

"Yes, I can't wait to marry this man." Holly stared up at William.

Wilder thought how 'very ready' he was to spend the rest of his life with Kate. Yes, it was fast, but it felt right.

After they had gotten home from the bomb scare, they'd had a long, honest talk. Nearly losing Kate had made everything clear to Wilder: he wanted to live together right away.

Fortunately, she felt the same way. She'd asked him to move into her house, but they both agreed to wait until the next weekend, after his brother's wedding. They didn't want to take away from William's big day.

Today, Wilder was simply going to enjoy the July Fourth festival with all of his friends.

It still felt strange to him. He'd left this town ten years ago, alone, with no word of farewell, and yet here they all were, welcoming him back. And even though he didn't know Nick or Zach that well, they were accepting of him. Zach was still a scary fucker, especially when giving him side-eye, but Kate explained he was like a protective brother.

"Hey, guys. Mind if I join you for a bit?"

Wilder glanced up to see Joey chewing on his lip.

The group was quiet for a minute. Then Chase stood up.

"Of course. Come here, man." He pulled him in for a hug. "How are you doing?"

Joey smiled. "Better. It's a long road, but I've been clean six months, and I'm determined to stay that way."

"Here, have a seat with us," Harmony invited.

Joey sat on the blanket and looked at Nick. "I don't think we've officially met. I'm Joey." He held out his hand.

"Nick. Nice to meet you. You know, I caught a lot of hell when I first took the detective job."

Joey chuckled. "Sorry about that. My dad wasn't ready to tell everyone what was going on with me, so the rest of the town didn't have the full picture."

"*I* gave him the most hell." Chase grinned at Nick. "Sorry about that."

"We're all good now," Nick said slapping him on the back.

Wilder wondered what had gone on but was happy to see everyone smiling now.

Joey frowned at Wilder. "You were undercover the entire time? I really believed you were an ex-cop."

"Detective," both Wilder and Nick said at the same time. Wilder glanced at Nick and smiled.

Joey snorted. "Well, I'm glad that's all over. All this time, I thought I owed Melia something, but it turns out I was wrong." He shook his head.

"What do you mean?" Wilder asked.

"Remember I told you she saved me that night by paying off my dealer?"

"Yeah."

"She didn't pay my dealer to save me."

"I'm not following. And how do you know this?" Wilder asked.

"I went looking for Simpson and found him and a whole lot of officers down by the diner yesterday. He showed me a photo of some guy named Brogan. I didn't recognize him... but Martin did. Apparently, so did Mr. Finley."

"They did?" Nick asked, leaning in.

Joey nodded. "He was Melia's high school boyfriend. When he saw the picture, Martin turned bright red and looked like he was going to punch something. Simpson explained to us that Brogan was the dealer Melia was working with."

"And how does that relate to you?" Nick asked.

"I thought she'd paid off my dealer that night to save me, to get me off of drugs. But I found out she'd already been in contact with Brogan and was selling for him. Buying something from my dealer was no big thing to her. I'm sure she resold it that night."

Melia didn't strike Wilder as the type who would work for someone else. But he once overheard her on the phone referencing a boss. Although now that he thought about it, that was likely part of her setting up Frank.

"Heads up. Martin's coming this way," Harmony warned.

Wilder glanced up to see Martin storming over, a scowl on his face.

"Hey, glad to see the police force having a good time," Martin snapped. "Does this mean you've found and arrested that asshole Brogan?"

Nick stood up and faced Martin. "Not yet, but the King County Sheriff's Office is working on it."

"King County? Why not you?" Martin crossed his arms. "I'd bet money that Brogan conned my cousin. There is no way she'd willingly sell drugs."

Wilder held back a scoff. Martin was clearly clueless about Melia; that woman knew exactly what she was doing.

"Why do you say that?" Nick asked.

Fisher shook his head. "That asshole was Melia's high school boyfriend."

"I'm guessing you didn't like him," Nick arched a brow.

They already knew he didn't as Joey had already relayed as much.

"No one in the family did! The guy was a loser. Melia was a great student, got straight A's. But this guy, skipped school any chance he could and drank every night. She started to do the same thing to be with him."

"Why did they break up?" Nick asked.

"His dad got a job in Idaho, and the whole family moved. Good riddance. Melia was pretty upset about it, but she got over it. Or so I thought."

"Idaho?"

"Yeah. Oh *shit*. Melia said her ex was from Idaho!" Martin looked gobsmacked. "But she said she had a restraining order against him. If he hurt her, I'll—"

Wilder held up a hand. "I've already searched the system, and I found no evidence of a restraining order. I'm not sure why she told you that."

Martin frowned. "How would she have gotten in contact with him? They moved years ago."

"We don't know," Nick said.

Martin shook his head as he stared out at the crowd. "Yeah, you don't know a hell of a lot."

Nick crossed his arms, clenching his jaw. "Look, I know you're worried about her. Once I know, I'll let you know. Okay?"

The other man sneered, "You do that." Then he turned and left.

"Asshole," Wilder muttered under his breath.

"I'd also love to know why she got caught up with Brogan," Nick admitted. "From everyone I've talked to, she was doing well as a real estate agent. It doesn't make sense that she'd give it all up to live on the run."

"When Martin canceled my contract, he said his houses weren't selling like he'd hoped. Maybe Melia wasn't doing as well as we all thought she was," Kate said from her spot on the blanket.

Nick pursed his lips. "You're saying we're going to have a bunch of vacant houses sitting around?"

"Great," Chase rolled his eyes. "Looks like we'll be busting some teenage keggers soon."

Holly frowned. "Why do you assume that?"

Chase laughed. "You didn't hang out with the party crowd in high school, did you?"

"Party crowd?" Nick asked. "I figured the entire school partied. What else is there for teenagers to do around here?"

"Hey! I had my sewing club," Holly responded.

Nick opened his mouth to respond but then his face lit up. Wilder followed his stare to see Lauren approach. She was carrying a small cooler.

"I brought water if anyone wants some." She opened the lid of the container and handed out several bottles.

"Thanks, babe." Nick took a water. "Okay, so Melia wasn't earning a lot as a real estate agent. But to turn to selling drugs?"

"You'd be surprised what people do for love," Wilder said.

"Give up her friends? Family?" Nick pressed.

"Isn't that what you did?" Harmony retorted. "By staying in Fisher Springs?"

Nick shook his head. "Nah, I traded up for a better life."

"Aw!" Lauren said. "That's so sweet." She leaned in to kiss him, and Nick turned it hot and heavy quickly.

"Hey! This is a family event." Chase hit Nick across the shoulder.

They broke apart.

Nick grinned. "Sorry. Couldn't resist."

"Hey, sorry we're late," Zach said as he approached with Jessie.

"Glad you made it," Kate said.

Zach laid out a blanket next to Kate, and the couple sat down.

"Hey, Jessie, you still have contacts with the King County Sheriff's Office?" Chase asked.

"No."

Nick frowned. "None?"

"Oh, I do, but I know where you're going with this, and no."

Chase flattened his lips. "And where am I going?"

"If I had to hazard a guess, I'd say it's about a case, and you want all the answers," Jessie countered.

Chase laughed. "You know me well."

She winked. "I know you well enough to also guess you asked Nick the same question already."

"He did and I said no," Nick confirmed.

Chase turned to Wilder "Can you find out if that gang intends to still use Fisher Springs as a gateway for its drugs?"

Wilder nodded. "Already on it. Once Simpson knows something, he'll tell me."

Chase pointed at Wilder. "See? He gets it. Thank you, Wilder."

He did get why Chase was worried.

Simpson had sworn to him that the FBI had arrested everyone involved in the bombing plot; it had to be the FBI, since they'd crossed state lines to do it. And apparently, by arresting their own undercover agent, they helped him gain more credibility with the gang.

But all of those men would be released until their trials as the undercover agent is gathering evidence of their drug operation, not the bombing. And someone had to take over where Melia left off. He hoped like hell whoever stepped up wasn't in Fisher Springs.

Chapter Thirty-Seven

Kate and Wilder watched from the lawn of the Chanler mansion as Holly and William stood in a receiving line, smiling at all their guests.

"I'm glad we eloped," Kate murmured, leaning close so only Wilder heard.

He laughed. "Yeah, me too."

She looked over at him, wanting to catch his smile, and took another moment to stare.

His hair was combed back, and he had just enough stubble on his face for it to be sexy as hell. Add to that he was wearing a tux, and all she wanted to do was drag him inside and find a bedroom.

He gave her a wolfish grin. "I know that look. Better behave, or I'll find us a tree to hide behind."

She laughed. "A tree? I was thinking inside."

He cocked his head. "I guess that would be more practical."

She snorted and shook her head, then went back to observing the happy couple. The receiving line before them grew as guests made their way from the backyard to the front.

"Uh oh," Wilder grunted.

"What?" Kate asked, but then she followed his line of sight and saw Detective Simpson walking up the driveway.

"Quite a few guests here, huh? I had to park up on the road," Simpson said as he approached. "Any way I could talk to you for a moment?" His eyes scanned the crowd and caught on someone that made him smile. "Nick Moore? Is that really you? I'm sorry I missed you the other day in all the craziness."

Nick walked over and shook Simpson's hand. "Detective now, is it?"

Simpson grinned. "It is. And look at you, loving small-town life. I heard you live in this monstrosity." He nodded at the mansion.

Nick laughed. "I do. I live here with my wife."

"Wife?" Simpson asked. "Ah, now I get why you stayed. Some of the guys bet it was a woman." He nodded. "Good for you."

Kate didn't want to be rude, but she wondered why Simpson was crashing the wedding. "Did you have something you wanted to tell us?"

His smile dropped. "Yes, I did."

Kate felt Wilder tense beside her. If the detective had come here instead of waiting until tomorrow, it must be important.

"I wanted to tell you in person that... the town is safe!" He chuckled. "I had you worried, didn't I? My contact at the FBI called. According to their agent, the group in Idaho is moving Melia's supply north."

Kate sighed in relief. "North?"

"Out of King County," Simpson clarified.

Nick nodded. "There's more of a market for those drugs up north."

"So it's still a problem, just someone else's problem?" Wilder summated.

"That's about right, yeah. Well, I'll let you get back to the wedding. Sorry to interrupt and I'm sorry this case took so much of your time. But thankfully we got it wrapped up before the nuptials."

Kate couldn't help but wonder if the man realized by coming here he was taking even more of Wilder's time from his family.

"Thank you for telling us. I really appreciate it," Wilder said.

"Have a good one." Simpson nodded as he walked back toward the driveway.

"I'm going to walk him out," Nick said, following.

"North," Wilder said turning to her.

"North," she said smiling.

While she wished the drugs would just go away, she was relieved. Summit County was south; at least that put Wilder further from this for now.

Taking his hand, Kate led Wilder to the receiving line, which had shortened considerably. Most people were standing in groups, mingling on the front lawn.

The reception was to be held in the backyard, where the wedding had taken place. There were workers out there now, moving chairs and setting up tables as fast as they could. That meant the guests could take their time out front.

By the time Kate and Wilder reached the newlyweds, Holly had tears in her eyes.

"No, don't cry! Your makeup," Kate lamented as she leaned in for a hug.

"I know. I can't help it. I'm just so happy."

"We both are," William said as he leaned in to kiss her cheek.

"Oh, there you are!" Wilder's mom walked up and pulled Kate into a big hug, then she did the same to Wilder. "You two are next, you know. And don't think you can run off and elope this time!"

Kate stepped back, trying to smile. While she knew she wanted to be with Wilder for the rest of her life, the idea of a wedding like this held no appeal.

Wilder grabbed her hand and gave it a squeeze, practically reading her thoughts. "I don't know. I really liked our wedding in Vegas. I'd be up for doing that again."

His mother shook her head. "No eloping this time. When you two are ready, let me know. I'll set up everything." She glanced around. "I wonder if we could do it here. How fabulous would that be?"

Kate swallowed the lump in her throat. Not only would she be subjected to a big wedding, but it would be planned by her mother-in-law?

"Okay, Mom," William interjected. "Let's not get ahead of ourselves, they only just started dating again."

She stared at the mansion. "I know, but I can see it now."

William turned to Kate and Wilder and mouthed, "*Go!*" gesturing toward the cars.

Wilder didn't hesitate. He tugged on Kate's hand, and they bolted away. Next thing she knew, they were hiding out in her car, giggling at the fact that they'd run from his mom.

Unfortunately, they couldn't go far; the car was blocked in since she'd parked at the front, figuring she'd be there for the entire reception.

"Well, looks like we can't leave," she said.

Wilder laughed. "We're already going to hear about this. Can you imagine if we *left*?" He leaned in and kissed her. "You're so beautiful."

Kate arched a brow. "Are you coming onto me in a car?"

Wilder glanced at the back seat, then down at their clothes. "I'd love to, but I'm afraid it would be obvious by the time we made it back to the wedding."

Kate reached up and touched her hair protectively. It had taken an hour to get it all pinned up. "You knock one hair out of a place, and you'll pay," she threatened with a mock-scowl.

When he didn't laugh, she turned her body toward him.

He was staring at her so intently.

"What's wrong?" she asked.

"Do you want a big wedding like this?" he asked.

She took his hand in hers. "No I don't. I'd rather have a quick wedding and spend our money on an elaborate honeymoon."

"A honeymoon, huh. We never really had one."

She squeezed his hand. "Have you forgotten? The night at the hotel in Vegas."

"That was it?"

She shrugged. "Suppose it was."

He shook his head. "This time, we'll do it right."

His words caused butterflies to flutter in her stomach. "This time?"

He turned back to her, grinning. "Yes, this time."

"Wilder, are you proposing?"

"Nope." He winked.

"*Ugh!*" She shoved at him.

"But I plan to," he added. "Got to keep you on your toes."

She swatted at him, though she was smiling.

This man. She loved him... and always had. How she had lived ten years without him, she'd never know.

He leaned forward until their lips met. Within seconds, their kiss turned hot and heavy.

Then someone banged on the window, and startled, they jumped apart.

"Hey, this is a family-friendly event!" Zach's voice boomed outside the car.

Kate laughed when she realized the windows had begun to fog up. "I feel like a teenager," she whispered.

Wilder chuckled. "Me too."

"We should probably go back now."

"Yeah, sounds safer than whatever that giant might do to me."

Kate snickered. "Zach's harmless."

Wilder's brows shot up. "He doesn't look harmless," he said as she opened her door.

"I'm *not* harmless. Don't forget that," Zach jabbed a finger at Wilder.

Next to Zach, Jessie rolled her eyes. "He's harmless."

"Woman, what are you doin'?" Zach asked.

Jessie shrugged a shoulder. "Just keeping it real."

He grumbled under his breath, then said, "We'll meet you at the reception."

As they walked away, Kate could still hear Zach insisting he was dangerous.

"I like those two," Wilder said as he stood by the hood waiting for her.

Kate walked up and looped her arm through his. "That's good. Because you'll likely be spending a lot of time with them."

"Guess I'd better get on his good side, then."

She squeezed his bicep. "You'd better."

Chapter Thirty-Eight

Melia

Melia finished off her Mai Tai and slammed the glass down on the table with one hand while the other scrolled through the headlines on her laptop screen. "Why isn't there any coverage on this?"

"What's wrong, baby?" Brogan asked.

"There's nothing in the news about Frank Waters."

Brogan's brow furrowed. "Who's that?"

Melia sighed. "The mayor of the town I came from."

"And why would you expect him to be in the news?"

She smiled. She hadn't told Brogan that she'd set the man up; no, there was no need for Brogan to have any idea what she was capable of — especially now that he was questioning her choices.

Once upon a time, she'd loved this man, but at this point, she couldn't see why. Had he changed? Had she?

"Your friends were threatening to bomb the town. I figured that would at least make the news. And the mayor likes to hear himself talk, so I was sure he would make a statement."

"Huh. Well, if it didn't make the news, maybe the guys changed their mind." Brogan took a long sip of his drink. "Or maybe they realized you left town and are looking for you instead."

The man spoke so casually, as it if were no big deal if they were looking for her.

"Have you heard from them?" she asked.

He didn't respond.

She looked away from her screen. "Brogan?"

He finished his drink. "Only my brother."

Melia took a breath, trying to remain calm. "You spoke to your brother?"

"Uh huh."

"What did you say?"

Brogan shrugged as he rolled his empty glass between his palms. "I wanted to check in and find out how my mom was doing. She's good, by the way. Then Gunnar mentioned that the guys figured out the mayor didn't steal anything—you did."

Melia sat up taller.

Brogan set down the tumbler and leaned forward, lowering his voice. "You didn't mention you were setting a man up for what you did."

Melia closed her laptop and stared out at the ocean as the warm breeze brought the smell of the salty sea air. Everything about this place was beautiful; she really hoped she could stay.

"Did he mention what they thought your role was in this?" she asked.

"Not really. Gunnar just warned me that they were going to come looking for you."

Melia had been careful. She had purchased the airline tickets in cash, obtained a fake passport the month prior, and had flown into Ibiza without anyone even giving her a second glance.

But Brogan... had he followed those instructions too?

After meeting up at the motel in Fisher Springs, they'd each gone separately to the airport, and then to their destination, just in case.

"Brogan, did you ever get a fake passport?"

"Hmm?" he asked, looking up from his phone. "A fake one? No, I ran out of time."

Dammit! Why hadn't she listened to her gut and ditched this guy when she had the chance?

Thankfully, she'd already researched where to go next if she had to run.

Trying to remain calm, she stood and grabbed her laptop. "I'm all sweaty from sitting out here, I'm going to go back to the room and take a shower. Why don't you pick a place for dinner?"

Brogan smiled. "Sounds good. I'll be up in a bit to shower too. I want to tan my back first." He flipped over on his stomach on the lounger.

"Sounds good."

Melia walked as fast as she could without drawing attention. Once back in their hotel room, she packed up her laptop and grabbed her bag.

Since arriving earlier today, she hadn't bothered to unpack. Thank god. She wasn't sure how much time she had before they'd be found, but her gut told her it wasn't much.

"Welcome to Casablanca, Mrs. Waters. Please let us know if we can bring you anything." The valet set her suitcases on the bed.

"Thank you. I will."

He gave her a nod and then left the room.

Once she was alone, Melia fell back onto the bed and pulled her phone out of her bag. It was a burner she'd picked up before leaving the United States, and only Brogan had the number.

Part of her felt bad for leaving him, but she had to.

If only he'd followed my instructions…

But no, he'd been lazy. And now it looked like he was pissed.

Brogan: *Where the hell are you? You left? Why?*

Brogan: *Shit. I saw Pete at the front desk. How the fuck did he find me?*

Brogan: *Where are you? I'm heading to the airport. I'll fly wherever you tell me to.*

That was the last message, left four hours ago.

She closed her eyes. Odds were he never made it to the airport.

She couldn't believe Pete had flown all the way out to Ibiza to get Brogan. He always made everyone else do his dirty work.

Of course, not everyone was so bold as to steal two million dollars from him—which was how she knew someone would be coming for them. Considering Brogan's lack of messages, that someone had likely already found him and confiscated his phone and was now trying to track down hers.

Which meant she didn't have much time.

She left her room and made her way to the pier. A large cruise ship was docked there, and several people were walking toward it.

"Gabriel, come on. The boat is leaving soon!"

Melia watched a mom try to rush her oblivious child toward the ship.

Pretending to be looking the other way, Melia ran into the woman, slipping the phone into her large tote bag as they collided. "Oh, I'm so sorry. I was looking at the ship."

"That's all right," the woman said. "Come on, Gabriel."

The boy was bent over, tying his shoe, and completely ignoring the woman nagging him.

The ship's horn blew.

"That's our warning," the woman pressed, still trying to get her son's attention.

Melia asked, "Where's the ship going?"

"Our next stop is Ibiza. We will arrive tomorrow morning. I can't wait!"

Melia smiled. "It's beautiful. You'll love it."

"Thanks," she replied.

The boy finally stood up and ran to his mom, who practically dragged him to the ship.

Melia watched as they got on, and the ramp was pulled up right behind them. "Have fun tracking that phone, Pete."

When she got back to the hotel, she began the letter she'd already written in her head several times. Frank would probably get it in a week; if he chose to join her, she'd see him in less than two weeks. He wouldn't need long to wrap up his loose ends.

She knew he'd be pleased about her choice of destinations. Most of the places without extradition treaties with the United States were so dreary. But Morocco... it was perfect.

Chapter Thirty-Nine

One year later

"How many times are you going to rearrange that?" Wilder asked, leaning against the wall.

Kate laughed. She had rearranged the photos and knickknacks on their mantel three times. "Until it feels right."

They'd bought a new, larger home together two months before, and Kate was determined to get every box unpacked before the baby was born. Wilder had already gone to work on a list of projects; his favorite had been replacing the simple stone mantel with a much more elaborate wood one. Kate loved it and wanted to make sure it was decorated in a way that drew visitors' eyes to it.

Wilder spotted their wedding photo on a chair and picked it up. "This has to go in the center."

Kate laughed. "Are you *trying* to piss off our parents?"

He grinned. *Guilty as charged.*

Against both of their parents' wishes, they'd flown to Las Vegas and eloped again. But this time, they did it right: Elvis married them, and then let them take a photo with him to prove it.

Wilder placed it in the middle of the mantel. "Perfect. Now why don't you sit and let me rub your back?"

Kate didn't argue as she sat down on the couch with her back to him. Now that she was in her third trimester, she was experiencing more back pain. "How much time do we have?"

Wilder glanced at the clock. "Ten minutes."

She sighed. Ten minutes, and their new home would be filled with family and friends. Holly and Harmony were throwing them a combination housewarming party and baby shower.

Wilder had rolled up his sleeves to start her massage when the doorbell rang.

"Well, so much for that." Kate shifted and leaned back on the couch.

"I'm sure it's Holly, ready to decorate." Wilder smiled as he headed to the door.

Holly had asked to come over twenty minutes before the party to do some quick decorating.

But his smile dropped when he found his mother stood on the other side.

"Mom, you're early." He leaned in and gave her a hug. "Where's Dad?"

"He's bringing in the gifts around back."

Wilder stepped aside to allow her in, and he saw the moment she noticed the wedding photo.

Her body tensed. Then she shook her head. "It was bad enough that you did that again. But now you taunt me with that photo? I just can't." She walked through the house to the backyard.

Most of the party was supposed to take place there, but as far as Wilder knew, his mother was the first one in attendance.

"We should probably head to the backyard now," he said.

Kate let out a sigh. "You're right. You know she's going to bring up our wedding for years."

"Yes, she will. And so will yours."

"So much for making it easier on ourselves," she grumbled.

She stood up, and he took her hand. When they got outside, they were surprised to find that most of their guests had already arrived — everyone except Holly and Harmony. But what surprised him even more was the sight of Kate's parents talking to each other and *smiling*.

After news of the mayor's affair with Melia had spread through town, Martha kicked Frank out of the house and consulted a divorce attorney. There was even talk that he should step down as mayor. But none of that happened, and neither Wilder nor Kate knew why.

He figured it wasn't his place to ask, and frankly, the less he knew, the better. He'd stay out of their business, and hopefully, they'd stay out of his and their daughter's.

"We made it!" Harmony singsonged as she and Holly walked into the backyard.

Holly was carrying a large cake.

"Let me help you with that," Zach offered. He took it from her hands and brought it to the table.

"Sorry we're late." Holly looked at her watch. "Wait, why is everyone early?"

"We couldn't wait to celebrate with the happy couple," Lauren said.

Nick and Chase stood toward the back, talking amongst themselves.

Wilder knew the real reason everyone was there; they hoped that he and Kate would finally reveal if the baby was a boy or a girl.

They had said they were going to wait until the birth to find out, which he hadn't expected to be a controversial subject, but it was. His mother had been upset, fretting about what she could buy the baby before it arrived. He had told her anything she wanted. That didn't sit well.

"Is this one of those gender reveal cakes?" Zach asked.

Wilder glanced at the one-layer sheet cake and bit his lip to keep from laughing.

Zach had been one of their more vocal friends when it came to wanting to know the gender. This didn't surprise Wilder. His first impression of Zach had been completely wrong; the guy was basically a giant softie, but he was fiercely protective of Jessie and his friends.

"No. We told you all, we're waiting until the birth," Wilder said.

Everyone groaned.

"Wow. Really?" he asked.

"Sorry," Harmony shrugged, "we all really want to know."

Chase and Nick made their way forward.

"Wilder, if you won't tell us about the baby… maybe you can tell me if you have heard any more about Joey?" Chase asked.

He had been asking this off and on for the last year, and every time, Wilder had to tell him no. But Wilder finally found out what had happened to Joey and wanted to tell Nick and Chase what happened.

Wilder nodded for them to follow him.

The three of them went in the back door and he led them into the living room. Wilder glanced around, making sure they were alone.

"I just got clearance to tell you. Joey testified against the gang in Idaho. He actually knew more than we realized."

"Shit. They'll go after him," Chase said, running a hand through his hair.

"They won't find him; he entered the witness protection program. That's all I can say."

Chase's eyes widened. "He did?"

Wilder nodded.

"So... that's it? We won't ever see him again? Shit, Dunin won't see him again?"

"I'm afraid not."

Chase fell back onto the couch.

"Sorry, Chase. But this gives Joey a fresh start. It'll be good for him."

He nodded. "Sure. I only wish I'd had a chance to say goodbye."

Nick coughed, clearly uncomfortable in the emotional moment. "So, uh... What's going on with Kate's landscape design business?"

Wilder was thankful for the change of topic. "It's going great actually. Thank you for connecting her with Springton Development. It's a much better opportunity than Martin would have ever provided her."

"Springton? Why does that sound familiar?" Chase asked.

"It's run by my friend Brian Springton. I've probably mentioned him before," Nick said.

Chase nodded.

"Hey, what are you guys doing in here?" Holly stood in the doorway, arms crossed.

Wilder grinned. "Just talking a little shop. Let's head back outside."

They walked out, and Wilder spotted Dane.

"Dane! You came." He walked over and hugged the man.

"Of course. I'm dying to see what you're doing for the gender reveal."

Harmony and Holly groaned.

"What?" Dane asked, looking back and forth between them.

"They still aren't revealin' the gender," Zach supplied as he sipped on a beer.

"Lame, guys. So lame," Dane shook his head.

Wilder laughed as he stepped up behind Kate and wrapped his arms around her belly. "Should we break it out now?" he asked her quietly.

She nodded.

He kissed her cheek. "I'll be right back."

Wilder went inside, to the kitchen, and opened the refrigerator. He was nervous as he grabbed the box, though it didn't matter if they were having a girl or boy; he would be happy either way.

He returned to the backyard. "Okay, everyone! We have a surprise for you. Inside this box are two cupcakes, one for me and one for Kate."

"Oh, please let this be what I think it is!" his mother pleaded.

He smiled at her, then announced, "Inside the cupcakes will be either pink or blue frosting. While we originally wanted to wait, we changed our minds."

"Yes!" His mother shouted.

Zach let out a whistle while Harmony clapped.

Wilder chuckled at how happy the crowd was over their change of heart.

"Where are our cupcakes?" Chase shouted.

"You get cake," Nick retorted. "You don't need a cupcake too."

Wilder pulled the two cupcakes out of the box and handed one to Kate. They were chocolate with chocolate frosting, and all he could see was brown. The bakery had been very careful not to leave any trace of the revealing frosting outside.

"Stop starin' at it and take a bite already!" Zach snapped.

Wilder laughed. He'd also learned that the guy would revert to an Irish accent whenever he was upset or nervous.

"Okay, ready?" he asked Kate.

She held the cupcake up to her mouth and nodded.

"I'll count!" Zach declared. "One... two... three!"

Kate and Wilder bit into their cupcakes at the same time, and then pulled them away from their mouths to show off the damage.

Blue frosting filled the center and now ran down Kate's chin.

"A boy! It's a boy!" her mother yelled.

There were cheers from their friends, followed by a round of congratulations.

Wilder soaked it all up. He thought he'd lost his chance at all of this, but here he was. Nothing would ever come between him and Kate again.

He leaned down and kissed her. She wrapped her free arm around his neck.

Someone coughed.

Zach yelled, "Okay, you can save that for later. Time to open presents!"

Wilder broke their kiss on a laugh and pressed his forehead to hers. "I love you."

She beamed up at him. "I love you, too."

Epilogue

Two months later.

"I can't believe I'm a father," Wilder said.

His dad slapped his shoulder. "Me either. I'm so happy for you, son."

"Two Americanos for Wilder," the girl behind the counter called out.

Wilder grabbed the two coffees, and he and his dad began the walk back to the maternity ward.

"You'll be living on that stuff for the first few months," the older man warned. "But it's worth it."

Wilder was happy his dad was here with him now. They'd had a rocky few months after he moved back to town; both had wanted to work on the relationship, but neither knew what to say. He was glad they'd gotten past that stage.

While his dad still wasn't thrilled that he and Kate had eloped, he overlooked it when Wilder changed his last name back to Loprete.

It had been a hassle at work with all the paperwork, but Captain Nelson understood.

"Look, before we get back, there's something I want to say," his dad said, then motioned to a bench.

They both sat down.

"I feel some responsibility for your divorce from Kate. I think that was why I was so harsh on you."

"Why would you feel responsible?"

His dad sighed and leaned over, resting his elbows on his knees. "This wasn't anything I ever planned to discuss with you or William, but it looks like I should have. All those years ago... your mom didn't cheat on me. At some point, I realized that was what you thought was going on, but I wasn't ready to tell you the truth."

Wilder's mind raced. "The truth? But... she was next door a lot."

His dad nodded. "Yes, but it wasn't cheating. We have an open marriage."

Wilder stood up and walked a few steps away before turning around. "You what?"

"You heard me."

"But I heard you arguing. You were upset she'd been with that guy."

"I was upset because she was developing feelings for him. That was a hard rule of ours—no feelings. We argued because she didn't want to cut it off with him. But she finally did, and things got better between us."

Wilder couldn't believe this. How had he never known?

Well, why would I? I shouldn't know about my parents' sex lives. Not even now.

He took a breath and calmed down.

"I'm sorry. Maybe if I'd been honest with you about it all you wouldn't have had such a strong reaction to what happened with Kate."

Open marriage?

Wilder thought through all his memories of their arguments. He never would have guessed that. And now he kind of wished he didn't know.

"Dad, the choices I made back then were mine. You tried to tell me to give it more time and I wouldn't listen. But what's done is done. What's important now is that Kate and I are back together."

His dad's eyes were glassy. "I'm so happy about that. And about that sweet baby boy of yours. You want to get back to him now?"

Wilder nodded. He did. He really did. And to his beautiful wife.

He'd always dreamed of a family with Kate; it might have come ten years later than he wanted, but it had been worth the wait.

They walked back to Kate's room in silence. When he entered, Kate's eyes went straight to the coffee.

"Oh, thank you," she exhaled in relief. "I need that so bad."

Wilder handed her the coffee, and she took a few gulps while he stared at his son in the bassinet.

His son. He still couldn't believe it.

The little guy was sleeping, and as much as Wilder wanted to hold him, he knew to let sleeping babies lie.

"Kate, dear, you should be careful. I'm not sure you should have that much caffeine while you're breastfeeding," her mother advised as she folded the clothes that had been tossed haphazardly into Kate's suitcase.

Wilder had known they were supposed to pack an overnight bag, yet they didn't. That meant he'd thrown in some random items last night while Kate had slowly made her way to the car. There had been no time to fold.

"It's fine. I researched it," Kate said as she took another sip.

Her mother pressed her lips together. "Hmm. Maybe you should ask the doctor when she comes in."

Kate's eyes found Wilder's and grew pleading.

"Would you two mind if I had a few minutes alone with Kate?" he asked.

Her mom frowned.

"Of course not," his dad said. "Martha, let's give these three some time to bond as a family."

Martha set down the sweater she was holding. "Okay but, Kate, you call me if you need anything."

"I'm sure she will." Wilder's dad led Martha out of the room.

Wilder sat on the edge of the bed. "How are you doing?"

"Better now. Please do not allow that woman to come home with us. She's driving me crazy."

He laughed. "It will just be the three of us, I promise. How's that sound?"

She smiled. "Wonderful. Thank you."

"Anything for you, Kate. Always."

Danielle Pays

Trusting Her Hero **Playlist is on Spotify**

1. Setting the World On Fire – Kenny Chesney, Pink

2. You Give Love a Bad Name – Bon Jovi

3. Holding Out for a Hero – Bonnie Tyler

4. Falling – Harry Styles

5. Don't Know What You Got (Till It's Gone) – Cinderella

6. You Are The Reason – Calum Scott

7. Stay – Post Malone

8. Just for You – Sam Cooke

9. No One Compares To You – Jack & Jack

10. Shallow – Lady Gaga, Bradley Cooper

11. My Boo – Usher, Alicia Keys

12. It's Your Love – Tim McGraw, Faith Hill

13. Timber – Pitbull, Kesha

14. Sunday Morning – Maroon 5

15. Love On the Brain – Rihanna

16. You're Still The One – Shania Twain

17. Making Memories Of Us – Keith Urban

Trusting Her Hero

Other books by Danielle Pays

The Dare to Risk series
Deceived
Pursued
Played
Consumed
Captivated – A Holiday Novella

The Dare to Surrender series
Chasing Her Trust
Taking Her Chase
Saving Her Target
Trusting Her Hero

Trusting Her Hero

About the Author

Danielle Pays writes steamy romance novels with a touch of suspense. She enjoys romance as well as mystery and suspense and blends them both using her beloved Pacific Northwest for inspiration with its mix of small towns and cities.

When she's not writing her characters into some kind of trouble, she can be found binging Netflix shows, trying to convince her children to eat her cooking, or drinking wine after battling said children at dinnertime.

Follow her at www.daniellepays.com or on Facebook at https://www.facebook.com/daniellepays/

Trusting Her Hero